Secrets OF HER HEART

By Karen Klyne

2025

BUTTERWORTH
BOOKS

This trade paperback is published by Butterworth Books, UK

CATALOGING INFORMATION
ISBN: 978-1-915009-82-1
CREDITS
Editors: Victoria Villaseñor & Nicci Robinson
Cover Design: Nicci Robinson
Production Design: Global Wordsmiths

Acknowledgements

Well, it's been a long time coming, but here it is at last! After months of nagging and persuasion, I've managed to produce this book. Eight months of typing, pacing, snacking, and s urping muchas vino. Voilà! A finished manuscript! Or so I thought.

When I triumphantly reread it, I smugly thought, "Aha! Nailed it this time—barely any edits needed!" But alas, I was wrong. Very wrong. Turns out, as per usual, I omitted to expand on emotion. Thankfully, I have Victoria, my amazing editor, who calmly reminds me that, yes, emotion is important in a romance novel! Thank you, Victoria, for your honesty, patience, and for making my words shine. You're one in a million and are probably deserving of a medal—or several bottles of Guinness.

Nicci, my cover designer, production wizard, marketing genius, and occasional therapist—what can I say? You make my books beautiful inside and out. Thank you for your creative magic and for somehow keeping me (and this project) on track. And thank you, Global Wordsmiths, for keeping the entire operation running like a well-oiled machine.

To my ARC readers: you are the heroes behind the scenes. Your patience, thoughtful feedback, and lovely reviews mean the world to me. Thank you for sticking with me through this wild ride.

Margaret, I'm forever grateful for your proofreading skills and meticulous attention to detail. Without you, I'm certain there would be far more typos.

Thank you, Hayley, for showing me this amazing coastline. All the wonderful scenery remains vivid in my mind.

Finally, to my readers—you beautiful, brilliant people What would I do without you? Your reviews, support, and enthusiasm make this all worthwhile. You're the reason I keep doing th s (well, that and the fun of inventing quirky characters). Thank you from the bottom of my heart. Here's to the next one!

Dedication

For Hayley,
who continuously nagged me because apparently,
"books don't just write themselves." A massive thank you.
Here's your book, Hayley—may it be worth all the
sighs, eyerolls, and not-so-subtle hints.
Enjoy... and next time, try patience!

Chapter One

EMMA BRIGHT SCANNED THE unfamiliar surroundings of her small flat. The contrast between this modest space and the large house she had shared with her wife, Brid, was stark. Every room in the house echoed with Brid's presence, each corner holding a memory. Here, the silence was a bottomless pit threatening to swallow her whole.

She'd resisted the move for a long time, clinging to the life they had built together, but the house had become a shrine, filled with the remnants of their shared life. Now, sitting alone in this tiny, sparsely furnished box, Emma felt the weight of her loneliness more acutely than ever. The quiet here was different—no longer the silence of a house too big for one person, but the oppressive hush of a space that had yet to feel like home.

Two weeks had passed, and there were still boxes that remained untouched, mocking her with their presence. However, today she would finally hang the picture of Brid. It had remained wrapped in newspaper, buried at the bottom of a box marked "Fragile." Whenever her friend phoned to check in, she made the same excuse: "I've been so busy buying new furniture that I haven't had time to unpack the personal stuff." It was partly true. She had spent hours at furniture stores picking out the perfect couch, the ideal dining table, the most comfortable bed. But in reality, those shopping trips were a way to avoid facing the more difficult task of unpacking the boxes filled with memories.

Her gaze wandered down to the photograph she held in her hands. Brid's face beamed with joy as she stood beside her beloved bicycle. The photo was taken on their last cycling trip together, just months before her death. She kissed her index finger and pressed it to Brid's face, then hung it on the picture hook beside her bed. *Oh, Brid. Why did you leave me?* It didn't matter that she knew Brid hadn't left her by choice.

Emma's eyes filled with tears. She clenched her fists and rubbed them against the cool fabric of her jeans. "What now, Brid?" she whispered as she stared at the photograph. "What do I do without you?"

"Put your Lycra on and get on your bike, Emma." It was as if she was still guiding her, urging her to find a way through the darkness.

Taking a deep breath, Emma complied. She went to the wardrobe and pulled out her cycling gear. The Lycra felt tight and unfamiliar after the few years of neglect, but she didn't care. She needed to feel that connection again, to honour the memory of the woman who had loved her so deeply.

She walked to the bike shed and ran her hand along the handlebars that connected her to the past, one that seemed impossibly distant. She remembered the exhilaration of their rides together and the sense of freedom that had always filled her heart.

As she wheeled the bike out of the shed, the morning sun greeted her, casting a warm glow over the busy road. She crossed over onto the cycle track. She'd only moved to Westleigh a few weeks ago but had already discovered that the town was criss-crossed by cycle tracks. It was such a bonus. If only Brid could experience it with her.

She mounted her bike and headed up the hill, and for the first time since Brid's death, Emma felt a glimmer of hope. She may be riding alone, but Brid's spirit was with her. Her words were a constant reminder that she should keep moving forward, keep living. Her new flat may never feel like home, but it didn't have to. Home wasn't a place but a feeling, a memory, and if she carried Brid in her heart, she would never truly be alone. As many times as she'd told herself this, this was the first time it felt like it might be true.

It had been a long time since she'd cycled, and her breathing became more erratic. The hill was proving to be both a mental and physical challenge, but as she got into a rhythm, she steadily climbed the gradient.

She was determined she wouldn't get off, and a mental dialogue urged her to keep going and conquer the incline. Just a little further, a few more turns of the pedals, and hopefully, as promised in the review she'd read, she'd be reaping her rewards. "A view to die for."

And there it was, a beautifully clear vista across the bay to a small island and to the hills beyond. It was the sort of place she could sit for hours, gazing out over the water, watching the multitude of different boats, yachts, ships, and sports enthusiasts. It looked like a perfect spot for a picnic, and she made a mental note to do that one day soon. Maybe she'd come here to watch the sunset. She promised herself she'd make a stop on the way back to take some photos. She'd need the break, because the ride back up looked like sheer hell.

At last, the descent on the other side came along. She coasted down towards the beach and the promenade. Saturdays always meant a hell of a lot more traffic, but the warm sunshine had obviously brought the day trippers out, making it even worse today. She slowed down when she saw the temporary traffic lights change to red and became slightly wary as cars drifted into the cycle lane where the road narrowed.

A passing motorhome missed hitting her by a lick of paint. "You bloody idiot," she shouted and jerked the handlebars a little too hard. The bicycle tyres whirred against the curb, and she began to wobble. She instinctively gripped the handlebars tighter, attempting to regain control, but the bike twisted beneath her. Try as she might to correct it, the bike had developed a mind of its own, and it veered back towards the curb. She mounted the pavement with the front wheel, but the back wheel skidded. The handlebars jolted from her grasp and then her mind went totally blank…until she heard a loud crack as she slammed hard onto her left knee.

She couldn't fathom how she'd got there, but she was in a semi-kneeling position. She swayed slightly when the pain kicked in, making her light-headed. *Don't pass out. Stay conscious.* It was difficult obeying the voice in her head, but she knew she had to.

There was a clanging noise behind her, and a woman crouched down to her level. She put her hand gently on her shoulder. "I'm calling for an ambulance. Hang on in there."

Emma nodded as she saw a group of people gathering around her. A few of them had phones at the ready, but the woman informed them she'd already made the call.

"Be back in a minute," the woman said. She returned with an umbrella and held it over her. "Not much, but it'll shade you from the sun."

Emma managed a thank you. She hadn't moved an inch. She couldn't. She just knelt in that same position, waiting and praying to hear the sirens from the ambulance.

An athletic-looking man clad in a red T-shirt and shorts bounded up and came to a halt. "Saw it all happen. I was just on my way to work; I'm a lifeguard. Listen, folks, there's no way you'll get an ambulance. There's been a major incident on the M3. Massive pile-up."

Emma's heart sank. She put her hand to her forehead and rubbed it, and a small sob escaped. "Christ." She didn't think she could hold this position for much longer. She slumped slightly, and the woman steadied her.

"Then we'll just have to take you to hospital by car."

Emma moaned and shook her head. "Can't move."

The woman sighed. "I'm sorry, but there's no alternative." She removed the umbrella. "Can you adjust to a sitting position?"

Emma huffed. "I'm not sure. I'll try." She leaned back and

placed her hands on the ground behind her. She cried out in pain and slowly eased herself onto her bum. She held her leg bent in front of her and gasped for breath as she felt the blood drain from her face. The world spun and dimmed.

The woman placed a firm hand on her shoulder. "Try to focus. Take some deep breaths." Someone passed the woman a bottle of water, and she unscrewed the cap. "Here, take some sips and keep inhaling. Deep breaths, in and out."

Emma followed her instructions.

The woman frowned. "Okay, so we're going to try and lift you to the side so I can get my car out."

Emma shook her head. "No! I'll shuffle on my bum." She was adamant about that one. There was no way she could be lifted. She knew the pain would be too intense. She kept her left leg bent and pushed back with her hands behind her. She shuddered and whimpered with every move as the pain shot up her leg. She stifled the urge to vomit, but it seemed intent on moving upwards and outwards. She concentrated deeply and managed to shift from the driveway she'd landed on. She let out a deep sigh. Her head spun and a dizzy sensation engulfed her.

She took a lungful of air and barely stayed conscious. Then she saw the gates opening and out came a black car. The woman got out and opened the passenger door. There was no way she could do this. Her pain threshold was high, but this was like climbing Everest.

After a short discussion with the woman, the lifeguard and another guy came to her assistance. "Sorry, this is going to hurt, but it's the only way," the lifeguard said.

They each put an arm under each of her arms and took a leg apiece. Emma yelled, but somehow they managed to lift her onto the side of the seat. She slowly manoeuvred her legs in.

The lifeguard crouched down. "One day this'll make a great story to tell your friends. Driven to hospital in a Roller," he said and closed the door.

"I'll try and take it slow," the woman said.

Emma relaxed a little. "Thanks for this. I don't know what I'd have done without you."

The woman smiled. "By the way, my name's Thea. What's yours?"

"Emma. What about my bike?" It seemed a stupid question under the circumstances.

Thea laughed. "Don't worry, I promise I won't steal it. I'll put it in the garage."

"Thanks, Thea." Trying to be normal and polite took every ounce of effort, and she all but screamed when they went over a pothole.

Thea gave her a sidewards glance. "I take it you want to go to the local hospital? There is a bigger one, but it'll take an extra thirty minutes."

Emma snorted. "As if I know anything about hospitals. I've only just moved here."

"Everyone says this one is the best, and it should only take us about five minutes."

But it was the longest five minutes Emma had ever experienced. She closed her eyes and eventually the car came to a standstill.

"Shit," Thea said.

Emma opened her eyes to see a long queue of ambulances ahead of them.

"Guess they must have come from that accident." Thea swung out in front of them and took the driveway to the top. She pulled up and opened her door. "Don't go anywhere. I'll be back in a jiff."

Emma looked down at her busted knee; she wasn't going anywhere.

It wasn't long before Thea returned and opened the passenger door; she had a wheelchair and two paramedics in tow. Emma wasn't sure how Thea had managed it, but she was mightily grateful. They eased her out, and she gingerly hopped on her good leg before collapsing onto the chair. While Thea and the paramedics chatted, Emma looked at the car she'd arrived in. Now she realised what the lifeguard was going on about. Her transport was a gleaming black Rolls Royce.

"Right, let's get you booked in," Thea said.

Emma smiled. "Nice car."

"Yes. I guess it has its advantages, but sadly, it's not mine."

Thea wheeled her forward. The automatic doors whooshed open and a smell of antiseptic assaulted Emma's nose. The bright lights and hustle of the accident and emergency room overwhelmed her and made her stomach lurch again. The reception was sheer chaos. They approached the front desk, and the receptionist eventually looked up from her computer screen.

"We need help," Thea said.

"I'll need some details," the receptionist said, barely looking up from the screen.

Emma supplied her with the relevant information.

"If you take a seat in the waiting area, triage will call you."

Thea grimaced at all the people crammed into the small area. "What's the estimated time?"

The receptionist raised her eyebrows. "As you can see, it's busy. I'd say between three and four hours."

Thea shook her head. She wheeled Emma around the corner and found a small space. "I'll be back shortly. Just going to park the car."

Emma glanced around. The area was filled with a diverse mix of people, each with their own ailments and anxieties. To put it mildly, it resembled a zoo. She held her head in her hands and tried to magic herself to another place. Any place, just not in a hospital.

Thea returned clutching a large carrier bag. "I'm so sorry. I'm going to have to leave you now. I've got to collect my boss's children from a party." She handed Emma the carrier bag. "This should keep you going for a while."

Emma peeked inside the bag to find two bottles of water, two packs of sandwiches, some fruit, a large bar of chocolate, and a bag of mints. She gasped and smiled. "You're amazing, Thea. Thank you so much for your kindness."

"I wish I could do more. We should swap mobile numbers. You can let me know if you need anything, because you might be stuck here for some time, and you can let me know how you get on."

"Of course." Easier said than done. No one remembered their phone numbers anymore. She had to think hard, but eventually she gave her number, and Thea rang it.

"There you go. Hope all goes well, and I'll text you later." She waved at the door as she left.

Emma caught her breath to stop a sob from escaping. Her only friend—a complete stranger—had gone. She'd likely never see or hear from her again. Her head slumped. Grief, an old and unwelcome friend, washed over her. A voice in her head whispered, *Don't give up because of one bad chapter in your life. Keep going. Your story doesn't end here.* Wise words, she supposed, but how many more chapters could she handle?

Chapter Two

T HEA SPRINTED BACK TO the car park after checking her watch. She was going to be late picking her kids up. Still, she knew they were safe, and they'd stay put.

She got into her car and banged her fist on the dashboard. "You twat." *Why did you tell her the children belonged to your boss?* Force of habit. She'd learned the hard way not to trust people, and she'd never divulge her life to anyone ever again. Once bitten and all that crap. There was no way she could sugar coat this shit, and she wasn't about to play pretend.

Did Emma really look like a woman who couldn't be trusted? Thea didn't think so at all. She'd had an accident and landed on her drive; she hadn't planned it. She could very well be a lovely person. She could also be mad as a hatter. She couldn't take the risk.

A vision of Emma formed in her mind. She had the kind of presence you didn't forget. She was certainly attractive. Thea laughed to herself. And hadn't she landed on one knee? It was a bit like a proposal. Emma must have been in agony, and it was a scene Thea would never forget, though if she didn't know better, she'd call it destiny.

She set off from the car park, and the bad memories loomed up in her mind. Momentarily, she lost concentration and nearly careered into a bollard. She told herself off and tried to get back into the zone, but the negative thoughts remained. She'd felt this crap so many times before, it was like déjà poo.

How stupid she'd been to trust Riva. Just the taste of her name on her tongue nearly made her vomit. She'd allowed her attraction to rule her head, and it made her easy bait.

A perfect mark.

She huffed and shook her head, trying to escape from the nightmare. It was time to put on a smiley face for her children. She lowered her window, pressed the intercom and waited for the gates to open. She parked and made her way up the steps to the front door and rang the bell.

The owners of the stylish house were aware of her circumstances. Still, she'd done her research on the parents before she'd allowed her children, Lyra and Sebastian, to come to their daughter's birthday party. Everyone was vetted at the private school she'd chosen for her children. They were all super-duper wealthy people who seemed to have the same fears as her. The difference was, her fears had once been realized.

When the door opened, Lyra and Sebastian ran into her arms and nearly sent her flying.

Lyra pulled back and shook her finger at Thea. "You're late, Mum."

Thea dropped her head and faked a small sob. "I'm sorry, honey. Wait 'til I tell you why." Thea looked up at the woman who'd accompanied them. "Thanks, Patty. I hope they've behaved themselves."

Patty laughed. "Your children have impeccable manners, unlike some of the other brats we've had here today."

"Thank you, and thanks for inviting them to your daughter's birthday party." She couldn't think for the life of her what Patty's daughter was called.

They said their goodbyes, and Lyra and Sebastian jumped into the back seat of the car. Sebastian was a quiet boy. He was only six, but he wasn't anything like as boisterous as most kids his age. All he seemed to do was stick his head in a book. She couldn't imagine where he'd got that from. Maybe his father. She didn't know anything about him to say anything with certainty. "You okay, Seb?" She loved her son's full name, but he insisted on it being shortened. She imagined he was teased at school. Children could be so cruel.

"Fine. Too many screaming girls." He rolled his eyes.

Thea nodded. "Ah, sadly that's what some eight-year-old girls do when they get together."

"Well, I'm never getting married to one."

Thea laughed. "Don't blame you, but you may change your mind later."

"Never."

Thea ruffled his hair. "We'll see."

Lyra waved her arms in the air. "Tell us what happened, Mum. Why were you so late?"

"I'll tell you on the ride home." She tucked them safely into the car and began the drive home as she relayed the story. Seb didn't seem in the slightest bit interested, but Lyra could hardly sit still.

"Poor lady. Is she okay?"

Thea shrugged. "I hope so. I'll text her later to see if she needs anything."

Lyra bounced in her seat. "You could invite her to our house. We can look after her."

"Slow down, sunshine. She's a stranger, and you know how we feel about those. She might have a family of her own to take care of her." Shite, she hadn't even asked if there was someone she could call for her. But then, she hadn't asked her to either.

When they got back, Seb went straight to his room. She wasn't sure if he was old enough for Enid Blyton, but her mum had passed *The Famous Five* books on to Seb. Thea remembered that she was about seven when she started reading them. Seb was younger, but he absolutely loved them.

Lyra flopped onto the floor in front of the TV. "Can I watch *How to Train your Dragon?*"

"Yes, but only for an hour."

Lyra pouted. "Ah, Mum. I won't get to finish it then."

"Well, you can finish it over the holidays." The answer seemed to meet with Lyra's approval. Either that or she couldn't think of an objection, and she said no more.

Thea went into the kitchen and prepared a chicken salad for herself since the kids had eaten at the party. She poured a small glass of wine and sipped it as she stared into space.

Riva reared up in her mind again, and she couldn't stop herself from drifting into the memories she tried hard to keep at bay... She'd met Riva at her local gym in Shepherd's Bush. It was only two years ago, but it seemed like yesterday.

There she was, on the treadmill beside her. Even with just a sideways glance, Thea saw how gorgeous and sexy she was.

But all hell let loose when Riva began her run on the machine, and she tripped all over the place.

"Aargh," she screamed, "somebody help me!"

Damsel in distress alert. Thea paused her program, leaned over and pressed the emergency stop button on Riva's treadmill.

Riva slumped forward and held tightly onto the rails. She looked over at Thea. "Oh my God, that was scary. Thanks so much. I thought I was going to fly without wings."

Thea laughed. "Are you okay now?"

Riva ran her hand across her forehead. "I think so. You're my hero."

Thea liked the idea of that. "Might be a good idea to have a trainer show you the ropes first."

Riva nodded. "Yeah, you're right, but it looked so easy. I've never been to the gym before. Never had the time. I've just moved here and thought I'd start as I mean to go on."

"Good idea, in principle. Listen, I'm just about done here. Do you want me to introduce you to Dani? She's brilliant."

"Oh, please. You don't mind?"

"Of course not. Follow me." Thea introduced them, and Riva booked a session for later that week.

Riva placed her hand on Thea's arm. "After saving my life, the least I can do is buy you a coffee. If you're free?"

Thea's parents had been looking after the kids. *I am currently unsupervised, and the possibilities are endless.* "That would be great."

And that was it. Coffee, followed by lunch, followed by dinner, followed by sex. All in one day. If it hadn't been for the kids coming home, Thea may have gone the whole hog and asked Riva to move in immediately, in true lesbian cliché style.

The thing was...Riva was perfect in every way. Apart from being stunning and fit, they had so much in common. It had been unbelievable.

It *was* unbelievable.

Thea sighed, brought back to the moment by shrill laughter on the TV. The memories always left her feeling dulled and oily. It had all been a big, fat lie.

Chapter Three

After four hours of unattended agony, and after being assessed by triage, a nurse wheeled Emma into a cubicle.

A doctor arrived and conducted a thorough examination. "We're arranging some X-rays. I'll see you later," he said and made a quick exit.

Surprise, surprise. Time seemed to stretch as she awaited the results, the pain and discomfort a constant companion. She'd eaten her sandwiches and fruit. At least she still had an appetite. That had to be a good sign. She opened her second bottle of water and took a long slug. What a Samaritan she'd found in Thea. However, right now, her mouth tasted like the bottom of a budgie's cage, so she sucked on a mint.

She lay in the cubicle, struggling not to writhe in agony. The excruciating pain shot through her leg with every slight movement. They obviously heard her groans and sent a nurse in with paracetamol. She needed something a lot stronger, but it did ease a little.

She watched the group of medical staff sat at a desk in front of her. She assumed they were discussing her case as they kept looking over. They glanced again and smiled. Somehow, the smiles looked like sympathetic ones for bad news to come.

"Hello, Emma. My name's Doctor Aswan. I've looked at your X-rays, and I have to say, you've done quite a good job on your knee. It's a nasty fracture, so we're going to put your leg in a cast. We'll see you again in a months' time and do some more X-rays. If it's knitted well, we'll change the cast for a leg brace."

She wasn't sure if that was good or bad news. "Can I go

home?"

Doctor Aswan shook his head vigorously. "Out of the question, I'm afraid. We'll get you sorted out with some help first. Maybe in a few days."

She sighed, a little more than thankful, because how the hell was she supposed to cope alone?

Shortly, a couple of nurses applied her cast. At first it was snug, but as they continued layering the strips of soggy plaster around her leg and it began to dry, it got tighter and tighter, and she felt as though an implosion may be imminent.

After that long and drawn-out procedure, a porter wheeled her away.

"Sorry, love, there aren't any beds available on a ward, so lucky you; you have your very own room in the trauma unit."

Within minutes, he helped Emma onto the hospital bed, and she lay there, her leg encased in a heavy plaster cast and her mind in a state of utter chaos, physically and emotionally shattered. The claustrophobic, clinical room offered little comfort. But at least she wasn't side by side with other people. A tiny bit of privacy meant she could let her tears fall in solitude.

As nighttime moved into the early hours, the ward suddenly came alive with a cacophony of suffering beyond her door. Emma stared at the ceiling, trying to block out the sounds that penetrated the thin walls. She was utterly alone and with no one to call, no one to sit by her side and hold her hand through the torment. No one to tell her it was going to be okay.

More tears welled up in her eyes. She was no cry-baby, but she couldn't stop them. No friends. No family. Should she call her best friend? No, she couldn't do that. Jen was in Ohio on her first trip in years to see her sister. Emma wasn't going to ruin that for her. Should she call her sister? She doubted Colly would respond. They'd had a fall-out nearly twenty years ago and hadn't spoken since. Emma had emailed her a few years ago when Brid was in palliative care, stupidly thinking that would put an end to their feud. She couldn't have been more wrong.

It seemed Colly would never forgive their parents for dying in a car crash. She'd given up her nursing training to look after Emma, who was seven years her junior. Emma sympathised, but it wasn't her fault, and she'd lost her mum and dad too Then there was the thing with Brid.

No, there was no one to call.

The nurses were kind but overworked. They came and went with brisk efficiency, assuring her she was safe, but offering little in the way of comfort. She longed for a familiar face, a gentle touch, anything to remind her she meant something to someone.

She closed her eyes, willing herself to be anywhere but there. She imagined a peaceful beach, the sound of waves gently lapping at the shore, and the warmth of the sun on her skin. Her shoulders dropped ever so slightly, and the feeling of dread receded just a little.

Her phone pinged, and she opened her eyes. She was still lying in a hospital bed, far removed from the beach she'd conjured up. This was her new reality.

Emma sniffed and grabbed a handful of tissues. She wiped away the tears and blew her nose. She checked her phone and smiled when she saw it was a text from Thea. That made her want to cry again, because a virtual stranger was the only person who knew she'd been in an accident.

Hi Emma. How are things? Any news?

A bad fracture. In plaster cast. Not sure what's next. It's a Bank Holiday so someone will see me Tuesday. Thanks so much for your help. The goodies were a lifesaver.

So sorry. Do you need anything? Perhaps I could come and see you?

Emma wondered if she really meant that. But why would she ask or even contact her if she wasn't being genuine? She was under no obligation. Regardless of Thea's reasoning, Emma desperately needed a friend. *Would welcome that.*

Great. I'll come see you on Tuesday afternoon. Sorry I can't make it before, but I have two energetic children to entertain. What's your surname?

It's Bright. Look forward to seeing you.

Bright by name, and bright by nature.

Emma inserted a smiley face emoji. *Thanks again xx*

Too late to remove the kisses; she'd already sent it. Anyway, there was no harm, and she meant them. She couldn't for the life of her remember what Thea looked like. She hadn't really noticed, most likely due to the pain fogging every other sense. She did remember her dark complexion and hair and her glossy brown eyes. Well, that was a start.

Emma made a silent vow to survive this and to find a way to rebuild her life, to find new connections and new reasons to keep going.

The long weekend was endless and boring. She fretted constantly about losing complete contact with the outside world. She had no phone charger and no clean clothes. If she'd had the sense to have a premonition, she'd have made a list and packed the essentials. Luckily, a nurse eventually found a charger in lost property, giving her something to concentrate on other than her crappy situation.

They moved her into a small ward with two other women, but apparently, they were visiting Earth from another planet. They spoke nothing but gobbledegook in a weird language only they seemed to understand, nodding and laughing together. Emma had no idea what they were rabbiting on about.

Bev, who had become her regular nurse, seemed to find it hilarious. "Sorry about this. We'll try and move you to another bay in a couple of days."

"Thanks. In the meantime, do you have a phrase book I could borrow?" She wasn't sure how she'd managed to maintain her sense of humour, but she was mightily happy she'd got one.

In the day, it was gobbledegook and at night, they sang. *All* night.

Well, if you can't beat them, join them. She found out that the two alien's names were Alice and Ilsa. Alice dragged Ilsa out of her bed to show Ilsa what was happening with *her* bed. From the little Emma could understand, Alice was convinced that her bed was leaking copious amounts of water, and she feared she'd float away into the sea, never to be seen again. From Ilsa's expression, Emma could see she shared Alice's concern. By now though, Emma hoped both their beds would be carried away to sea.

Perhaps she was being unkind. After all, they were well into their eighties, both suffered from some form of dementia, and both had taken a spill, landing them here, and people were being crammed into any area where a bed was free, no matter the condition.

Mental note: Don't have an accident at the weekend, especially a bank holiday weekend.

By the afternoon, Bev settled Ilsa and Alice into their beds for a nap, but as soon as she left, Alice burst into hysterical sobs.

Oh my God, not the water again. Of course, Ilsa left her bed and joined Alice. More of the gobbledegook. Then Ilsa sobbed too.

Emma called out their names and patted her bed. "Come and sit with me."

Ilsa and Alice walked over without hesitation and sat on Emma's bed but continued to sob.

Emma grabbed their hands. "I'm here to help."

Alice shouted, "It's the water! It won't stop."

Her frail shoulders shook, but at least Emma could understand now. She nodded. "That's why I'm here."

Alice gasped. "You'll stop the water?"

Emma smiled. "Yes, it's my job."

Alice hugged Emma. "Thank you, God. How?"

"I know where the tap is," Emma whispered. "Shh, they don't want me to turn it off."

Alice and Ilsa pressed their fingers to their lips.

Emma kept her voice low. "Now listen to me very carefully, I shall say this only once." *Wasn't that a line from a famous comedy drama?* Oh well. "You must both go back to your beds and pretend to be asleep. You must close your eyes very tightly. Have you got that?"

They nodded again.

"Go."

They followed her instructions, and soon, both were snoring. Emma didn't get much sleep, but at least there was no more wailing.

But the peace didn't last.

"What about the boxes?" Alice cried.

Emma sighed. "What boxes?"

"I packed my belongings like my daughter said," Alice mumbled, "but now I'm stuck with them."

Emma rubbed her brow. "We'll store them."

Alice shook her head. "No space."

Emma winked. "Wrong. I found a cupboard down the corridor that'd be perfect for your boxes."

Alice gulped. "It won't be big enough."

Oh yes, it bloody will. "How many boxes do you have?"

"About ten."

"No problem." Emma smiled. "It holds twenty."

Alice relaxed. "But someone might steal them."

"Don't worry, Alice. I have the key."

Alice sighed with relief. "Thank you, dear."

Emma could only hope that Ilsa hadn't got ten boxes too. Still, she could always find another storeroom. She felt bad for them. How terrible, to be so frightened of things your own mind was conjuring up. They only seemed to have each other. And Emma knew just how that felt.

Over the long weekend, she'd managed to keep control of the situation but knew it couldn't last forever. Maybe today was the day they'd move her. Anywhere. She'd be happy in the storeroom.

She wasn't in pain as long as she didn't move. That was a plus, and she needed as many of those as she could. However, the same thoughts kept popping up in her head. *What if?* What if she hadn't moved? Had she made a bad decision? What if she hadn't gone out on her bike that day? The thoughts depressed her. She had to face the facts. She *had* moved home, and she *had* gone out that day. The accident *did* happen, and she couldn't turn the clock back. If she could, then she would also change the fact that Brid had died. She breathed in deeply. She had to come to terms with it, though that was going to take time.

After breakfast, she had a visit from another doctor.

"Good news, Emma; you can go home."

Emma clapped her hands. "Wonderful. When?"

"The physiotherapists will assess you. Could be today or later in the week. I can t be more precise because we're so busy."

As she shuffled awkwardly in her bed in that awful hospital gown, the news of an extended stay sank in, and a wave of devastation washed over her. A mix of frustration, fear, and a profound sense of being upended. At last, she'd got off her ass to explore her new surroundings with a view to making new plans and having a way forward—but it was all disrupted by the unforeseen need for medical care.

There was some good news: Alice was being discharged. It was sad, really, because she was being moved to a dementia home. One minute she was there, and the next minute she was gone.

Ilsa looked forlorn. She sat on Emma's bed and cried. She was such a sweet old lady. Just like her, she didn't have any visitors. Emma began to imagine that one day, she'd be back here after losing her mind, and she'd have nobody who cared either. She put her arm around Ilsa and cried with her.

A few hours later, Ilsa was moved back to her residential

care home, and Emma was overcome with the loneliness. She didn't think she'd miss Alice and Ilsa, but it was all so quiet, and melancholy engulfed her. Before she could fully wallow in her situation, two young women burst through the swing doors.

"Hello, Emma. Good to meet you. My name's Maddie, and this is my partner in crime, Deb."

Emma tried to be cheerful. "Good to meet you both. Are you releasing me?"

Maddie tipped her hand from side to side. "As soon as we can." She rubbed her hands together. "Got some questions first, then we can draw up a plan."

Emma nodded. "Fire away."

"It says on your records that you live in a ground floor apartment. Do you have any relatives or friends who can help you?" Maddie asked.

Emma shook her head. "I'm afraid not. I've only just moved here from Leeds. I haven't had time to meet anyone, let alone make any friends."

"No worries. We'll provide you with some equipment and put a care package together. That involves carers coming in three or four times a day, you know, to help get you up and get some breakfast and at lunch time to prepare something to eat. Teatime will be much the same, and then you'll get one visit in the evening to help you into bed."

"Do you really think I need all that help?"

Maddie laughed. "Frankly, yes. Listen, it won't be for long."

They checked her leg and even got her out of bed briefly, but she quickly grew dizzy and the pain made it hard to breathe. After she was settled again, they made some notes in her chart.

"We'll get back to you in a couple of days." They waved and disappeared.

Emma pressed the remote on the side of her bed and the mattress slowly went flat. She closed her eyes. She'd never imagined she'd be lying in a hospital bed only weeks after moving into her new place. She felt the tears welling up again. Outside her window, the world was moving on, oblivious to her personal turmoil where time stretched endlessly. It was all about the uncertainty and the unanswered questions about the road ahead. Her future had become a series of question marks.

She was startled out of her depression when she heard tapping on the door window. She opened her eyes and for the first time in days, she smiled. She'd only seen Thea once, but there was no mistaking that beautiful face.

She pushed the door open and peeked around. "Are you up for a visitor?"

Emma grinned and beckoned her in, then hit the button to put the bed back into an upright position. "I sure am. Especially when it's my favourite Samaritan."

Thea laughed. "You mean you have more than one?"

Emma shook her head slowly. "No. You're the one and only."

Thea gave Emma a big hug. "You look a heck of a lot better than the last time I saw you."

She was taller than Emma remembered. She looked so good in denim cropped jeans and a vibrant blue T-shirt with a dragonfly print across the chest along with the words, Let it Be. Emma's eyes lingered a little too long at the picture of the dragonfly...or was she staring at Thea's breasts? *Oh my God.* What was she thinking? Had she ever ogled anyone other than Brid like that? Nope, she was almost sure she never had. She averted her eyes and gave a little cough. Emma chuckled, trying to put the moment behind her. "Thanks, I sure hope so." She ran her fingers through her hair. "God, I must look dreadful. I haven't even got a brush or anything."

Thea clicked her tongue. "You look great to me."

Emma's cheeks burned. She was sure Thea wasn't eyeing her up in the same way as she'd done. She was just being polite and making her feel better.

Thea glanced at the plaster cast on Emma's leg. "What's the

verdict?"

"It's going to take time, but I think they're optimistic. A couple of months or something like that. Maybe a bit longer. It's just so annoying. How could I let this happen?"

"Ha, I don't think you had a choice. Life is like toilet paper. You're either on a roll, or you're taking shit from some asshole."

Emma couldn't help but laugh, which was just what she needed.

"Anyway, look on the bright side; you met me."

Emma nodded. "That's very true."

Thea reached into her big shoulder bag then began to unload all sorts of stuff onto Emma's bedside table. "Lemon and Barley, chocolate, and an assortment of magazines. I didn't know your taste in reading, so I brought you one of each."

Emma touched Thea's arm lightly. "You are a true gem, Thea."

"It'll get better once I know you." Thea frowned. "Shall I go and get you a hairbrush? In fact, give me a list of essentials. The shop downstairs sells most things."

"Are you sure you don't mind?" Emma didn't want to push a stranger's kindness, but it wasn't like she had anyone else lining up to help.

"Of course not. I know how I'd feel."

Emma fumbled awkwardly in her bedside cupboard for her phone. "I have some cash. I'm old fashioned." She took a twenty-pound note from the back of the case and handed it to Thea. "I hope that's enough. If it isn't, I promise I'll repay you."

"No worries. So, hairbrush. What else?"

"Toothbrush and toothpaste and some soap and a sponge." She'd really like a pair of PJs but was sure the little shop wouldn't run to those, and twenty pounds wouldn't be enough for that anyway. She hated the hospital gown, though, and couldn't wait to get out of it.

"No problem. Be back in ten." Thea gave a little wave and left.

Emma found solace in the familiar warmth of Thea's voice.

It was going to be a long and challenging journey, but Thea's presence seemed to ease her emotional burdens and help her to cope. She wasn't *completely* alone.

Thea returned in no time and placed everything on the top of her cupboard, along with the change. She rummaged in her bag and pulled out a pair of earbuds. "Just in case you want to listen to some music or something." She pulled out a tissue from the box and went over to the small sink. She wet the tissue and wiped the earbuds. "Almost as good as new."

"You're a lifesaver. Honestly, I can't tell you how much I appreciate your help."

Thea made herself comfortable in the chair and pulled it closer to the bed. She glanced around the bay. "Hey, you're lucky to have this to yourself."

Emma shook her head. "You have no idea what it's been like." She related the story to Thea and when she'd finished, they both fell into fits of laughter.

Thea leaned back into her chair. "So, what's your story?"

Emma raised her eyebrows. "My story?"

"Yeah. Tell me about yourself." Thea stared at Emma and waited. She slapped her thigh. "Jeez, I'm so sorry. I just want to know who you are, but I can see I'm being intrusive."

Emma shook her head and waved away the concern as well as the feeling of grief that hit her yet again. "I'm so sorry, Thea. You're not being intrusive. I've just lost the art of conversation. I've been on my own for a while. I do talk to myself, but it's not the same." She laughed. It was true, she couldn't remember the last time she'd had a real conversation with a human being. The only person she videoed with was Jen, her best friend. In fact, her *only* friend. She'd known her since she was six years old, and they had a business together. She'd loved her work; it had been her passion and her saviour. Jen knew her almost as well as Brid had. But that was history and a closed book...along with her other interests.

She supposed it was unfair to say she only had one friend. Brid's friends had been supportive both during and after Brid had passed away, but they weren't *her* friends; they were Brid's. Emma lived to work, whereas Brid worked to live. She was a supervisor in the call centre with British Telecom. Sometimes Emma had wondered how Brid had ever reached those dizzy heights. After all, she was hardly ever there and gained the name of sick-note Brid. She either had a hangover or a cold. They agreed very early on in their relationship that they'd continue with their own interests and never hold each other back. It worked, and they fit like two books on a shelf. They were soulmates.

She felt so guilty when Brid's friends called and texted her. She didn't really know them, apart from the odd get togethers at birthdays and Christmas. Sometimes she'd respond, and sometimes she forgot. In the beginning, they came around to see her. They brought food and kind words, but she wanted neither. She wanted to be left alone. She was so wrapped up in her grief that she didn't want to let anyone else in. She'd felt detached, whirling in the eye of a tornado. She'd never experienced loneliness before, but the permanent numbness was like she had taken a straw and sucked all the emotions from her body and mind. On reflection, maybe she should have let them in. Maybe then she wouldn't be relying on a stranger to get her a toothbrush, for fuck's sake.

Perhaps it was time to change all that and open up a little. "Before I begin, do you think you could open the window? I keep asking, and they keep forgetting. It's so stuffy in here. Trust me to be missing this beautiful sunshine."

Thea pushed the window to its fullest opening. As she did so, her T-shirt rose up, and Emma caught a glimpse of her tanned back. Bloody hell, she was doing it again! She looked away, baffled at her inability to behave like a sensible human.

Thea returned to her seat.

"I'd lived in Leeds all my life." Emma chuckled. "I bet you don't even know where Leeds is."

Thea laughed. "I believe it's north of Watford. I think I passed Leeds once on the way to Harrogate."

Emma nodded. "Well, it's nothing like Harrogate. But it was home, and I loved it."

"It's a long way from Westleigh."

Emma nodded. "True. I woke up one day and thought, it's time to move on. So that's what I did."

Thea leaned back in her chair. "Why Westleigh?"

Emma laughed. "I stuck a pin on a map and that's where it landed."

Thea laughed. "I don't believe you."

"I'm serious. My best friend, Jen, asked me what my priorities were. I told her I'd like to be by the sea. North was too cold, east was way too windy, and west was too wet. She knew I hated the cold weather, so it had to be south. She told me to close my eyes, placed a pin between my fingers, and said, "go." Of course, I didn't think she was serious, and nothing was written in stone. But I did what she said, and the pin landed on Westleigh."

"Wow. So, what happened next?"

"Jen went onto Rightmove, chose some properties, and arranged viewings for the following weekend. She booked us into a hotel and that was basically it. Frankly, I didn't know what I was doing, but I knew I had to make this move. I found an apartment that I liked, and Jen did the rest."

"I take it Jen lives in Leeds, otherwise she'd be here, I'm sure."

"Yes, but she's on holiday in the States at the moment."

Thea raised her eyebrows. "Huh, typical. These things often happen at the most inconvenient times. Anyway, did you love the place as soon as you set eyes on it?"

"No. I liked it. It was close to the sea and to cafes and supermarkets, and I thought, if I'm going to live anywhere, this is the place."

Thea shook her head. "I'm gobsmacked." She paused and

stared at Emma as though debating something internally. "Okay, let's go for it. Why did you feel so compelled to leave your hometown, the place you said you loved."

Emma closed her eyes. This was going to be painful, but somehow, she felt at ease with Thea and knew she could tell her. "I was married to the most wonderful woman. She was the love of my life, but she died."

Thea covered her face with her hands. "I'm so sorry, Emma. I should never have pushed you."

Emma shook her head. "Honestly, it's fine. I think it's time I talked about it." She eased up the bed and tried to get more comfortable. "I'd grieved for nearly two years. I knew I couldn't start a new life there. Yes, I could have sold the house and bought somewhere nearby where I could begin making different memories, but I just couldn't do it. It was all too familiar. I had to find me again."

Thea gently touched Emma's hand. "You're so brave."

Emma laughed. "Or stupid." She spread her hands out palms up. "And look where I've landed."

Thea pursed her lips. "It could always be worse."

Emma shrugged. "Could it? Maybe somebody's trying to tell me something. Perhaps I shouldn't have left." Emma looked down at her hands in her lap, then she smiled and looked up. "I'm being stupid. I made the right move. I feel it in my bones—even the broken ones."

Thea slapped the bed with her hand. "Exactly." She laughed. "Hey, if you hadn't flown off your bike onto my drive, we may never have met. We'd be missing this new friendship."

Emma would like to think that was the case, but she'd had too many sleepless days and nights, and right now, she couldn't see many positives. However, she was pleased she'd met Thea. She seemed bubbly and cheerful, which was just what she needed right now.

Thea poked Emma's arm. "Don't you agree?"

Emma shook her head. "Pardon?"

Thea laughed. "I must really have made an impression on you...*not*."

Emma clasped Thea's wrist. "I'm sorry. I was in a bit of a dream. You've made a wonderful impression on me, and I don't know what I would've done without you."

Thea grinned. "That's better." She tilted her head to one side. "Can I ask you how long you'd been married?"

"Seventeen years."

Thea raised her eyebrows. "Wow."

Emma nodded. "Yep. We met, and a year later, we got married. Then she was taken away from me."

Thea took Emma's hand and squeezed it. "But nobody can take away the eighteen years of happiness."

Emma smiled. "You're right, but you always want more. You know, I look at some couples and wonder why they're together. Why don't they just go their own sweet ways. So, forgive me. Sometimes I feel a bit sorry for myself and wonder why she died when what we had was so perfect." Emma lifted her hands. "I know why she died, of course. She had cancer. She was always so full of life and laughter. I just don't understand why they take such lovely people and leave the miserable ones behind."

"Perhaps because there's a better place for the special people. I don't know. All I know is, we were put on this earth for a reason. I believe it's because we must experience both happiness and sadness. I like to hope that happiness outweighs the sadness in the long run."

Emma inclined her head. "You seem very wise for someone so young."

"Ha, young? I'm thirty-six. And trust me, I'm not wise."

Emma laughed. "Thirty-six. That's roughly how old I was when I met Brid."

"How old was she?"

"When I met her, she was fifty-five," Emma said. "Big age gap."

"I bet you hardly noticed it."

"You're right. Even when she turned seventy, it never showed. She was so young at heart." Emma chuckled. "Much crazier than I am. She was always like a big kid."

"That's good to hear. Life is for living. It's also about having fun and enjoying every day."

"Ah. So speaks the voice of experience."

Thea put her hands to her cheeks. "No way. I've made some poor judgements, but I hope I've learned something from them."

"I can't imagine you making bad decisions, given the way you've rushed in to help me. Anyway, it's your turn. What's your story?"

Thea glanced at her watch. "My turn next time. I wish I could stay, but I need to pick the kids up. Would it be okay if I visit again on Thursday?"

"That'd be great. You're just the sort of company I need."

"Likewise." Thea stood and almost ran to the door, then she turned. "See you soon."

Emma waved. "Thanks for everything," she said as the door slowly shut behind Thea. As soon as Thea disappeared, the thicket of loneliness returned. She almost missed Ilsa and Alice. Almost.

Melancholy came back to haunt her. She missed Brid so much. She was always the strong one. She knew exactly what Brid would say. *You stood on your own two feet from the age of thirteen. You knew what you wanted from life, and you chased it. You built up a successful business. You don't need me anymore, but you do need a life. You need to laugh again. You need to love again.*

Emma jolted upright. *What's that about love?* Why had she imagined that Brid would say that? Because that's what Brid would say. They'd had many conversations about it. She wasn't a jealous woman. She knew that Emma loved her with all her heart, but she'd always said, "Life goes on, and when I'm gone, I want you to find happiness again."

It was all so stupid really. She'd had an accident and met a great person, but that didn't mean she was the right woman. She might even be married to a man and have seven kids. Anyway, Thea was way too young. She heard Brid laughing in her mind. *She's thirty-six. Much the same age that you were when we met.* She brushed the thought away with her hand. In her weak and vulnerable state, her mind was playing tricks on her. All the same, whenever she thought about Thea, a warm feeling engulfed her. She probably just had a fever.

Chapter Four

THEA TOOK OFF LIKE a mad woman. If she wasn't careful, she'd be late again. Lyra and Seb wouldn't be impressed, and they'd tease her something rotten. Well, Lyra would. Seb would occasionally look up from his book and agree with Lyra at the right moment.

She parked outside the school gates right on time, and the kids jumped into the back of the car.

Lyra fanned herself with a magazine as Emma began the drive home. "Phew, it's hot in here, Mum. Can we have the air conditioning on?"

Lyra was right. It was hot. A rainy June had led into a roasting July. She loved the warm weather though. It was in her blood, and although she'd lived most of her life in England, she craved the sun on her body.

"Did you go visit the lady in hospital?" Lyra asked.

"The lady?"

"Yes, the lady who had the accident outside our house. You said you were going to visit."

"Did I?" Thea glanced through the rear-view mirror and saw Lyra elbowing Seb in the ribs.

"Ouch." Seb yelped. "What did you do that for?"

Thea looked back again to see Lyra folding her arms across her chest.

"Mum said she was visiting that lady in the hospital, didn't she?"

"I think so." Seb flipped a page in his book and continued reading.

"See, Mum, Seb heard you too."

Thea laughed. "That's because you poked him."

Lyra grinned. "How is she?"

If Thea didn't answer soon, Lyra would go into a sulk. "Her leg is in a plaster cast. The good news is, they'll let her go home as soon as they've fixed up some help for her."

"Poor lady. I hope you cheered her up."

Thea nodded. "As best I could."

"Are you going again?"

Thea shrugged. "Maybe on Thursday."

"Good. What's her name?"

"Emma."

Lyra made a swooning sound. She leaned back into her seat and closed her eyes. "Awesome. There's a new girl at school called Emma; she's so cool. Do you think she'll become your best friend?"

Thea nearly choked. She laughed. "Quinn is my bestie."

"We love Quinn, but you hardly ever see her."

That was true. "Anyway, why are you so interested?"

"You seem lonely. You should have more friends."

"Ha. Have you been talking to Yaya? You sound just like her."

Seb had their grandmother's smile. Lyra had her way with words, and her precociousness often made her sound far older. *Having a weird mother must build character.*

"Well, she's right. You hardly ever go out anymore. You're in a rut. It's time you stopped beating yourself up about the past."

Thea nearly choked and couldn't help but laugh out loud. Those words were definitely right out of her mum's mouth. Of course, they were both right. She *was* in a rut, and she was finding it almost impossible to climb out of it. Her mum was forever making quotes about life, particularly Thea's. "A rut is like a coffin with the ends knocked out," she'd always say.

Thea knew the cause, but she just didn't know the cure. Perhaps doing something different and breaking away from her routine was the answer. It didn't have to be something big.

Strangely, she found herself longing for Thursday. Was it natural to feel excited about meeting someone new? Of course it was, even if the circumstance of their meeting wasn't great. The conversation had flowed, and it'd been so easy to talk to her.

But then, it wasn't like she had a good track record, was it? She felt the car closing in on her and bile rising in her stomach at the thought of Riva. She drank some water, but it didn't take away the bad tang.

Not all her relationships had been bad though. Quinn: her buddy, boss, and true bestie had always been there for her and never asked for anything in return. She laughed. Well, apart from sex, that is. She guessed it wasn't a relationship in the true sense, more of a freelationship, which suited them both. Quinn was already married—not to a woman, but to her job. She was an army lifey, not a wifey. When it had all kicked off with Riva, Quinn had been the one to pick up all the pieces. She'd dropped everything, managed to get leave from the army, and rushed to her side. She helped Thea rebuild her life and start again. They loved each other to bits, but neither wanted anything more than a friendship with benefits.

Wednesday seemed to last more than a week. She found herself wishing that she could spend longer than an hour with Emma, but for the time being, that would have to suffice. It was stupid really because she knew her neighbour Fee would collect her children from school if she asked. Her fear was silly because she only lived next door, but Thea would never forgive herself if something happened to Lyra and Seb.

She parked and went into the M&S food store in the hospital before she went up. Thea glanced through the window into the ward. She didn't want to go in if Emma was busy with nurses. Luckily, nobody was there, and Emma was listening to something on her phone. Thea was pleased she was using the earbuds she'd given her, and it made her feel like she'd done something useful to help.

She had this weird feeling in the pit of her stomach. Was it excitement or fear? Was the attraction scary or awesome fun? She hoped it was the latter, but it was hard to tell. Riva had obliterated Thea's trust in her own instincts.

She pushed the door open and waved.

Emma immediately pulled the earbuds out and moved herself up the bed to a sitting position. "It's so good to see you, Thea. I wasn't sure if you'd make it."

"Wouldn't miss it for the world." Thea bounded over and gave Emma a hug, which she then second-guessed and pulled away from quickly. Were they in a hug stage already? She flushed and put the bag down on the table. "Thought you might like some fresh fruit. I saw these fruit kebabs and couldn't resist."

Emma's eyes widened. "Oh, wow. Those look fabulous. I love fruit. I hope you're going to help me with these?"

Thea shook her head. "No way. I'm sure they'll keep fresh a while. Thought it might make a nice treat after dinner."

"You bet. Thanks so much."

Thea watched Emma put them in her bedside cupboard. The way she moved her body was so graceful, despite her restrictions, and she looked so happy to receive such a small gift. The way she looked even in that hospital gown...gorgeous, captivating, sexy. How could anyone look so hot in what was essentially a paper shawl? Common sense told her that beauty was in the eye of the beholder, and Thea certainly saw beauty. She realised she'd been staring for way too long when Emma began to look uncomfortable. "So how are you? Any news on your escape yet?" She wished she could've come up with something smarter.

Emma grimaced. "I wish. I heard on the grapevine that the physio might be around to see me tomorrow. I'll believe it when I see it. I just hope they don't forget about me."

"I doubt they will." Thea looked around the ward, which was empty apart from Emma's bed. "At least you have the ward to yourself again."

"Only just. Several patients have passed through today, and they tell me I'll have long term company later." Emma shook her head. "I really can't imagine what I'll be landed with next."

Thea frowned. "Let's hope it's somebody who's lucid."

Emma shrugged. "I can only hope." She patted the seat at the side of the bed. "Come and sit down. It's your turn to tell your story."

"Not much to tell really." That wasn't anywhere near the truth, but Thea was nowhere near ready to open up. Her story would have to be selective. Perhaps if she stretched it out and began with her family background, she'd never get to the bits that continued to terrorise her.

Emma tutted. "I don't believe you. Somehow, I get the impression you've led an interesting life. Tell me about your work."

Thea chuckled. "Long story. Shall I begin with my first job?"

Emma rubbed her hands together. "Oh, please. Distract me for as long as you can."

"Brief background. My father is Greek. When he was a young man, he came over to work in the family restaurant, which was owned by his aunt and uncle. He met my mum, who's English. Long story short, they got married and had three children, and I was the last to come along. Mostly, I grew up in Shepherd's Bush, though we'd go visit family in Greece often. When I was a kid, I worked in the taverna along with my two brothers, Christos and Nicholas. I liked being in the kitchen, playing with food and cooking traditional dishes. It was second nature to me. I hated school. I was crap at most subjects. I bolted home every day, back to my haven in the kitchen. When they were old enough, my brothers returned to my grandparents' taverna in Zakynthos." Thea looked directly at Emma, wondering if she was actually interested in her entire family background. "Don't suppose you've ever been there?"

Emma shook her head. "No. I've been to Corfu and Rhodes, and of course, Athens. I have heard of it though. I've always said

I'd like to explore some more of the Greek Islands."

Thea smiled. "You should. It's not that far from Corfu, and it's well worth it." Thea briefly closed her eyes and travelled back in her mind to her beautiful island. She vowed to go back one day for more than a holiday. She opened her eyes. "Anyway, I think I was a bit of a disappointment to my family. They hoped that I'd go to catering college and take over running the restaurant when I was old enough, get married, have loads of kids, and keep it in the family. Instead, I joined the army."

"Oh my God." Emma said laughing. "What on earth possessed you? Not that I'm saying it was a bad choice. It's just so far removed from your haven."

"Well, I can only blame the recruitment officer who came around to our school. I had a massive crush on her and somehow thought I'd impress her by joining up. Of course, I never clapped eyes on her again. Saying that, it wasn't such a bad idea because I wanted to be involved in cooking, so I joined the Royal Logistics Corp as a chef. Well, a trainee. I signed up for four years. After all, what was four years of my life when I was that young? The pay was good, and I thought I'd get to do some travelling too."

"How did your mum and dad react?" Emma asked.

"They went ballistic. Then my mother cried for days. All she could visualise was me in a desert in a tent, somewhere in Afghanistan. Of course, that was always a possibility which I'd largely ignored when I was signing up. Luckily, I spent my time equally between here, Germany, and Cyprus." Thea smiled. "I loved Cyprus. It felt a little like home, and I could speak the lingo too." She laughed. "Not to mention the weather."

"You make it sound like a sanctuary, but you're not still in, are you? Or are you planning to go back?"

Thea tilted her head. "Too old for that. But I did sign up for another four years. It was a good life."

"Bloody unsociable hours by all accounts," Emma said.

"Too true. At first, I didn't think I could hack it. I was always tired and thought I was missing out on socialising. But I got used to it and most of my friends were doing the same. We were all young and had no commitments, so we organised our social life around our job. The army catered for us very well." Thea grinned. "Mostly we had ourselves a ball."

Emma laughed. "I bet you did." She stroked her chin with her fingers. "So why didn't you stay in?"

Thea looked down at her watch. "I'll save that for next time." She leaned back quickly. "That's assuming there will be a next time?"

Emma crossed her arms. "Well, there certainly better be. You don't think you can just leave me in the lurch like this, do you? Unfinished stories are the worst."

Thea smirked. "I knew if I held back the second part, you'd invite me again."

"Ha, very cunning."

Thea picked up her bag and sighed. She really wished she could stay. It had been a long time since she'd felt so relaxed in another woman's company. But she'd been invited back, and that was a big plus. She gave Emma a hug. It lasted a bit longer than the others, and Emma didn't object. If anything, she sensed a kind of intensity and a small bit of desperation in Emma's hold. Thea wanted to kiss her cheek or forehead but decided against it. It was too soon, even for friendship. She pointed at Emma. "If they move you or send you home, be sure to text me, won't you?"

"I promise you'll be the first to know." Emma gave a soft, sad laugh. "Not as though I have anyone else to tell."

Thea frowned. "I'm sorry." She wondered if she could manage a visit sometime over the weekend. She got her phone out and flipped to her calendar. Wouldn't Emma wonder why she didn't have time to herself? Surely her employers would want to spend time with their children over the weekend. She'd better build that into her story. "Normally I have the weekend off, but the children's parents have a business meeting in London. But the kids are going indoor climbing on Sunday with the school. Can I do a short visit then?"

"I'd love that. It'll give me something to look forward to."

Thea's insides glowed warmly. "See you then." She almost skipped out of the ward. The happiness bouncing around inside her right now was off the scale. For once, there was an absence of pain. For once, she was looking forward instead of back.

Why though? It'd been so long since she'd had these feelings that they were hard to accept. And could they last? After all, she wasn't being totally honest with Emma. But protecting her children made that necessary. She'd become such a pessimist over these last few years that she hardly dared believe they could. They never had before.

Chapter Five

EMMA LEANED ON HER elbow and watched Thea leave. She already couldn't wait for her to return. Why did it matter so much? Because she wasn't just a normal visitor; she was special. Emma couldn't qu te put her finger on why, but did there have to be one? That was the person Emma was. Brid constantly told her she over-analysed everything. Emma put it down to her strange upbringing. She was always trying to resolve uncertainty. She sought perfection, but mostly she was trying to avoid mistakes. Maybe because Colly consistently told her she mace bad choices. All it did was give her a bad attack of anxiety. Maybe it was time to stop questioning and start accepting. Well, she could try. There was no doubt in her mind, she really liked Thea and was looking forward to seeing her again.

Bev deliverec her washing bowl and towel. She couldn't manage a shower until her cast was off and even then, Emma wondered if her life would return to normal. She drew the curtains around her even though there were no other patients in the ward. Granted, it wasn't like people were lining up to see a broken, middle-aged woman taking a sponge bath, but still.

Bev tossed the soggy flannel to her. "Great news; you'll be having company very shortly."

Emma winced and gave Bev the death stare. "I can't imagine. So far, apart from you lot, I haven't met anyone near sane." She laughed. "And frankly, I'm not sure about you either." She tossed the flannel towards Bev's head.

Bev laughed out loud and threw the towel back at her. "Just be careful, or I'll lose this one and send Alice back."

"Don't tell me Alice is already back?"

"Yep. She slipped off the loo in her care home and cut her head open."

Emma sighed. "Aww...poor lady. I hope I never get to that point. Getting old with dementia is a horrible thought. I think I'd prefer to be put down." It sounded harsh, but it was true. After watching Brid struggle with her lack of independence, she knew she didn't want to go through the same, ever.

Bev giggled. "That can be arranged if you continue being rude to me."

"Tell me the worst. Who is joining me?"

"A woman. Bit older than you. Multiple fractures." She shrugged.

"A bit more information might help. Like, is she lucid?"

"She's verbal," Bev said.

Emma scowled. "What exactly does that mean?"

Bev pressed her forefinger against her lips. "I've said enough already. I assure you she's mentally sound."

Emma shook her head. "Why don't I believe you?"

Bev drew back the curtains and collected the wet towels. "Because you're incredibly mistrusting. I think you've been in here too long."

"Too bloody true. I may not be a celebrity but someone should get me out of here."

Bev smiled. "The sooner the better. We need your bed."

Emma lurched from meal to meal, but the fairly tasty and varied food was one positive thing about this hospital. It was another warm day, so she chose a turkey salad and followed it up with one of the gorgeous fruit kebabs Thea had brought her. It felt like eating a hug, and she blinked away the stupid tears. Fruit wasn't something to cry over. She was probably just overtired, so she closed her eyes.

Enter her new ward mate. She heard her way before she saw her. A high-pitched voice gave out imperious orders. The woman was wheeled in, and the porter aimed for the bed to the side of Emma.

The woman waved her arms in the air. "No, no, darling, not there. I need a bigger space." She pointed to the bay opposite Emma. "That's much better. If they have to hoist me out, there's much more room.'

Emma could see the sense in that. The woman had her arm in a sling and no doubt other injuries, or she wouldn't be in hospital. She was larger than life, not only in voice but in stature too. Yes, the bay across the way was much more sensible.

They pushed the woman in along with all her belongings. It looked like she was setting up house. Her side table was full to overflowing with fruit, chocolates, biscuits, and juice, as well as a phone and iPad.

In the meantime, her sheet had almost slipped off to expose her. "For heaven's sake, draw the curtain, darling," she shouted to the nurse. "We don't want all and sundry to see my fat arse, do we?" She howled with laughter.

Emma giggled. At least she seemed to have a sense of humour.

The commotion continued behind the curtains with lots of orders and a list of requests. Eventually, the nurse drew the curtains back. The woman sighed loudly, and she held out a hairbrush to the nurse. "Be an angel and just run this through my hair, will you? It's impossible to do it with my arm in this sling."

The nurse, one Emma hadn't seen before, obliged.

She put the brush down on the side cabinet. "Right, Margot. Good luck, and don't forget to obey the physios, okay?"

"Oh, darling, you're not leaving me, are you? Why can't you swap wards?"

The nurse laughed. "Margot, that's not how it works. Anyway, I couldn't possibly deprive the nurses here of all that you offer." She blew a kiss and left.

Margot rearranged her sheets and raised her bed. She gave

a little wave to Emma. "Hello, sweetie. Nice to meet you. My name's Margot Templeton-Smythe, though I do tend to drop the Smythe since my divorce. Bloody bastard ran off with the vet. Her bills were outrageous. She obviously had expensive tastes."

"Hi, Margot. My name's Emma."

"Lovely to meet you, Emma, though the circumstances could be better." She pointed to Emma's leg cast. "Ooh, that looks nasty."

Emma raised her eyebrows. "It could be worse. I came off my bike."

"Motor or push?"

"Push bike. I wish I had got off and pushed instead."

Margot cackled. "You wouldn't get me on one of those things for all the gin in the Netherlands."

Emma doubted if Margot had been anywhere near a bike in her life. She was clearly used to better modes of transport. Margot reminded her of someone, but she couldn't place her. She squeezed her eyes shut, trying to recall. Then it came to her. Yes, yes, it was Hyacinth Bouquet from that old TV comedy. Perhaps louder and larger, but nevertheless, a distinct likeness. "You look like you've been through the wars yourself."

Margot held her hand to her forehead dramatically. "You wouldn't believe it."

Emma was sure she wouldn't, but she was about to hear the story anyway.

"After his lordship got vetted, I had to sell our five-bedroomed house in Axington. You know Axington?"

Emma shook her head. "I've only just moved here from Leeds."

Margot closed her eyes and swooned. "Beautiful village. One of the prettiest and most prestigious. You know that woman who reads the news? Well, she lives there. Anyway, go it must. Couldn't afford to run it, and he wanted his share too. Found this delightful little bungalow in Westleigh, and then at the last sodding moment, it fell through." She jerked her head back.

"Distraught. Virtually homeless, I was. Fortunately, my sister came to the rescue. In hindsight, I'd have been better off in a tent in the middle of the motorway. However, needs must. So off to Della's I went. Dire is the only word that springs to mind. Terrible place. She means well, but—anyway, long story short."

This is the short version? Emma couldn't help but smile. It was good to have the quiet cell filled with some life again.

"First morning, and I took a shower. Well, I say a shower, but it was just one of those make-do things hooked on the wall over the bath. Climbed out but there was bugger all to hang on to. Stupid slippery tiles. So bloody small too. Couldn't swing my effing pussy around, let alone a bloody cat." Margot cackled again. "Lost my footing and toppled, landing arse over tit in a crumpled heap. Bloody forty-nine years old and a cripple."

Emma could picture it and couldn't suppress the laugh that popped out. "Oh dear. That's terrible."

"The pain, sweetie. You can't imagine. Fractured my hip and shoulder. They had to give me a new hip, but they say the shoulder must heal naturally. I really can't fathom how I'm going to cope because—"

"Afternoon, Margot," a nurse said as she came in. "I've come to sort out your medication." She checked Margot's notes at the end of her bed. "Would you like your morphine now or can you wait until later?"

Margot held her shoulder. "Now, please, dear. I'm in agony."

The nurse nodded. "Okay, can you give me your full name and date of birth?"

"Of course. Can you draw the curtains?"

"Sure, if you really want me to." She frowned and drew the curtains. "Name and date of birth?"

"Margot Templeton-Smythe." Margot lowered her voice to a whisper. "Twenty-fifth of August, 1963."

Emma wasn't intentionally listening, but she had incredibly good hearing and couldn't help it. By her calculation, that gave her a full decade over her earlier claim. Emma laughed quietly. Frankly, she couldn't give a damn how old Margot was, but that was typical Hyacinth Bouquet.

The nurse pulled the curtains back.

"Have you heard from Dudley yet?"

"Your brother-in-law?" The nurse scratched her head. "I don't think so."

Margot pointed to her bottle of orange squash. "I can't drink that. I need fresh."

Of course she did. Emma figured she could expect family to do things like that.

"He said he'd bring it in."

The nurse made her way to the door. "I'll check with the nurses' station." She returned quickly, clasping an Asda plastic carrier bag and passed it to Margot. "He left this about half an hour ago."

"Thank you." Margot raised her eyebrows. "Asda! Hasn't he heard of Waitrose?" She removed the contents and placed them on her table. The last item was a small plastic bottle, which she quickly put into her bedside cabinet. "That's worn me out. I'm going to shut my eyes for a while."

It wasn't long before Margot was snoring loudly. Emma thought it was preferable to another round of commentary, at least for the moment. When there was a pause in audible breathing, Emma nodded off, only to be awoken by a rasping, wheezing snore-fest. She looked at her watch. Only another hour until her next feed. Like an animal, meals were the only thing she had to look forward to, apart from seeing Thea, that is.

Over dinner, Margot quizzed Emma about her life. She gave her a brief account, telling her about her marriage to Brid, her bereavement, and how she'd found herself living in Westleigh.

Margot's eyes lit up. "How fascinating, sweetie. Of course, I've met some lesbians in my life, but I've never shared a room with one." She looked positively enthralled.

Emma felt her face redden. "I can assure you, Margot, you're perfectly safe. I've only ever been out with one woman, and she was my wife, and my life."

"Oh, sweetie. I was only joking. Anyway, I'm not averse to a little dabbling."

You won't be dabbling with me. Margot was certainly not her type. Possibly Thea, but never Margot. She wasn't quite sure why she'd added Thea's name to that thought.

The next few days passed by quickly. In between loud naps, Margot imparted her life story. She spared no details, particularly the intimate ones about her ex-husband, Hugo. She'd obviously led a colourful life and loved to share her experiences, unlike Emma, who kept her cards close to her chest. She wasn't the sort of woman who enjoyed discussing her private life. Luckily, Margot did, so they never ran out of conversation.

The physios visited on a regular basis and finally, they supplied Emma with crutches. They weren't as easy to use as she'd imagined, but as soon as the cast was removed, she'd be put into a brace and would be partially weight-bearing. That would make it a little easier. It was all a question of time, they told her. As for Margot, Emma couldn't see a bright future. Try as the physios may, they could hardly get her out of bed. The hoist seemed to aggravate her condition, particularly as she couldn't use her arm to keep her balance. She was obviously in pain, and they gave up. Poor Margot ended up in tears. It was sad to see, but Emma couldn't think of anything positive to say. She'd used up all her positive platitudes during Brid's slow decline.

On Saturday afternoon, Deb the physiotherapist popped her head around the door. "Great news, Emma. Everything's in place, and you'll be discharged on Tuesday. We'll be following you in the ambulance with your appliances."

Emma raised her arms in the air in jubilation. "Fantastic. When you say appliances, what do you mean?"

"An assortment. Perching stools, a trolley to push around, you know, so you can carry your food, etcetera, and a safety rail for your loo. You'll be having intermediate care, which means a team will come in three or four times a day to assist you. Shouldn't be long before we just check up once a day. See you Tuesday."

"Thanks, Deb. What time?"

"Depends on transport. Possibly the afternoon."

When Deb had gone, Emma held her stomach to calm the swarming butterflies. It was happening, and suddenly the fear gripped her. Somehow, being in hospital, as bad as it was, provided security. When she was home, she'd be totally alone.

Margot pouted. "I'm going to miss you, sweetie."

Emma nodded. "Yeah. Me too."

Margot could be irritating, but they'd formed one of those hospital bonds, and it would be lonely without her.

"We should swap phone numbers. Are you on WhatsApp?"

"Of course. Wonderful. We can do video calls."

That wasn't quite what Emma had in mind. She'd been thinking about texting and the odd call. How selfish. Emma was planning on making a speedy recovery, but poor Margot could be stuck in the hospital for weeks, even months. "Absolutely. We can even meet up when you're well again."

"Oh, yes. Let's do that."

That seemed to do the trick, and Margot's mood improved. However, it didn't last long, and Emma's concern grew. Margot didn't touch her lunch and wasn't her normal bubbly self at all. Emma watched her, feeling like something was wrong.

And then it was.

Margot clutched her chest and struggled for breath, her eyes wide with fear. Emma pressed the emergency bell. Nobody came, so she grabbed her crutches, propped the door open, and shouted for help. Two nurses came running and closed the curtains around Margot. Then a doctor followed. Eventually a porter came, and they wheeled her from the ward at full speed. Margot didn't look good, though that could have something to do with the oxygen mask covering her face.

One of the nurses remained to clean up the small mess they'd made in their hurry to help.

"Is she okay?" Emma asked.

"Hopefully." The nurse looked around. "I don't suppose you saw her drinking anything other than the liquids on her tray?"

Emma glanced down at her lap. The last thing she wanted to do was tell tales, but she had seen Margot surreptitiously pouring something into her orange juice. "I think she has a plastic bottle in her bedside cabinet."

The nurse searched through the small cupboard. Margot must have hidden it well, but eventually she found it and sniffed the contents.

"Thanks, Emma," she said and hightailed it towards the door.

Emma felt guilty, but if it was going to help save Margot, it would be stupid to conceal it. She'd thought it was odd when Margot had hidden it. And what would anyone mix with orange juice, other than alcohol? Alcohol and morphine could be fatal, something she'd learned through Brid's illness. How stupid! She reminded herself that she shouldn't make judgement. Margot may seem like a happy, sparkling person, but she didn't *know* her. She didn't know her problems, and she didn't know her life. She prayed that her roommate would recover.

Later that evening, her prayers were answered. Margot returned and didn't seem too bad, though she was a little sheepish. She blew a kiss to Emma then snuggled down under her duvet and quickly went into snoring mode.

Margot slept most of the following day but by lunchtime, she was back to her normal, chirpy self.

Emma had been worried that she might take a downward spiral and breathed a sigh of relief when she woke. "Hell, Margot. You really scared me. Are you okay?"

"Thanks, sweetie, I'm fine now. I think it was a combination of the wrong drugs. Too much morphine and paracetamol."

Emma nodded. The alcohol was none of her business, so she dropped the subject. "Will your sister be visiting today?"

"Oh lordy, lord. One hopes not. N double O C, do you know what I mean?"

Emma frowned and shrugged. She hadn't got a clue.

Margot lowered her voice. "Not of our class, darling."

Emma raised her eyebrows. "But didn't she save you from being homeless?"

"Oh, her heart is in the right place, all right, but I suppose it's all about who you meet in life. More to the point, who you marry! Dudley came from one of those council estates." Margot held her hands up. "Don't get me wrong, I've nothing against them, but he just never made anything of himself. Had a strong aversion to work in his teens and never changed. Bit of a scrounger."

Scrounger or not, they took her in when no one else was stepping up. Not many people would have done that, especially when they were looked down on and treated like second-class citizens. Margot reminded Emma of Colly. All through her early life, Colly lectured her about the people she mixed with. Emma had to lie when she was going out with Jen. Colly despised her because she came from the wrong side of the tracks. How wrong she was. She was always up her own arse, and Emma doubted if she'd ever changed. "Sometimes people don't get the breaks in life, Margot."

Margot wrinkled her nose. "Mm, perhaps I *am* being too harsh." She laughed. "I'll try and be more altruistic in the future."

Emma laughed too. "Yes, give it a whirl, Margot."

"At least we're in the same boat. No visitors for either of us."

Emma looked at her watch. "Well, I may be getting—" There was a rap on the window. Emma looked around and grinned, then she beckoned Thea to come in.

Thea came in and kissed Emma's forehead.

She smiled and tried to ignore the sweet feeling that came from the platonic kiss. "Great to see you, Thea." She pointed across the room. "This is my new friend and roommate, Margot. Margot, this is my friend Thea. Remember, I told you how I was rescued by my good Samaritan."

Margot waved "You're a star, Thea. Lovely to meet you."

"Good to meet you too, Margot." Thea dug around in her bag and pulled out two Magnum ice creams. "Mint or salted caramel?"

Emma licked her lips. "Oh, joy. Mint, please. My dream on a stick."

Thea smiled. "Somehow, I put you down as a minty person." She handed it to Emma and stared down at the other before she walked over to Margot's bed. "Would you like one?"

Margot dramatically placed her hands on her chest. "Oh, darling, how sweet. That would be lovely. Are you sure?" She reached out and grabbed it before Thea could retract her offer.

Thea smiled. "Absolutely. I'll go down and get another." She winked at Emma. "Back in a minute."

"What a lovely girl," Margot said.

Emma tilted her head. "Isn't she just. That was such a lovely gesture."

Thea could have sat down, and they could have both tucked in. She'd never met Margot before.

Thea returned and unwrapped her ice cream. When she bit into it, she somehow made it look seductive. Emma tried to ignore her thoughts and concentrated on her last mouthful of mint chocolate. "That was delicious. And it was really nice of you to give the other one to Margot."

Thea looked surprised. "I suppose that was the way I was brought up. My mum would have killed me if I'd done anything different."

Emma smiled. "Mine too, but thanks anyway."

Thea finished, squidged her stick up into the wrapper and tossed it onto the tray. She leaned forward and used her finger to remove some chocolate from the side of Emma's mouth then left her finger there. "You missed a bit."

Emma laughed and considered licking the chocolate from Thea's finger. Their eyes met. Oh my God, what was she thinking? Her face heated like a furnace.

Thea looked down then put the wrappers in the bin. "Any news yet?"

Back to normal. Though Emma felt anything but normal. "I'll be going home sometime Tuesday."

Thea pouted. "So I won't see you again."

"Why on earth not?" Panic surged through her.

Thea shrugged. "Well, you'll have your carers around and be able to get back to your life."

That was true. She didn't *need* Thea to come around anymore. Was it selfish to wish she'd stick around? "I thought you'd become part of my life. There's no reason why you can't visit me at home... if you want to." Selfish or not, Thea was her only real contact outside these walls. And she genuinely liked her.

Thea raised her arms in the air. "Of course, I bloody do. I wasn't sure if you wanted me to. I mean, I'm just the person who brought you to the hospital."

Emma waggled her finger at Thea. "You don't think you're getting away that easy? In the meantime, I'm waiting for part two of your story."

Thea slumped. "It's so boring. And I can't remember where I left off."

"You were about to tell me why you left the army."

"Ah. So I was." She fidgeted in her seat until she looked comfortable. "It wasn't that I didn't like army life, but when my term came to an end, it would mean I'd have to sign on for another four years. I decided it was time to return to civilian life and see where that took me. I went back to the family restaurant and my flat above it. I'd bought an apartment in Hammersmith, but I'd already let it out."

"Wow, that was quite an achievement."

Thea laughed. "I'll be honest; Army pay is damned good. I hardly spent anything, so I managed to put a hefty sum as a deposit with an affordable mortgage, and the rent covered that easily."

Emma winked. "Very shrewd."

"Thanks, Emma. Not many people acknowledge that."

"Well, I can, because I had to work hard for everything I got."

Thea nodded. "Anyway, I was so much better at cooking, especially for large numbers, so everyone was happy to see me. It was fun, but somehow, I wasn't totally fulfilled." Thea paused and looked over at Margot. "Does she realise she still has her audio book playing at full blast? Surely she can't hear it over her snoring."

Emma raised her eyebrows and chuckled. "I'm sort of used to it now. It is a bit annoying because she does the same late at night. I don't really want to listen to her historical romances, and worse still, the narrator is terrible."

Thea laughed. "Why don't you tell her?"

"I nearly did. Last night she turned the volume up by accident. It made me jump. She said, 'Sorry, were you sleeping?' I wanted to say, 'No, I'm training to die.' But I just smiled. Anyway, I figure she needs it. After all, I'm off home on Tuesday, and I doubt she'll see her home in a very long time. Though I don't think she has one as she's staying with her sister and brother-in-law." Emma lowered her voice to a whisper. "She may be bubbly, but I don't think she's a happy lady. I feel sorry for her."

"You could always take her in."

"No!" Emma winced and lowered her voice. "I don't think so."

Margot stirred and snorted, then her snores continued in a regular rhythm.

Emma and Thea giggled.

"C'mon. Continue."

Thea tutted. 'We mostly had regulars at the taverna. It was that sort of place. You know, homely."

Emma nodded. "I can picture it." From what she knew, food was an integral part of Greek culture. She had fond memories of her time spent in Greek restaurants; there was always a cosy atmosphere, almost as though you were part of the family. The meals seemed to last for hours. Just thinking about it took her back in time and gave her a warm, happy feeling.

"There was an older Greek couple who came in on a regular basis. They were also from Zakynthos, so there was a big connection. They were from the other side of the island, but they were almost like family. My aunt and uncle knew them well and obviously, they'd talked a lot about me to them. Apparently, their daughter and husband were visiting and told us they'd be bringing them next time. They seemed really excited about it. They were a lovely family. Never stopped talking and laughing. When we finished early in the kitchen, we used to join our family in the restaurant and chat to the customers." Thea licked her lips. "This is thirsty work. Do you mind if I help myself to a glass of water?"

"Go ahead. There's a can of Coke in the cupboard if you'd prefer."

Thea shook her head. "Water's fine." She poured herself a glass and took a long gulp. "Long story short, we spent the next few evenings chatting. They asked if I'd join them for coffee on their last evening together. Their daughter and husband were going back home the following day, and they wanted to offer me a job."

Emma sat up straight. "Let me guess. They wanted you to look after their children."

Thea nodded, and an expression flitted across her face before she shook her head and moved on. "Right in one. You see, I love children and although I had some reservations, I agreed to come to Westleigh to meet them all on their home ground. Thing was, they travel all over the world on business. Of course, I fell in love with the children and took the job as a live-in nanny."

"It seems quite a responsibility."

Thea rung her hands together. She seemed rather tense. "I do get time to myself. I know it doesn't look that way, but in school holidays, they spend most of their time with their other grandparents in Greece."

Thea seemed almost defensive, which was strange. There must be more to the story, but Emma wasn't about to push. It wasn't her place. "That all sounds wonderful."

"I guess that's what made it more attractive." Thea seemed to relax a little. "Do you like children?"

Emma shrugged. "They're okay in small doses. It never came up with Brid and me. At her age, it was way too late to think about children. She would've cringed at the thought of being a parent and dropping off her five-year-old at the school gates. Everyone would think she was the grandmother." Emma laughed. "Brid was way too vain for that. Her motto was, 'Life is short. Take the trip, buy the shoes, eat the cake, and drink the champagne.' She certainly lived by that. I never looked back on my childhood as a wonderful experience, and I'm not one to handle deep issues. Of course, I was thirty-five, and I'd worked hard to get my dream. So we never talked about it."

Thea smiled, though it seemed a little forced. Had Emma offended her?

She touched Thea's hand. "Hey, it's great you've found your perfect job. There's nothing wrong with loving children; we're all different."

Thea still looked a bit peeved, though she had no idea why. She checked on her watch. "Jeez. I got carried away. I'm so sorry, I'll have to go. Are you serious about me visiting you at home?"

That was a welcome lifeline. "Of course I am. When can you come?"

Thea checked her mobile. "Is Thursday afternoon any good?"

Emma laughed. "I don't think I'll be going elsewhere. It'll give me something to look forward to."

"Me too. Will you text me your address?"

"You bet. Now off you go, or you'll be late again."

They hugged, and Thea placed another soft kiss on Emma's forehead. It was the most beautiful and tender feeling. It wasn't just comforting, it was caring, something Emma desperately needed. It had been a long time since somebody had made her feel protected. Nothing would come of the budding attraction, of that she was certain. But it felt awfully nice to be the focus of someone's attention after all this time.

Chapter Six

THEA SAT IN HER car and thumped her head on the steering wheel. It was becoming a habit, and she feared she'd end up doing some permanent damage...as if she wasn't damaged enough already.

The lies had flowed so freely. She'd rehearsed her story for Emma beforehand, but nevertheless, it left her with a feeling of deep shame. What had happened to the trusting Thea of old? Riva had happened. Riva and that terrible two years after. She desperately wanted to move on, but the pain and the shock of it all never let up. The vile taste in her mouth reared up. She vowed she'd make it up to Emma one day, if their friendship continued. She'd come clean as soon as she learned to trust again. For now, she did what she felt she needed to in order to keep the kids safe. So be it.

She met her children inside the climbing centre and smiled at one of the kids' teachers.

Seb ran towards her and jumped into her arms. "Mum! It was fantastic. Can we sign up? Please, can we do it again?"

Seb only got this animated when he was talking about one of his favourite books, so she latched onto it. "I don't see why not."

He jumped up and down excitedly. "Cool."

"Where's Lyra?"

He wrinkled his nose. "Talking to some boy she fancies. She says he looks a bit like Hiccup from *How to Train Your Dragon*."

Thea wondered if her daughter saw herself as Astrid. "Oh. Right." She spotted Lyra and beckoned her over. She hugged her daughter. "So, how did it go?"

"It was awesome, Mum."

Seb lurched forward and punched her arm. "It wasn't. You fell off."

Lyra protested. "No, I didn't fall. I lost my footing. It was slippery."

Seb sneered. "You only like it 'cos that Adam likes it. I saw him showing off to you."

"He wasn't showing off. You're only jealous because he's better at it than you."

Seb pouted. "I'm only six. He's nearly nine."

Usually, Seb made a point that he was nearly seven. Obviously, it didn't suit this situation. Apparently, sins of omission were a family trait.

"Well, Adam says he's going to teach me how to climb the big wall. You won't be able to do that because you're only a little boy."

Over my dead body. "I reckon you should progress slowly and see how you like it first."

"I love it, Mum. You ought to come and have a go. There are lots of old people here, and you could join them."

Thea coughed to hide her laugh. Who was the mother here? Anyway, it had been a success. It was a natural thing for kids to love climbing. She remembered how much fun she used to have shimmying up trees when she was young. She loved taking risks. She loved all the make-believe escapades, and she loved competing with the other kids. It built up strength, flexibility, and balance, but above all, it taught kids to mix, bond, and accept help from others. That's what the army had done for her. "We'll see. Maybe later when you get into the course."

"Does that mean we can put our names down?"

Thea put her arms around their shoulders. "Come on. Let's do it now."

Two happy children skipped along beside her with beaming faces. Letting them loose a little was a scary prospect, but she hoped it was good that she was taking a step forward and letting go of a little bit of fear.

They all sat down for a meal, and they told her all about the climbing, schoolwork, and their classmates. As always, they challenged each other and pushed each other's buttons, and Thea gently played referee. It was a school day tomorrow, so she put them to bed early, glad for the silence that would allow her to think about her own life. And about Emma.

Thea poured herself a glass of wine. She took it outside and settled onto a sun lounger after selecting some relaxing music. It was a warm evening and lying by the pool calmed her mind. She closed her eyes and drifted off.

She awoke to the sound of her mobile ringing. It stopped. Had she imagined it? Finally, she sat up after it rang a couple more times. She glanced over and saw it was Quinn. "Hello, stranger."

"No wonder I'm a fucking stranger. You never answer me. I called loadsa times this afternoon."

"Jeez, Quinn, I'm really sorry. I forgot to check for calls."

"Well, you had me worried. Make sure you check in future. Anyway, what's new, kitten? What's captured your attention?"

It had been a while since she'd heard that friendly voice. Thea smiled. Kitten was Quinn's pet name for her. She always said that Thea used her as a scratching post. "I was visiting a friend in hospital."

Quinn sniggered. "Friend? Since when do you have friends... apart from me, that is?"

"Since a stunning woman crashed her bike onto my driveway."

Quinn laughed. "Tell me more."

Thea filled her in on the events of the last couple of weeks.

"Wow. You're moving along. I'm proud of you."

Thea shook her head. "No. I've done something bloody stupid." She added in the bit about the lies she'd told.

"You're a fuckin' idiot, Thea. I take it you've got the hots for her."

"I mean, I think so. She's good looking and has a wicked sense of humour. But she's also been in hospital, and it's not exactly a great time to hit on someone, is it?"

"She sounds normal and nice. You've got to tell her the truth and see where it goes."

"I know, I know." Thea sighed. "But she doesn't like children."

"Uh? What do you mean?"

"I asked her. It's important to me that Emma understands how I love my children. They're the most important thing in my life."

"But it was hypothetical. She didn't know they were *your* kids."

"Yeah, but that doesn't change anything. I wouldn't want her pretending to like my kids just to spend time with me. This way, I know she doesn't like them, and that means there can't be a romantic future."

"Aargh!" Quinn's tone suggested a definite eye roll would be in progress. "You're not giving her a chance. Listen, Thea. Nice women don't come along too often. If you're interested in her, then you should keep the door open. Maybe she'll change her mind."

Thea sniffed. She didn't answer but knew Quinn was right. She just hated to admit it.

"Are you still there?" Quinn asked.

"Yes, I was thinking. I'll come clean when I next see her."

"And when might that be?"

Thea grabbed a cushion and groaned into it. She was glad Quinn hadn't insisted on a video call. She dropped the cushion. "Thursday."

"Make sure you're honest."

Thea raised her eyebrows at Quinn's imperious tone. "Yeah, I will." She cleared her throat. "So, what's happening with you, babe?"

"Much of the same. It's gonna be a busy week. I'm cooking for some VIPs at a state ceremony next weekend," Quinn said. "I've been offered another posting in Cyprus."

Thea rubbed her fingers across her lips. The thought of Quinn being so far away scared her. "That's terrific." She wished she'd put some more enthusiasm in those words.

"Hey, you can get on a plane and be with me in four hours."

Thea rocked back and forth on the lounger. "I might just do that."

Quinn laughed. "No, you won't. You're too hooked up on your new girlfriend."

"I'm not. I hardly know her. Jeez, Quinn, I wish you were here right now."

Quinn growled. "Sex cures all. We could always swap to video."

Thea wasn't sure if she wanted to do that. Normally, she'd jump at the suggestion, but not this time. "We could, but —"

Quinn laughed. "I know you well, kitten. That's a definite refusal."

"I'm sorry. It's not that I don't want you."

"For fuck's sake, don't say sorry. We've always had a freelationship. You need something more than that. Something more permanent. Shame, 'cos I'm sure as hell horny." Quinn laughed. "Shit. I was due to meet the guys in the bar. Best go before I talk you into it."

Thea tilted her head. "Thanks, babe, and thanks for listening. Go have one for me. I mean the drink, not a hookup."

"Lighten up, Thea." Quinn's tone softened. "Your girl will understand. Be honest with yourself and with her. You deserve to be happy."

Thea nodded. "I will. I promise." She was full of good intentions, so why did she doubt herself? Because letting people in causes chaos, and chaos leads to heartbreak.

"We'll talk before I go."

"Go where?" Thea asked, confused.

"Cyprus. Remember that conversation?"

"So, it's imminent then?"

"Yep. Next month."

Thea slumped. "That's too soon."

"Honey, it's Cyprus, not the back of beyond. It has internet. It's the same as being in the UK."

"You're right." Thea chuckled. "I'll keep you posted. Kisses, babe."

Quinn made the sound of blowing a big kiss and hung up.

Could she really cope without Quinn? She'd have to learn. It wasn't like her days weren't full, and Quinn wasn't around all the time anyway. It was just the idea of being alone that made her shudder. But she'd be fine. She was always fine.

The next few days dragged by, and Thursday drew closer too slowly. She busied herself with paperwork and booking some flights to Zakynthos. They weren't cheap because of the school holidays, but money wasn't an issue. She'd just finished when she received a text.

Got home late last night. What an ordeal. Comfortable and enjoying being waited on by my carers...NOT! Address: 7 Montgomery Court, 120 Deen Road, Westleigh, WL16 3RA. Press the intercom and I'll let you in. Looking forward to seeing you. Emma xx

Me too. See you about 2pm xx

So Emma hadn't changed her mind. No matter what happened between them, she could have a friend—as long as she was honest with her. And soon.

Thea got up bright and early on Thursday morning. The sun was shining, and she felt refreshed and happy. That was quite a novelty. She jumped in the shower and she let the warm water cascade over her body longer than usual as she thought of Emma's laugh and the way her arms had felt around her. Before she could take that visual any further, she turned the water to cold, dousing the embers so they didn't turn into more. She got dressed and hammered on Lyra and Seb's doors. "Come on, you lot. You're not going to school without breakfast."

Both of them moaned. She put some music on and sang along with Pink.

Lyra sat on a barstool and narrowed her eyes. "Somebody's happy today. Have you won the lottery?"

Thea laughed. "I hope not. We'd have to pick yet another charity to patronise."

Lyra tapped her fingers on the worktop. "There are lots of poor people around. My teacher said they're homeless, and they have to sleep in doorways, and under bridges, and stuff. Can we send them something for Christmas?"

"I know. We'll do something before Christmas."

"So why are you chirpier than usual?"

Here we go again. There was no point in keeping it from them. Seb joined them and grabbed a banana, which he passed to his mum. She chopped it up and added it to his cereal. "I'm going to see Emma today. She's just come out of hospital, and I think she still needs a friend."

Lyra looked up from her cereal. "Are we ever going to meet her soon?"

Thea considered the question. "Yes, of course. When you come back from your holidays with Yaya and Papou."

Lyra and Seb spent their summer holidays with their grandmother and grandfather, along with the rest of the family.

"You are staying with us, aren't you, Mummy?" Seb asked.

"For two weeks. Then the same when I pick you up."

"Cool," Seb said.

Lyra tucked into her cereal. "Will you hang out with Emma while we're gone?"

"Don't speak with your mouth full, Lyra. And wipe that milk from your chin."

Lyra wiped away the milk with a wadded-up napkin. "Will you?"

Thea spread her arms out. "I have no idea." She looked up at the clock. "Come on, get your stuff ready, and let's get off to school." That seemed to stem the questions, though there were the usual huffs and groans as they left.

Thea punched in Emma's address on the sat nav to find it was ten minutes away; nothing was very far in Westleigh. Although it was technically a town, it was more like a large village. She decided to stop off at Deli Kaz, a few minutes away from Emma's, where she picked up two coffees and an assortment of Danish pastries. There was nothing wrong with taking food to a friend, she repeated to herself as she worried over what Emma might like.

Emma buzzed her in at the front door of the building, and she made her way to Emma's apartment. It took a few minutes before the door opened.

Emma gave her a broad smile. "Hey you. Come on in."

Thea wanted to greet her with a hug, but Emma was hobbling on her crutches, and knowing her, she'd end up knocking her over.

Emma leaned her crutches by the side of her chair and flopped down. "Sorry, I still haven't got the hang of these yet, and it's exhausting trying to figure them out. It's so good to see you. Take a seat."

Thea put her stash down on the small table beside Emma. "Coffee and cakes."

"You little gem. That's just what I need. I'm fed up with endless cups of tea and salads, which is apparently all my care workers seem to know how to make."

Thea gave Emma a hug and lightly kissed her cheek. "You look different."

Emma wore a pair of shorts with a white T-shirt. They hugged her curves, and Thea had to pry her eyes away from Emma's breasts. The hospital gown hadn't done her justice at all, although Thea remembered how beautiful she looked even in that loose get-up. Her hair was combed, showing just the slightest bit of grey around the temples, and her eyes were bright.

Emma laughed. "So, hospital gowns don't do it for you?"

"Err...well, let's just say you look a hell of a lot better in that outfit." Even if Emma was wearing a frogman's outfit, she'd still fancy her. Mind you, rubber always had been a turn-on. Quickly, she batted that thought away. Thea wanted to say so much, but this was Emma's territory, and she suddenly wasn't sure how to start. "Pastries. We need plates, otherwise there'll be crumbs all over."

Emma pointed to a door behind her. "Kitchen's in there, if you don't mind. Plates are in the cupboard, and the kitchen roll is near the microwave."

It was a lovely little kitchen. Everything was orderly, just as Thea had imagined. With two kids in the house, hers wasn't nearly as clean and organized. She found what she needed and put two pastries on each plate. "I hope you like white coffee. Do you need sugar? I doubt it, you're sweet enough." *Oh my God. What a crap line.* She'd never ever said that to anyone before. What on earth had come over her?

Emma smiled. "As it comes, thanks."

She prayed she'd not come out with any other shite and sat down opposite Emma with her coffee and cakes. "How's it going? And don't hold back."

By that time, Emma had a mouthful of pastry. She covered her mouth with her hand, until she'd finished eating. "Sorry, I must look like a gannet. The carers did my shopping, and all I've eaten so far are microwave meals, bananas, and leaves of some description." She pressed her finger on the plate and captured some crumbs. "I've been craving some decent coffee and calories."

Thea stood. "Do you want me to go and do some shopping for you?"

"Thanks, but no thanks. I've done an online order, and it'll be here tomorrow."

Whilst Thea was up, she looked around. "You have a cool apartment. It's so cosy."

Emma laughed. "That's the word I use too, plus bijou. Brid would say it was like a rabbit hutch."

"No way. It's beautiful." Thea glanced at a picture on the wall. "Is that your wife?"

"Yes, but it's not a great one. We were on holiday, and I think she was drunk."

Thea stepped closer to the picture. "She looks like a fun person."

"Absolutely. She loved life."

What must it be like for someone to talk about you with that kind of love in their voice? The thought brought a lump to Thea's throat. She glanced down at the photos on the sideboard. Should she ask about those or would Emma think she was a nosy bitch?

"It's okay. You can look at them. I don't have many, but that's my mum, dad, and sister."

Thea chewed one of her nails. She wanted to ask questions, but everything seemed so personal.

"My mum and dad aren't around anymore. They died in a car crash when I was thirteen." Emma chuckled softly. "Don't get too worried; not everybody dies when they meet me."

"What about your sister?" she asked, hoping there wasn't a tragic story connected to her too.

"She's definitely alive...as far as I know."

"I'm so sorry about your mum and dad. I can't imagine growing up without parents." Thea sat back down. "If you don't want to talk about it, I'll understand."

"It was over forty years ago. I've come to terms with it, but you're right, it was hell at the time. I was brought up by my sister, Colly. She's seven years older than me. She was training to be a nurse in London when it happened. Not being able to finish that possibly contributed to her not liking me, although we'd never bonded even before our parents died. I guess seven years is quite a gap when you're growing up."

Thea frowned. "I'm sure it was. There are only a few years between me and my two brothers. We had a great relationship, but they were always overprotective."

"I wish. I suppose she could have let the social services take me into care, but she was getting half an inheritance and half the house when she was twenty-one. Same with me. When she reached twenty-one, she was allowed to sell the house, and she bought a smaller place with her share. Mine went into a Trust." Emma laughed. "She charged me rent though."

"Bloody hell. Who charges a fourteen-year-old kid rent? Is that even legal?"

"No, but I didn't know that at the time. I hardly got any allowance either. She was so tight with the purse strings. She seemed to punish me for everything bad that had happened. I really suffered through school. I had lots of emotional problems, and nobody seemed to take them on board. Consequently, I left school with no qualifications whatsoever."

"Jeez. Wasn't there any counselling?"

"If there was, my sister blocked it. I was too messed up to question anything. Even at our parents' funeral, she never hugged me. One hug would have made so much difference." Emma smiled, her expression wistful. "Anyway, I survived, and life wasn't always unhappy. My bestie through school was Jen, and that friendship continued despite Colly's protestations. She said I shouldn't mix with her because she came from the wrong side of the tracks."

"How cruel. She sounds like a real cow."

Emma giggled. "She was. She nearly flipped when Jen and I got a job stacking shelves in Tesco. As soon as we'd saved a bit of money, we moved into a small flat together."

"That's brilliant. I take it you didn't pursue a career with Tesco?"

"Ha ha. No, I had a dream." Emma took a sip of her coffee.

"That must be cold. Shall I pop it in the microwave?"

"Thanks, but I often drink tea and coffee cold."

Thea sat on the edge of her chair. "So, c'mon, what happened next?"

"Jen and I never had any spare cash, so we bought all our

clothes from charity shops. We were both pretty good at making alterations, adding something quirky and making them unique. And that was my dream."

"What, you mean a clothes designer?"

Emma roared with laughter. "No. I wasn't that clever. I saw a niche in the market. Skiwear was so expensive, and so were golfing clothes. So I thought, why not open a nearly new shop specialising in those? That way, we could also have some designer clothes... In fact, we could sell anything we wanted. We ended up with handbags, jewellery, watches. Before we got up and running, we did a lot of buying from car boots and fairs. One day, I bought what I thought was a copy watch for fifty pence. We took it to jewellers and discovered it was a real Rolex. We sold it for seed money."

"Wow, that doesn't happen every day."

"No, but it didn't stop us from hunting for that kind of miracle to happen again. We looked around for premises, and as soon as I hit twenty-one, we began our venture. We called it Second 2 None. It was amazing how many people wanted to get rid of stuff. Loads of people take up a hobby and then pack it in, or they want to start something but can't afford to. It just grew and grew, and we bought our second shop. We ended up with five. Then there was the advent of the internet, and we decided to try our luck with a website."

"That's an amazing story, Emma. What's happened to all that now that you're here?"

Emma looked down at her hands. "When Brid died, I lost all interest and decided to retire. We kept two shops and our web business, all of which Jen runs now. We also have some great employees."

"Sounds like she's the best thing since cookies. Does she have time for a personal life too?"

"Yes, she lives with a guy called Steve. I vaguely remember him from our school days. He's a few years older than us." Emma laughed. "It's funny. He's retired from the police, and we spent so many years running from them. Once, we got caught for stealing a cotton reel. Anyway, now he's her soul mate. He has his interests, and she has hers, and it really works."

"Lucky Jen. That's quite a story. You should be proud of yourself."

Emma laughed. "It's just another rags-to-riches story, I guess. But it feels good to have done it."

Thea wished she'd made her fortune on her own, instead of winning the lottery. "Was Colly proud of you? Or did she resent your success?"

"The latter. She didn't like to be proved wrong. She always said I wouldn't amount to anything."

Thea tilted her head. "Do you still see her?"

"I'm afraid that's another story."

"I have time. The children have a swimming class after school."

"It's a bit one-sided and boring. I haven't stopped talking. Your life must be more interesting."

"You're joking," Thea said. "I want to know everything about you." Because the more she knew, the more she could trust Emma. The more she heard, the more she liked. Emma was genuine, a hard worker, and had made something of herself despite terrible circumstances. There was an awful lot to admire.

Emma chuckled. "Well, the next stage is quite amusing, but I need some liquid refreshment first. Would you mind, Thea? I'd love a Coke. There are some cans in the fridge."

Thea returned with two cans, and Emma took a gulp.

"Okay. Colly qualified as a nurse and climbed the ladder in the NHS in Leeds. She married, but it didn't last. Surprise, surprise. She'd been plagued with fibroids and ended up having a hysterectomy. We were still on speaking terms twenty years ago, so I visited her in hospital. It was unbelievable. She seemed so happy and full of life. I'd never seen her like that before, and it blew my mind. At first, I thought it was the relief of the operation, but I was wrong. It was to do with the person in the next bed. And that was Brid."

Thea clasped her hand over her mouth. "No way."

"She was laughing, joking, and to be honest, it was a new Colly. Brid was in for the same operation but for different reasons. Brid and I hit it off too. To be honest, I wouldn't have visited again, but I have to say I was drawn to Brid. We all got on so well and had some good laughs. Colly came out of hospital, and I thought I might see Brid again as the two of them were going to get together. I was invited around once. I thought that was it, and I'd never see her again."

"Colly wanted to keep her newfound friend to herself?"

"Yep. But I got a massive shock when Brid turned up in the shop. She asked me for dinner, and that was that."

Thea frowned. "I can't imagine Colly was thrilled about that."

"No. When she found out, she never spoke to either of us again. Never. I tried to reason with her. I couldn't see why the three of us couldn't be friends. I contacted her when Brid died, but she didn't reply."

"Jealousy is an ugly thing."

Emma looked sad. "I thought it might bring us together." She perked up. "But that's the past. I can't change it, so I moved on."

Thea nodded. It was high time she moved on too. No time like the present. She cleared her throat. "Emma, I have something to tell you. You may not be very happy with me when I confess, but I really—"

Emma's mobile rang, and she glanced at it. "I'm sorry, Thea, I have to take this; it's the physio."

Thea nodded and wandered out onto the patio to give her some privacy. *Typical.* Could she now go back in and start again, or should she take this as being saved by the bell? She glanced at her watch for the umpteenth time. Fifteen minutes had passed, and it was getting close to her leaving to pick Lyra and Seb up.

Emma called out for her to come back in.

"I'm so sorry about that. She wants to start my program but needed to go through some exercises for me to do before she gets here. She's sent some videos through, but it took forever." Emma laughed. "Anyway, come and finish your confession."

Too late. There was no way she could tell her everything and just leave. However, she did have to tell Emma about her forthcoming trip. "It's the school holidays soon, so I'm taking Lyra and Seb to be with their grandparents in Zakynthos. Then I'll spend some time with my mum, dad, and brothers...and all my other relatives."

"That'll be lovely," Emma said, her tone flat.

"I'm only going for two weeks, then I'll be back. It's not that long really, and I can't wait to see them all. It's been a long time since I was there."

"Lucky you. It must be so exciting. I'm sure I can cope without seeing you for a few weeks." Emma laughed. "Was that it then? I thought you were going to tell me you were married or something." Emma coughed. "Not as though that would affect our friendship."

It bloody would. What she *was* going to tell Emma was infinitely worse. Thea smiled. "No. I'm not opposed to it, but I've never met the right woman."

Emma tilted her head. "To be honest, you never actually said if you were a lesbian. I think I kind of just guessed."

"It didn't seem necessary." Thea chuckled and held up her hand. "I'm really into k.d. lang and Jodie Foster, and I watch re-runs of Ellen most nights. My favourite singer is Pink, and I really fancy her." She ticked the items off on her fingers as though it was a checklist to prove her gayness.

Emma burst out laughing. "I love Pink too. I'd love to go to one of her concerts."

Thea bounced in her seat. "Hey, that's something we could do when you're up and running." That sounded very much like an offer of a date, but Emma didn't even blink.

"Now that's something to spur me on. Brid wasn't a big fan. Anyway, when are you off?"

"The end of the week. I don't think I'll be able to see you before that. There's so much to prepare." Thea tried not to feel overwhelmed at the very thought of it.

Emma smiled. "It'll fly by. Hopefully by the time you get back, I'll be in a brace instead of this bloody thing," she said, pointing to her cast.

"So you'll be making a full recovery?"

Emma laughed. "I don't think I'll be on my bike, but they do say I'll be able to walk a little with crutches soon."

"Great. I'll be able to take you out. There's so much beautiful countryside to see nearby. We can go for some picnics."

Emma beamed. "Now you're talking." She paused. "In the meantime, much as I hate to lose your company, you're going to be late for the children."

Thea frowned. "You're right. I'd best be on my way." She stood and pointed at Emma when she looked like she might get up. "You stay put. I can see myself out." She collected the debris and took it to the kitchen.

"Just shove the plates in the dishwasher. It's to the right of the sink."

Thea did as instructed, feeling a little strange about moving through Emma's place with such ease. Their relationship seemed to have moved to another level. The openness of saying she was also a lesbian cleared that path, and there was something...a thread, a current, that was pulling her closer to Emma.

Thea leaned down to give her a hug. Her heart was pounding in her chest loud enough for the world to hear. Emma gazed back at Thea, her eyes holding what looked like a mixture of nervousness and desire, mirroring Thea's own emotions. Time slowed as Thea moved closer, unable to resist temptation. She cupped Emma's chin as she edged nearer and felt the warmth of Emma's breath on her mouth. Their eyes closed, and their lips met. It was like a dance, gentle and yet filled with passion. The world disappeared into oblivion. Time seemed to stand still, and the world around them faded away into a soft blur. The soft touch of Emma's lips ignited a spark, sending shivers down Thea's spine with an enchanting blend of tenderness and passion that left her breathless. As she pulled away, they both smiled. The simpl city of their first unforgettable kiss was a moment of pure magic.

Thea had kissed many women in her life. Usually, it was more of a snog, and it ended up in a marathon of sex. But this was the most beautiful and sensual kiss she'd ever experienced. She wanted more, but common sense got the better of her, and she eased back.

Emma squinted. "Go, or you'll get the sack."

Thea grinned and fluttered her eyelids. "Well..."

Emma laughed. " don't mean that sack—not yet anyway."

Thea couldn't think of anything else to say. She blew a kiss to Emma and left. She had no idea what she was doing, but damn, did it feel good to be doing it.

Chapter Seven

EMMA LEANED BACK IN her chair, closed her eyes and sighed. *Wow! That was unexpected.* The kiss left her with a feeling of floating on air. A combination of lightness and happiness, but most of all, freedom. She was unsure of the last one. Perhaps it was a sign of moving on. Her mind whirled with so many questions. All she knew was that kiss had been unbelievably wonderful, a rediscovery of emotion she'd locked away in a box. Sure, she'd been thinking almost non-stop of Thea, and some of those thoughts had turned the corner into fantasy, but she'd managed to convince herself it was one-sided, and that Thea was firmly positioned in the friend zone. But that kiss...

A voice in the back of her mind told her not to get carried away. Ha. That wasn't an issue. Thea was literally flying away. Maybe that was for the best. It would give her a chance to gather her thoughts. Yes, it was only a kiss, but that was usually the beginning of something more meaningful. She wasn't sure if she was ready for another relationship. She'd never imagined anyone could follow after Brid. She'd been her one and only. Brid's voice whispered, *Give her a chance.*

Later that evening, her phone rang. Her heart skipped several beats when she saw who it was. "Hi, Thea."

"Hey. I couldn't let that kiss go without saying anything. Are you okay?"

There was a hint of apprehension in her voice.

Emma chuckled. "Of course I'm okay. It took me a while to recover." She paused. "It was quite unexpected."

"Good unexpected? Or did I scare the shit out of you?"

"No to the latter. It was unexpected in a good way. A *very* good way."

"Phew." Thea sighed heavily. "I'd been wanting to do that for quite a while."

"Really?"

"Really. Getting to know you in the hospital was really nice. I mean, not nice that you were in the hospital. Oh, you know what I mean."

Emma took a deep breath. "The kiss was perfect. I didn't expect it, but I'm certainly not complaining."

Thea breathed out noisily again. "Good. I'm glad it happened. I guess we've crossed that 'friends' line now. How do you feel about that?"

"I'm happy with it. I guess we take it as it comes."

"Good. That's how I feel," Thea said. "It's a shame I'm going away. That's bad timing on my part."

"It is, but I'm going to be pre-occupied with physio for a while. I'm determined to get this bloody leg right again."

Thea laughed. "It's a beautiful leg."

"How do you know? You've only seen it in a cast." It had been a long, long time since she'd enjoyed flirty banter. Was she even doing it right?

"I saw it before that, though I wasn't looking at it in that way." Thea laughed. "Anyway, that beautiful, problematic leg brought us together."

Emma laughed. "I wish we'd found another way. It seems a bit of a drastic way to find a love interest."

"True, but at least you saw my Samaritan potential." Thea shouted something away from the phone. "I'm sorry, Emma. It's the children's bedtime. I have to go. I needed to talk to you though, to make sure we're good. And because I wanted to hear your voice."

"I'm pleased you did. Otherwise, I might have thought I'd dreamt it. Now off you go and do your duties." She'd have been happy to talk to Thea on the phone all night, like a teenager with a first crush. But they were both far from lovestruck teens.

"Thanks. It's going to be a busy week. I'll call you from Zakynthos, if that's okay."

"I'll look forward to it. Safe journey and speak soon." Emma hung up. She smiled at the prospect of things to come.

***

Emma thought the next few weeks would drag, but she was wrong. They flew by like a rocket. Her physiotherapy plan had begun, making her think she'd died and been dropped into Hell. She'd thought the break itself was painful, but it was nothing compared to what the physio was putting her through. She'd opted to go to therapy at the hospital, so twice a week, transport collected and delivered her to the unit. She thought it would be a good way to get out of the flat for a few hours a day, but she grew to dread the trip to the torturous unit. On her days off, she'd finish one set of exercises, have something to eat, then begin again, and that continued throughout the day. By the evening, she was popping painkillers like jelly babies.

The more she exercised, the more she questioned how strong her bones were. Would there be a weakness in her leg and would it fracture again? They assured her that bones repair themselves. Nobody fully understood it, because it was way too complex. The self-repair was spontaneous, natural, and sought no direction from the individual. She was told that as long as she pushed the physio to its limits, she'd make a good recovery.

Emma took them at their word and became their star pupil. There was no question that having the prospect of dates with Thea spurred her forward. She was quite apprehensive about their age difference, and she definitely wanted to be in shape to keep up with someone so much younger than her. She'd never really given the age gap between her and Brid a thought. Brid certainly hadn't; she'd been way too vain to give it a second thought.

Thea rang her most evenings. She sounded upbeat and was obviously having a fabulous time with her family. It was a busy time of the year, so she was helping out in the kitchen most evenings. Even though she was shattered, she always found time to ring. At a time in her life when Emma had felt so very alone, Thea made her feel like she wasn't totally lost in the world, and those calls kept her grounded in a way she didn't know was possible.

The crucial day of her follow-up appointment at the hospital to determine the next stage of her recovery arrived. If she could've paced the room, she would have. Instead, she hopped up and down the hall on her crutches. She was usually a patient person, but she was eager to get these results. She wore herself out and sat back down, looking at her watch and wondering if her transport would arrive on time. God, if they were late, she'd miss her appointment and have to wait for another month.

Her intercom buzzed, and she pressed the button to open the main door. Nobody arrived, and she began to panic. She slung her rucksack on her back and opened her door. That wasn't easy, because it was a fire door and sprang back, nearly knocking her flying.

A transport driver rushed down the corridor. "Sorry, my lovely. I'm new to this building and took a wrong turn," she said with a clipped accent.

Emma forced a smile. "It's okay. I hope we're not going to be late."

"Nah. I'll have you there in no time," she said and took Emma's rucksack from her. She roared with laughter. "Bloody hell, are you taking bricks to the hospital? I know it's a bit dilapidated, but there is a limit."

"It's just my lunch, water, and other bits. You may laugh, but I sometimes don't get collected for hours."

"I'll make sure we get you booked on my list. I'll come and

collect you personally, my lovely."

Emma smiled. "I'd really appreciate that. Thank you."

The trip was short but not sweet. It was a wonderful service, yes, but hospital transport was not built for comfort, and the bus lacked sufficient suspension. She held her leg firmly between her hands as the ambulance bounced up and down and from side to side. She prayed that her cast would survive the journey and not arrive in pieces. However, she did get there way before her appointment. Her driver, Giselle from Romania, wheeled her up to X-ray, booked her in and assured her she'd collect her later.

No one at the X-ray department gave her any information; they didn't say if her leg had disappeared in the cast or whether there was no hope. She opened a magazine but didn't see a word of it as she waited in the waiting room for the physician. What if the outcome was bad? What if she had to put up with carers for the rest of her life? What about her future plans? What if, what if, what if? She looked at the people sitting around her. Nobody understood what she was going through, but she had no idea about their problems either. Allowing herself to get maudlin and self-pitying wasn't okay.

She looked up when they called her name and headed down the hall to get the decision.

Later that evening, the phone rang. "I was getting worried. I rang earlier, but you didn't pick up. It's so busy here, and I've been rushed off my feet. Come on, tell me, how did it go?"

"I've got rid of my cast at last." Emma tapped her new leg brace.

"That's fantastic. So what happened? What's the verdict?"

"I am now the proud owner of a super-duper leg brace. It has this little dial on the knee which controls the degrees of bend in my leg. The bone is healing nicely, better than expected actually."

"Yay! That's brilliant news. Are you weight-bearing now?"

"Not totally, but if I keep up my rigorous exercise, it won't be long. I have my next appointment in three weeks. I phoned my physio when I got in, and she's going to try and get me into hydrotherapy. It'll really speed up the recovery time. I guess that's my reward."

"That's all brilliant. I bet it's a lot to take in."

"It is, but it's all good news." She couldn't really express how good it felt to have someone care about her and celebrate this small victory with her. That would have been too intense to say out loud anyway.

Thea didn't respond for a few moments. "I've missed you."

Emma laughed. "In between all my suffering, I've missed you too." She thought about asking Thea when she was returning but didn't want to sound too pushy.

"I'm back on Sunday. Do you fancy that picnic?"

"God, yes. I can't wait to get out into the fresh air. I'd offer to prepare something but—"

"No way. I can get some stuff on the way back from the airport. I'll pick you up about twelve thirty. Is that okay?"

"Magic. I'll see you then."

"Best go, I can see my mum approaching, I think she's going to give me the third degree." Thea laughed. "They keep asking who I'm speaking to each night, and I won't tell them. Mostly just to mess with them."

"Well, good luck and see you Monday. Safe journey." Emma sat with her thoughts, trying to parse out her emotions. Would Thea tell her mum about them? Or was it too early? Surely a single kiss and some phone calls didn't warrant telling Thea's family about her. She wasn't sure what she would do in the same situation, but she did wish she had a mum to confide in. It would have been nice to share it with her sister, but that was out of the question. The only person she could tell was Jen, but she hadn't even told her about the accident, let alone meeting a woman. Jen needed her vacation. And there was no rush. It was early days, and nothing might come of it anyway. What did she have to offer a woman like Thea? A broken leg, a tiny flat, no friends, and no business. She wasn't exactly a catch. Thea's interest might wane like the moon after a week of more time together.

It had become one of those rare summers when every day was bright and warm and Monday was no exception. Emma was up early, not only because of the prospect of seeing Thea again, but mainly due to the time it took to get ready. Her carers were down to two a day now: a morning carer to help her in and out of the shower, and one later to check if she needed any help with a meal or carrying anything around. As soon as she'd had her shower safely, her carer helped her find some clothes to wear.

Petra, her regular morning visitor, opened the wardrobe door. "What do we fancy today then? Something to impress?"

"Bloody hell, Petra, I'm only going for a picnic with my friend."

"Ha. Methinks your picnic date is special. You get a dreamy look on your face every time you talk about her."

Emma waved her arms. "Just give me anything; it doesn't really matter."

Petra removed a pair of scruffy denim shorts from the wardrobe and held them up. "These okay?"

"Stop teasing and give me the light blue shorts and the white T-shirt, please."

Petra obeyed and laid them on the bed. "I can tell you want me to piss off, so I'll leave you to make yourself pretty." She laughed. "I might see you later for a report. Otherwise, I'll have to wait until tomorrow." She waved and took her leave.

Emma dressed and was satisfied she looked presentable. She packed a small rucksack with a light jacket and her water bottle. She was ready an hour before, so she picked up a book and sat down to read, though it was hard to settle.

At twelve thirty, anxiety began to sneak in. That was the right time, wasn't it? Five minutes passed. Emma fidgeted with her phone, stealing glances every few seconds in case Thea had texted her. She checked her intercom phone to see if it was working okay. The seconds seemed to stretch into minutes as she waited for Thea to arrive. Was this a date? Whatever it was, Thea was late. Doubt gnawed at her. What if she hadn't come back from Zakynthos for some reason or other? Emma's life seemed to be filled with what ifs, and Thea seemed to be one of the bigger ones right now.

She sipped her cold coffee, though it did little to soothe her nervous energy. She glanced at her watch again. Maybe she'd misunderstood, and she was supposed to meet Thea in the lounge. Perhaps she was just running late. Maybe something had come up.

The intercom buzzed, and Emma jerked, sending her phone flying across the floor. It took her several precious minutes to retrieve it. She finally got to the intercom to let Thea in.

The doorbell rang a few moments later. "Come in, it's open," Emma said, her heart racing.

And there she was, large as life.

Thea rushed over, gave her a great big hug and kissed her cheek. "Sorry I'm late. I wanted to pick up some fresh pastries, but there was a hell of a queue."

"No problem. I hadn't really noticed." Small fibs like that were okay, weren't they? "Wow, you look amazing. What a tan." What she really wanted to say was how terrific her body looked in her white shorts and tank top, but it gave her an excuse to stare a little longer.

Thea nodded. "I only have to look at the sun, and I go dark."

It was funny how Thea had the ability to dissolve all her tension. It wasn't something new; she'd felt it right from the beginning.

Thea glanced at her brace. "Hey, that looks cool."

"Huh. I suppose it's better than the cast, and it's quite comfortable, considering."

Thea laughed. "I reckon you could start a trend, although not many people could look so sexy in a leg brace."

Emma's cheeks burned. "I don't know about that. I don't think I've ever seen myself as sexy in anything."

Thea's eyes widened. "Trust me, you do."

If anybody else had said that, Emma would've felt incredibly awkward, but Thea had a natural knack that made her feel at ease. The shared laughter and connection were still there and would make for an interesting first date, if that's what it was. "So where are you taking me?"

Thea crossed her arms. "It's a surprise. You'll just have to wait and see." Thea picked up Emma's rucksack. "Do you need to put anything else in here?"

"Just my phone." Emma passed it to her, and she slipped it into the front pocket. She rested her sunglasses on top of her head and reached for her crutches.

Thea hovered. "Do you need any help?"

Emma shook her head. "I need to try and be independent, but thanks anyway."

Slowly, they made their way through the lounge and into the car park.

Thea opened the passenger door. "I'll let you figure out how best to get in."

Emma stood back. "Is this the Rolls Royce you took me to hospital in?"

Thea nodded, her expression growing a little guarded.

"It doesn't look the same as a conventional one."

"No, it's a Cullinan. It's a four-wheel drive."

"I didn't know they made SUVs, and here I am, about to be chauffeured around in one for the second time."

Thea winked and clicked her tongue. "Lucky you. Actually, you're my first passenger, apart from the children."

"I'm honoured."

Thea took the crutches from Emma and laid them on the back seat. "Can you manage? You might find it easier if you sit your bum on the seat and gently swivel around."

Emma followed her instructions. "Nice. There's plenty of room to stretch my legs."

Thea slid into the driver's seat, then seemed to impulsively lean over and give Emma a quick kiss before returning to her chauffeur duty.

"So where are we going?" Emma asked, her lips tingling.

"A place called Rocky Cove. Do you know it?"

Emma laughed. "I haven't been anywhere. I arrived, unpacked, settled a little...and then I took my bike out. You know the rest of the story."

"Well, it's one of my favourite places. The children love it, and we often take picnics there."

"Then I'm sure I'll love it too."

Thea glanced at her briefly. "I hope you do. Once we get through the town and past the dual carriageway, you'll see some awesome scenery."

Thea wasn't wrong. After about a twenty-minute drive, they took a left turn and headed up into the hills. Neither of them said much, so Emma just took in the views. Emma softly nudged Thea's arm. "You weren't lying. This is truly spectacular. I'm surprised there aren't more tourists."

"It's Monday." She laughed. "I'm sure there'll be some locals around, but most of the tourists head off to the beach or other hot spots they've read about."

"I'm pleased about that."

Thea turned up a tiny lane with hedges on each side, and Emma was surprised that the car actually fit between them. Thea stopped in a pull-in to let a car go by, then slowly weaved her way around and around the tight corners. She seemed to know it like the back of her hand, which was a great relief. It probably required a lot of concentration, so Emma refrained from chatting.

They reached the peak, and Thea turned down a rugged track and pulled into a small car park. It wasn't so much a car park as an area covered in rubble and stones.

"We have arrived at our destination," Thea informed her in a robotic sounding voice. "Don't worry about the stones. I've reserved a perfect spot especially for you." She drew the car to a standstill on a piece of grass verge.

"I'm impressed." Not just by Thea's skill, but in the fact that she'd taken the time to consider how Emma would get around.

Thea wiped her forehead. "I was praying nobody was parked here. There are usually a few walkers out, but they generally park their cars over there." Thea pointed to an area at the back of them.

As she'd predicted, there were a couple of cars and a small motorhome. A man sitting by the side of his campervan looked like he'd fallen asleep in the sunshine.

"Don't move. I'll unload everything, then I'll come and give you a hand."

Emma stayed put, staring at the beautiful views across the cliff and still wondering if this was a date.

Thea opened the passenger door, and Emma gently swung her legs to the side. 'Take it easy. The ground is a bit uneven, but it's generally quite flat." Thea held out her arms. "Hang on to me until you're out and steady, then I'll pass you your crutches."

Emma eased her bum off the seat and slid down. It was quite high up, and she was glad she had Thea's arms to fall into, for many reasons. For a few seconds, they stared into each other's eyes and smiled.

Thea coughed and pulled away a little. "Hang onto the door a minute." She opened the back door and pulled out the crutches. "You okay?"

Emma wasn't sure. She felt a little unsteady purely because for the fraction of time Thea had held her arms, it had caused an earthquake in her stomach.

Thea guided her forward. "Take it easy. I'm here, and I won't let you fall."

Too late. Could she fall for someone so fast? Especially after... the thought of Brid cooled the heat in her cheeks and elsewhere. *Don't be daft.* Thea was like a mother hen, watching her every move until she eventually held the back of the chair, and Emma lowered herself into it.

"Phew. For a moment, I thought I'd made a mistake bringing you here. I'd forgotten how undulating the ground was."

Emma gasped as she swivelled carefully to look around. "Oh my God. The view is spectacular."

Thea smiled, as if she was pleased with herself. "It is, isn't it?" She pointed over the cliff's edge. "See? Rocky Cove."

"It's magnificent. I've never seen a better view." She stared in awe. "Can you get down to it?"

"Yes, but it's a tad treacherous. There's a lovely little beach down there. We, that is the kids and I, took our picnic there once. It took us ages to get down, but it was well worth it. Maybe one day, when you're back to one hundred percent, we could try it."

"Oh, I'd love to. That's something to look forward to."

Thea grinned. "In the meantime, I bet you're starving."

Emma laughed. "I could eat a horse."

Thea went around the back of the car and came back with a large wooden picnic table. She opened it and spread a red and white checkered tablecloth over it. Then she retrieved a picnic basket filled with a French loaf, a selection of meats, olives, cheeses, figs, dates, pastries, and fresh fruit. She opened a bottle of sparkling cider and poured two glasses.

"I thought this would go well. It's one of my favourites and fairly innocuous."

"This looks amazing, Thea. Thank you so much."

"I brought the feta cheese back with me, plus the fresh dates and figs, but don't report me to Customs. Honestly, they go so well together." She passed a glass to Emma and held up her own. "Here's to many happy days ahead."

Emma smiled and chinked her glass against Thea's. "Happy days."

She handed Emma a plate and cutlery. "Tuck in."

Emma took her at her word and helped herself to a little of

everything. "You're right, that feta goes so well with the figs. I had it in Greece once, but this tastes so much better. It's so fresh and tasty."

"One of my aunts makes it herself and supplies it all over the island. I'm glad you like it."

Emma shook her head. "What a talented family you have."

Thea grinned. "They are. I'm so lucky, and I never take it for granted. Family is so important. They're my life, and I cherish them." She winced. "I'm sorry, Emma. That was tactless."

Emma waved her hand. "Please don't apologise. But I would truly love a family like yours. I bet it was wonderful to see them all again, and possibly a wrench to leave them?"

Thea looked down. "Yes to both." She picked up her phone and scrolled through her picture gallery. "That's my mum and dad, and me, obviously." She showed it to Emma.

It was a picture of them sitting together in the restaurant. "They look like very proud parents."

Thea nodded. "They're the best." She scrolled through some more and showed her. "My two brothers, and their wives and kids."

Emma laughed. "There's an awful lot of them."

"Yeah, we're a big family."

She flicked along and paused at images that captured moments of joy and togetherness at family dinners, celebrations, and lazy afternoons by the shoreline.

"I'm almost envious."

Thea raised her eyebrows. "Only almost?"

Emma shrugged. "I've never experienced it, so I don't know."

Thea tilted her head slightly. "Do you think you'll ever make it up with your sister?"

"God knows, I've tried, but I don't think she'll ever forgive me. She thought I stole Brid from her, which was all a load of rubbish. It was such a shame, because we could all have been such good friends. Colly was always such a drama queen. Any opportunity, and she'd go off on one. She always made a mountain out of a mole hill." She tossed her head back. "When she played up, Brid would refer to it as 'Collywood.' Initially, Brid had liked her, but eventually she came to the conclusion that she was barking mad."

"Such a shame. Life is too short to hold grudges." Thea offered Emma some more food.

While chatting, they'd manage to polish off the vast majority of the picnic, and Emma held her hands up. "Honestly, I couldn't manage another thing. It was delicious. Thank you so much."

"My pleasure. I hope it'll be the first of many."

Emma smiled. "Me too."

Thea cleared the debris into the boot of the car and sat down beside Emma.

The sun hung high in the sky, casting a warm glow over the rugged cliff that overlooked the vast expanse of sea, and a gentle breeze whispered through the air. "This is absolutely magical." Emma breathed in deeply and licked her lips. "I can taste the sea."

Thea's gaze moved to her lips and then up again. "We're so lucky to have all this so close by."

"Aren't we just?" Emma fidgeted on her chair. She extended her injured leg and moved it back and forth.

Thea watched her with concern. "You don't look very comfortable."

"What I'd really like to do is remove my brace and stretch my leg out flat."

Thea sprang up and went to the car. She returned with some cushions and a vibrant blanket, which she laid out on the grassy ledge. "With help, do you think you could lower yourself onto the blanket?"

Emma laughed. "No idea, but I'll have a bloody good try." She put her hands on the armrests and eased herself up. Thea stood in front of her and held out her hands for Emma to hold. She guided her forward to the side of the blanket. "Okay, I'll lower you down gently. Trust me, I'll take your weight."

The warmth and strength in Thea's hands sent little shivers through Emma's body. She moved into a sitting position. Both seemed reluctant to part hands, but eventually Thea let go. Emma waited a few minutes, then eased her leg down and removed the Velcro straps on the brace. She put it to one side and sighed. "Oh, heaven. It's wonderful to feel the warmth directly on my leg." As she settled back on the blanket, Emma was finally able to really focus on the view. "I'd love some photographs, but my phone camera is pretty crappy. It wouldn't do it justice."

Thea picked up her phone. "If you like, I'll take some. I've just treated myself to the latest Samsung. It's got an awesome camera."

"If you wouldn't mind."

Thea clicked away, taking photos from every conceivable angle. She sat down close to Emma and flipped through.

Emma gasped. "You can even see the surface of the sea shimmering in the sunlight. And that one—you can actually see the sailboats dancing on the horizon and the trails of white against the canvas of the water."

Thea looked pleased with herself. "Pretty damned good, eh?"

"Definitely. I *must* have this phone. Can you send me the model name?"

Thea smirked. "Of course I will." She shuffled behind Emma. "We should take a selfie." She leaned in close, positioned the camera, and clicked several times. She showed them to Emma. A few of them were good and natural, but on several, they were both pulling funny faces. Their laughter mingled with the rhythmic sounds of the crashing waves below.

"I can't believe you found this spot," Emma said. Sunshine poured over Thea like she was something out of a mythological tale, and Emma couldn't quite tamp down the butterflies in her stomach.

Thea poured a small amount of cider into their glasses. "It's like our own little piece of paradise."

Emma nodded, thinking that it was Thea who made it truly beautiful. "It's perfect. I never imagined a picnic could be so enchanting."

They clinked their glasses together, toasting the beauty of the moment. The crisp cider was invigorating and added to the joy of her day. They exchanged stories about their childhood, memories of days out by the coast, and conversation flowed naturally like the symphony of the sea.

When their chatting slowed to a comfortable silence, they reclined on their blanket. What could be more perfect? *Another kiss.* The butterflies took flight in her stomach once again as she glanced at Thea chewing on a blade of grass. The sunlight played on her face, highlighting the smile that never failed to make her heart skip a beat. She was aware that Thea was stealing glances at her too.

Thea turned to Emma. "There's something I've been thinking about day and night when I was away," she said softly. She gently cupped Emma's chin and traced small circles on her cheek.

Emma's heart raced as Thea leaned in, and their lips met in a sweet and tender kiss. The kiss deepened, and her body hummed with pleasure as Thea gently parted her lips with her tongue and slid it into Emma's mouth. Emma responded. It was oh so delicious. Her heart felt as though it was floating alongside the wispy clouds.

They eased back out of the kiss, their faces still close together. Thea moved her head back slowly, as if to give Emma some space. They stared into each other's eyes and smiled. Neither of them spoke because it wasn't necessary. A sense of tranquillity seemed to wash over their little private space.

Thea intertwined her fingers with Emma's. "I could stay here forever," she whispered.

"Me too. It's like time is standing still." She rested her head on Thea's shoulder, wrapped in the magic of their first picnic.

On the drive home, Emma sat lost in thought, not seeing the

beauty of the passing scenery. The memory of their kiss clung to her the most. It had been a perfect moment, their lips meeting in a tender touch. Yet, as the warmth of the day faded into the cool of the evening, so did her sense of security.

Nineteen years. The number haunted her thoughts. She was fifty-five, a woman who had seen and experienced much of life. Thea, on the other hand, was brimming with exuberance and dreams. Their age difference was a chasm that she imagined would only widen with each passing day.

Emma couldn't help but feel the weight of her vulnerability. What if Thea eventually realised the disparity between their worlds? What if she woke up one day and realised that she was simply too old for her? The thought gnawed at her, feeding a fear she couldn't bury.

Emma sighed, running her fingers through her hair. Her thoughts drifted back to the picnic, to the way Thea had looked at her, eyes filled with adoration. It had been so long since she had felt seen, truly seen by someone. But along with that joy came the fear of losing it, of watching it slip away as Thea grew and changed.

Yes, Thea was mature beyond her years; she had more or less said that their age difference didn't matter. But what if Emma was a phase, a fleeting chapter in Thea's story?

Emma wanted to trust and believe, but her past experiences had taught her that life was fragile. She had loved and lost before, and the scars of those heartbreaks had left her wary, her heart guarded.

The fear of being emotionally hurt, of being left behind, was a shadow she couldn't escape. The fear of the future, of the unknown, meant it was hard to consider moving on.

As the night drew to an end, she knew that she would soon have to confront these fears with Thea. But what if she did and lost her anyway?

Chapter Eight

THEA DROVE EMMA BACK home. She gripped the steering wheel hard, her mind replaying the day's events over and over. The picnic had been perfect—laughter echoing in the warm air, and the taste of cider lingering on her lips. But it was the kiss that had left her in a state of exhilaration and confusion.

She glanced over at Emma, sitting quietly in the passenger seat, and couldn't help but feel a mixture of emotions. She was undeniably captivated by Emma and the way she made her feel both grounded and exhilarated. Yet, beneath her excitement, there was a current of uncertainty. What would happen when Thea told her the truth?

Despite those churning emotions, they spent the rest of the ride in a comfortable silence. She helped Emma out of the car and walked her back to her apartment. Once inside, she made sure that Emma had a cold drink.

Emma touched Thea's hand. "I'm sorry I had to be back so early." She laughed. "It's almost like we had to dash back before my mum caught us."

Thea kissed the tip of Emma's nose. "I understand, and I don't want you to lose your carer access. It wouldn't be fair."

"I know. I think they'll cut me down next week to one in the morning anyway, so hopefully it won't affect our time together much going forward."

Thea stroked Emma's cheek gently. "Are you happy with that?"

Emma nodded. "I think I'm ready. I only need the morning help because I need assistance getting into and out of the shower."

Thea's mind drifted momentarily to that scene. *I could help with that.* She coughed and attempted to remove the image from her mind when the doorbell rang.

She was forever being saved by the bell. Shame, because she didn't wish to come out of that particular dream.

"She's early." Emma frowned. "The door's open," she called out.

A woman bounced in with a wide grin on her face.

Emma shook her head and grinned a little. "I might have known it would be you, Petra. You're half an hour early. And how come I have the pleasure of your company twice in a day?"

"We're short staffed, so I volunteered." Petra smiled at Thea. "Aren't you going to introduce us?"

Thea thrust her hand forward. "Hi, I'm Thea."

They shook hands. "Good to meet you. I'm Petra, Emma's favourite assistant." She turned to Emma. "So, how was the picnic? You sure picked a good day for it. Wish I could have come with you."

Thea was pleased she hadn't. There would have been no sumptuous kiss, no feeling of slow-building romantic promise.

"It was wonderful. Both the food, and the views were to die for. And the company was pretty good too." Emma gave Thea a shy smile.

"I'd best go and leave you to it." Thea winked at Emma, though she was loath to leave. "I'll call you later." She bent down and kissed Emma on the cheek. If Petra hadn't been there, it would have been full on the lips, but she wasn't interested in having an audience when things were still so new and tentative. Now she'd have to wait for the next opportunity to come clean.

When she got back home, sadness crept over her. The house seemed so empty without Lyra and Seb, but she knew they'd be having a ball with their grandparents and uncles. She used to panic about leaving them. She didn't have a job she had to get back to, but she thought it was good that Lyra and Seb have quality time with their family, and she valued those few weeks of down time messing around and doing stuff beyond being a parent. She drove her mum crazy with the list of things she must do and not do, but Thea's main concern was always their security. *Somebody must always be with them...at all times. Don't let them out of your sight.*

"Even if there hadn't been the attempted kidnap, we would never leave them alone. Never," her mum repeated over and over.

She knew that, but she also knew that Lyra was sporty like her, and she was a fast runner. Something could catch her eye, and she'd be off in seconds. And what if she slipped off a cliff or something? *For fuck's sake, stop worrying.*

She unpacked the picnic basket and emptied the remnants of the cider down the sink. She needed something stronger. She took the half bottle of white wine left from last night out of the fridge, poured a glass and took a large gulp. A text notification disturbed her thoughts, and she eagerly opened it. It was a simple message from her mum: *We miss you, my love.*

A lump formed in Thea's throat. She thought about texting back, but instead she video-called. It was earlier than their usual chat time, but she found herself yearning to see them and hear all their voices. "Hi, Mum. I miss you too." It was hard holding back the tears that were forming, but she tried as she knew that upset her mum.

"Hello, my darling. I wasn't sure if you'd be back from your picnic with your young lady. How did it go?"

Thea laughed. "She's fifty-five, Mum."

Her mum's expression turned serious. "I know, but she sounds young and vulnerable in her soul. And you must take it steady with her. You don't want to run headlong into something and frighten her off."

"Mum, I don't intend to. I promise." But when she'd confided in her mum about Emma, she'd skipped the lies part, knowing her mum would go ape and say that it'd all backfire. She'd probably be right. "Is everything okay?"

"Yes, all is well. And don't change the subject."

"Message received. We had a great time. I took her for a picnic at Rocky Cove."

"Isn't that the place you took us to? It was so romantic."

Thea raised her eyebrows. "Yes, that same place."

"And?"

Thea looked away, remembering the simple beauty of the day. "And what?"

"Did things progress?"

"I kissed her." This really wasn't the conversation she wanted to have with her mum. She certainly wouldn't elaborate if the relationship developed.

"Oh, how lovely. I can just picture it."

"I'd rather you didn't!"

Her mum chuckled. "It's just so exciting. Wasn't it lucky she landed in your drive?"

"I'm not sure Emma would see it that way."

"But it was destined to be."

Thea rolled her eyes. "I know you're a big believer in destiny."

"I am indeed. I do hope you're going to bring her here. We'd all love to meet her."

Thea ignored that and took a sip of her wine. It was *way* too early for a meet-the-parents scenario. "How is everyone?"

"If by that, you mean your children, I'm afraid you can't talk to them right now. They've gone for a couple of nights with Nicholas and Anna. Remember, it's Zoe's birthday tomorrow. There's a big kid's party."

The room seemed to tilt a little, and her heart raced. She leaned back on the sofa. Something pounded against her chest like a hammer and chisel.

"Thea. Breathe."

Thea swallowed and took a deep breath. "I'm okay."

"Darling, I know you still struggle with this, but your brother and family are well aware of your anxieties. Lyra and Seb are perfectly safe with them."

Deep down, she knew they were, but it didn't stop her stressing. She'd started by leaving them with her family for a morning and taking a long walk. Gradually, she'd worked towards longer separations. She was confident when her children were with her mum and dad; they never took their eyes off them. "I'm sorry, Mum. I know they are. I just get worried if they're with lots of other kids. You know, in case they all run off and play hide and seek or something."

"I know you do." Her mum gave a tight smile. "Sadly, gone are the days when children could run around freely without fear of the unknown. But all the parents are there too, and they all love their children. They're very careful about not leaving them alone."

Thea nodded, slightly reassured. "Thanks. I know I'm overreacting. It's habit."

"We'll be over there tomorrow too. We're closing the restaurant for the day. Can't miss our granddaughter's birthday, can we?"

Thea sighed. Knowing her parents would be there made her feel a little better. "How's Dad?"

"He's good." Her mum laughed. "At the moment, he's waving his arms around trying to attract my attention. A large group just came in."

"Okay, I best let you go. Speak to you soon."

"You will, love, and don't worry."

"Okay." *That'll be the day.*

As the night wore on, Thea found solace in the memories and the digital connection she shared with her family. She flicked through all the photos and reminisced on so many great times. Her family made everything an adventure, and it had always been that way, especially in her childhood. Her dad was a great storyteller and if he wasn't reading from a book, he was inventing his stories. She guessed that was the reason her mum had fallen head over heels; she was a sucker for a good fantasy.

She dreamed of the day she'd return to the island, where the azure sea met the endless sky. Would Emma love it as much as she did? The story of her parents and their love made her smile. What Thea would give to fall head over heels as they had. That possibility with Emma unfolded in her mind. But the cruel reminder of the lies she'd told made her feel like she'd thrown up a wall between them.

Later in bed, she called Emma, wanting to hear the sound of her voice. "Sorry I didn't call earlier. My mum texted me and then we got into a long conversation."

"Please don't apologise. I think it's lovely you have such a great relationship. Thank you so much for today, it was a tonic and a half," Emma said.

"And for me too. I love being with you. Let's do it again. How about dinner one evening?"

"I'd love to."

"Are you free Friday night?"

"Err...let me check my social calendar. Guess what, I'm free."

Thea laughed. "Cool. What time do you like to eat?"

"Since my carers, anytime around six, but before that I used to eat around seven."

"I'll pick you up about six thirty."

"Lovely. I'm already looking forward to it." Emma hesitated. "Truly. Thank you for today. I've been stuck in a dark place for so long, and I feel like I'm finally moving toward the light again."

It was a lovely sentiment, but Thea wasn't sure how to respond to something so genuine. "Glad to be of assistance." She kept her tone light, but it still felt like a missed opportunity.

Thea spent a long time researching restaurants. There were a number that seemed acceptable, but she'd never eaten out in Westleigh, apart from places with the children, and they always picked those. Even when Quinn visited, they had dinner at home because Thea would never leave the children with anyone but her family. She feared that someone would be watching, lurking around behind some wall, waiting to pounce and take her children from her. She tried to be brave, but old fears replayed in her mind. *We're all brave until we realise the cockroach has wings.*

The following day, she saw a few of the mothers chatting outside Waitrose and figured it would be a good opportunity to get some local knowledge. "Hi, guys."

"Hi, Thea."

"I need your help. I have a friend over and want to take her for dinner somewhere casual but with great food. Any recommendations?"

They all gabbled away together discussing the pros and cons of several restaurants.

"Without doubt, the best is L'Union on Burn's Hill," Marcia, the tacitly agreed ringleader, said. "There's no parking so you'll need to take a taxi. Plus, they have an amazing wine list. The tables are nicely spread out, so there can be no eavesdropping from nosy diners, and unlike a lot of places, you can hear yourself talk. Cosy, intimate, charming...and expensive." She laughed.

"Sounds perfect. I knew you guys would have the answer." She left before they asked who she was going to dinner with. No need to add to the gossip train.

When she got home, she checked the website. It seemed trendy and popular, so she booked a table, not wanting to leave their first dinner date to chance.

It was a long wait until Friday, but when it eventually arrived, Thea spent several hours preparing. After a shower, she spread several outfits on her bed. She tried them on, discarded them, tried more on, and shook her head. She settled for a pair of black jeans and a crisp white blouse. A good, classic look. Why was she so nervous? Had she ever taken a woman out for dinner before? She frowned. Surely, she had. *Nope.* She and Quinn always either ate at each other's place, or they ate in the mess on base. She'd dated other women, but their meet-ups had been at pubs or clubs. That revelation threw her into a total frenzy, and she dropped onto the edge of her bed. This was Emma, not some random woman. She felt comfortable and could talk to her as if she'd known her all her life. No need to panic. They were taking things slow, and Thea didn't need to give herself extra pressure. She took a deep breath and smiled. She could do this.

She arrived at Emma's slightly early and rang the bell.

"Door's open. Come in."

Thea gave her a hug and a light kiss on the lips. This wasn't the right time for a real snog, although that's what she'd have liked. "You look terrific." Her light blue jeans and shirt complemented her own outfit.

"You look gorgeous yourself," Emma said and smiled.

Thea took Emma's hand. It felt sweet, romantic, and snug. She pulled her up gently and passed the crutches to her. "Thanks. Let's go and celebrate."

"What are we celebrating tonight?"

Thea winked. "Our first dinner date."

She helped Emma into the front seat of the taxi. She would've preferred to have sat close to her in the back, but it was too cramped, and Emma wouldn't be able to stretch her leg out.

The journey only took five minutes, and they were soon inside the fancy restaurant.

Emma glanced around and murmured appreciatively. "Looks like a wonderful choice, Thea."

Thea nodded, pleased with herself, even though she'd never stepped foot in L'Union before. The soft glow of ambient lighting filled the chic restaurant, casting a warm and intimate atmosphere.

A waiter showed them to their table, which was tucked away in a pleasant little nook. A gentle hum of conversations and the clinking of china echoed through the elegantly decorated space.

Thea and Emma sat across from each other at a candlelit table adorned with crisp white linen.

Emma's eyes widened. "I feel underdressed. I would have made more effort if I'd known we were going to such a swanky place."

"Trust me, you look terrific. Nobody dresses up now; just look."

Emma glanced at the other people around them. "I guess we blend in well. It's been a long time since I dined out."

A waiter approached with a friendly smile. He presented them with menus and described the evening's specials. "Can I get you two ladies a drink?"

Thea looked at Emma. "What about a cocktail?"

Emma's eyes lit up. "I can't remember the last time I had a cocktail."

Thea spread her hands out and looked up at the waiter. "What would you recommend?"

"Negronis are refreshing."

Thea rubbed her chin with her hand. "And that is?"

"Tanqueray, Campari, and Regal Rouge red vermouth."

"Sounds good to me. What say you, Emma?"

Emma laughed. "Why not."

When the waiter left, Emma clasped her hands together, as though unsure what to do with them. "I can't remember the last time I had more than a glass of wine."

Thea chuckled. "I had plenty of wine in Zakynthos."

Emma nodded. 'I bet you did."

The waiter returned with the cocktails. "Enjoy, ladies."

Thea held her glass up. "To our first real date." They clinked their glasses together.

Emma raised her eyebrows when she took a sip. "Whoa, that's pretty lethal."

"We're not driving, so it's okay, I think."

Emma nodded. "You're right, and why shouldn't we enjoy ourselves?" She put her glass down and picked up the leather-bound menu.

Thea stole glances at Emma over the top of her own menu.

Her eyes seemed to dance over the array of dishes, and Thea was captivated by the subtle play of emotions on her face. What would it be like to be so open? "I hope you like French cuisine."

Emma licked her lips. "I like all food, and I have a big appetite."

For a moment, Thea's mind wandered at the thought of Emma's big appetite. "What do you fancy?" *I know I fancy you.*

Emma tilted her head and caught Thea's eye, as though she'd recognised the dual inference. "I think I'm going with the cheese souffle, followed by the herb-crusted lamb roulade."

Thea grinned. "That's exactly what I want too." She swapped the menu for the wine list. "What colour do you prefer?"

"Red please, especially as it's lamb."

"Great, my choice too."

The waiter returned to take their order, and as they waited for their meals, the air was charged with the anticipation of what the evening might hold. They exchanged light-hearted banter about their preferences and favourite food.

Thea put her elbow on the table and leaned her chin on her hand. "What are your hobbies?"

Emma laughed. "You mean, apart from eating?"

"Well, that's a good start."

"Let me think." Emma leaned back in her chair. "I did like cycling, but I'm not sure I'll have the courage to get back on a bike again."

Thea took Emma hand and squeezed it tightly. "Of course you will. I'll make sure you're back on it as soon as they give the word."

"Do you like cycling too?"

"You bet. Lyra and Seb have bikes. They don't ride on the road cycle tracks, but we load them up in the car and go somewhere safe. There are some brilliant old railway cycle paths not far from here. They love it. When you're back in action, maybe we could all go together."

Emma rubbed her hands together. "I'd love that. I never got

around to checking those out. Perhaps if I had, I wouldn't have been run off the road."

"Who knows? Sometimes bad shit just happens wherever you are. A bear could have chased you or something."

Emma laughed. "Do you get many bear attacks in Westleigh?"

Thea chuckled. "No. We have bear bells."

Emma pushed her arm playfully, then let her hand slide slowly down to Thea's hand, never breaking eye contact.

When the first course arrived, the cheese souffles were a feast for their eyes. The waiter poured their wine and departed. Thea and Emma made subtle sounds of pleasure as they savoured each mouthful, occasionally stealing glances at one another with appreciative smiles.

Emma closed her eyes. "That was sheer heaven on a plate."

"Agreed. Next time I might have two."

Emma laughed. "I may join you."

"So it appears we also share the pleasure of living to eat."

"Oh yes, though unlike you, I'm a lousy cook."

"Well, I love cooking, but not to this standard. I can't remember the army chefs ever making dishes like these, certainly not for the squaddies. Did Brid do all the cooking?"

Emma nearly split her sides laughing. "God, no. She was far worse than me. Don't get me wrong, we always ate well, but it was either from M & S, Waitrose, or those meals you order online with all the ingredients supplied."

"There's nothing wrong with that. Keeps people in jobs." Thea sipped her wine, though she couldn't imagine not making her own meals regularly. "What else do you enjoy?"

"Music of all sorts. I can't live without it. Walks in the countryside and enjoying nature. You know, the physical world collectively...plants, animals, the landscape. In fact, I think I prefer all that to humans."

Thea nodded. "Definitely. Me too."

Emma stroked her chin. "I love reading too. It's my dream to curl up in front of a roaring fire with a good book...the physical ones of course. Kindles are brilliant for holidays so you can take lots of books, but there's nothing like the real thing."

"You're a woman after my own heart." Thea was realising that more and more. She wondered if Emma enjoyed sex. It wasn't a topic she could just throw into the conversation, though it had always been an important part of her life.

The waiter cleared their plates and returned with their main course. The lamb was accompanied by onion and herb stuffing, a puree made from Jerusalem artichokes, Dauphinoise potatoes, and a lamb jus.

He poured more wine into their glasses. "Bon appetit."

Emma took the first taste, and her eyes lit up. "I think this is the best meal I've ever had."

Thea felt smug. Okay, so it had been Marcia's recommendation, but she'd booked the table. "One of many I hope."

As the evening unfolded, their comfortable connection continued to deepen. The restaurant's food and ambiance became the backdrop, and the dinner date marked the beginning of something promising.

The waiter returned and removed their plates. "Dessert, ladies?"

Emma held her stomach. "I'm not sure if I could manage another bite."

"Oh c'mon, Emma. There have some awesome desserts."

Emma checked the menu. "Well, the Yorkshire rhubarb and almond tart does sound tempting."

"And the sticky toffee pudding for me, please."

"I don't know where you put it, Thea. You're so slim," Emma said.

Thea laughed. "I'll do a lot of jogging tomorrow."

They lingered over dessert, savouring the sweetness of both dishes and the growing relationship developing between them. Emma held up her spoon for Thea to try the rhubarb, and Thea took her time sliding it from the spoon and into her mouth, her gaze not leaving Emma's.

"How did you fill your day today?" Thea asked over coffee.

"I wrote a long email to my friend, Jen. She's still in America, but she's coming back in a couple of days. I haven't told her anything about my accident."

"Why not?"

"Because she would've got the next plane back. She's visiting her sister and family for the first time in yonks, and I didn't want to ruin that."

"Won't she go and jump on a plane now?"

Emma laughed. "No, because it's still in my drafts file. I'll send it when she's settled."

"Well, she won't be very happy with you." Thea shook her head. "I certainly wouldn't be if someone I cared about hadn't reached out to me when they needed someone."

"But the moment will have passed. I'm on the road to recovery now. Trust me, I know it's for the best."

Thea glowered. "Rather you than me."

Emma looked contemplative. "Did you ever meet Bev?"

Thea searched her memory but came up blank. "Bev?"

"She was a nursing assistant on the ward."

Thea shook her head. "Can't say I recall her. Why?"

Emma rubbed the back of her neck with her hand. "She was really supportive in hospital. She sat and chatted with me a lot and always made sure I was comfortable."

"So she paid you a lot of attention?"

"Yes."

Thea spread her hands, palms up. "And? I imagine this is leading somewhere, because you look a little disturbed."

"It was odd. She once said to me that she passed by my apartment. She laughed about it and said that she'd recognised the orange bistro table and chairs on my patio that I'd descr bed."

Thea narrowed her eyes. "But they're not supposed to have

access to your address."

"I know. But I guess you see it, don't you? I imagine she'd come across it in my notes."

"Has something happened?" She didn't like where this story was going.

"It was a beautiful morning, so after my carer had been, I took my coffee out on to the patio and suddenly she appeared, walking by with a dog."

Thea's mouth was dry, and her tongue stuck to the roof of her mouth. That kind of behaviour was something she was far too familiar with. She poured some water and took a drink. "Did she stop to talk?"

"Yes. She asked me how I was. She said it wasn't her dog, that she was walking it for a friend. Then she said the coffee smelt inviting."

Thea felt like her eyes were about to pop out of their sockets. "You didn't invite her in, did you?"

"No way. I thought it was odd. I said it was nice to see her, and I was waiting for the physio to arrive. I wasn't, but it was all I could come up with." Emma laughed. "It's probably nothing, but you know when you just get that sense—"

"She's a fucking stalker. You should report it to the hospital."

Emma's eyes widened. She glanced around, possibly because Thea had spoken rather loudly. "A stalker?"

"Yes!" Realising she must sound paranoid, she cleared her throat and lowered her voice. "My friend was stalked. It was scary beyond imagination."

Emma frowned. "Maybe you're right. I'll give it some thought."

Thea slapped her hand on the table. "No. No. Don't just think about it. Report her."

Emma held her hands up. "Okay, message received and understood. I'll do it tomorrow."

Thea leaned forward. "Promise you'll do it."

"I promise." Emma frowned a little, looking bemused.

Thea sighed. "I'm sorry, Emma. You might think I'm overreacting, but I've had experience of this."

"Thanks for your concern." Emma looked like she wished she'd never mentioned it.

For a while, it put the mockers on the evening, but they soon got back to normal conversation and talked about their favourite travel destinations. Still, Thea couldn't get the issue out of her head, try as she might to set it aside.

The bill arrived, and they had a friendly fight about who was paying before agreeing to share it. Their taxi arrived, and the night air greeted them as they stepped outside.

Emma shivered. "Brrr, it's gone a bit chilly."

Thea rued the fact that she hadn't got a jacket to slip around Emma's shoulders. She would've liked to wrap her arm around her, but Emma's crutches kept her from getting that close. Instead, she rushed ahead and opened the taxi door.

When they arrived at Emma's, Thea jumped out and held the door open for her. "Can you hang on five minutes?" she asked the driver. "I'll be right back." She wanted to stay longer. In fact, she would've liked to spend the night with Emma, but she'd prefer to do that on home territory, and she knew Emma's carer would be there bright and early. She also didn't want to move too fast. Emma had been through so much, and it was obvious she was still hurting from the loss of her wife. Thea cared about her and wanted to make their first night together special and hopefully free of the ghosts of both their pasts.

Emma unlocked her door, and they stepped inside. "That was an incredible evening, Thea. Thank you so much."

Thea looked deeply into Emma's eyes and stepped closer to her. Their lips met, and Thea parted Emma's lips with her tongue. She could taste a hint of blackberries from the wine as their tongues mingled. Thea placed her arms around Emma's waist, pulling her closer as the kiss intensified, and Emma tousled Thea's hair.

When they finally parted, Thea sighed deeply. "I suppose I'd better go."

Emma smiled, and her eyes sparkled. "I suppose."

"Are you doing anything on Sunday?" Thea asked.

"I don't think so. You're the only one on my schedule these days."

"What say I pick you up about four?"

"Perfect. I don't even need to ask what we're doing." She traced her fingertip along Thea's lips. "I just want to be with you."

Thea stepped back before her willpower splintered. "Don't forget to lock the door. And make sure your patio is locked too."

Emma giggled. "You think my stalker's going to creep in?"

Thea frowned. "It's no laughing matter, Emma. Those people are dangerous."

"Don't worry. I'll check all the doors and windows. Now go before your taxi gives up on you."

"Okay. See you Sunday."

Thea relaxed in the back of the car. Their dinner date had been all she'd hoped it would be, but the talk of a stalker made the wine sour in her stomach. The last thing she wanted was a repeat of the kind of drama she'd left behind.

Chapter Nine

IN THE QUIET SOLITUDE of her home, Emma lost herself in reflection, savouring the memory of a wonderful evening. A smile tugged at the corner of her lips. It wasn't just the setting or the cuisine that made the night special; it was the shared moments of laughter, the meaningful conversation, and the growing connection that made it truly unforgettable. With each exchange, they discovered shared interests that weaved a tapestry of common ground.

Emma had lit up when Thea mentioned her love of cycling. Emma wondered if she really meant it, about them all going cycling together. She'd never been around children, but cycling would be a good ice breaker, and she probably wouldn't need to make a lot of conversation. Did she really want to share Thea with the children though? And wouldn't their parents be a bit worried about Thea introducing the children to a stranger, let alone inviting her on their outings? The more she thought about it, the more she sensed that Lyra and Seb were a massive part of Thea's life. In fact, she seemed to love them as if they were her own. Emma realised she'd have to come to terms with that, but she was sure they'd have plenty of time on their own too.

Despite their discovery of shared interests, something niggled at Emma. It wasn't so much *what* Thea said, it was more what she *didn't* say, as if she was holding something back. Whatever it was, Emma couldn't put her finger on it. Maybe Thea was keeping bits of herself away. It was early days, and who was she to talk? She'd certainly avoided the *age* discussion. Sooner or later, she'd have to address that issue.

Anyway, it had been an amazing time and not once throughout

the whole evening, had she thought about Brid. Of course, Brid would say that was progress, but Emma couldn't help the pangs of guilt.

There was something else that nagged at her too. Thea's reaction to Emma's encounter with Bev had been a bit over the top. She supposed Thea was concerned about her welfare, but she'd been incensed by the story and acted totally out of character. Or had she? Emma didn't really know her at all, and Thea might just be showing her what she wanted Emma to see. Perhaps there was another side to Thea, one she didn't know. *Now who's overreacting?*

Despite all the thoughts tearing around in her mind, Emma's sleep was peaceful, occasionally filled with dreams of soft kisses and Thea's beautiful, bright smile. When Petra arrived the following morning, she was still fast asleep, but there was a key box in the shed so carers could enter without disturbing their patients.

She must have sensed a presence and when she opened her eyes, Petra was standing at the bottom of her bed with a mug of tea in her hand.

Petra laughed. "Good morning, sleepy head."

Emma yawned and smiled. "You're early. What time is it?"

"I'm late and it's eight thirty."

Emma whistled. "I certainly slept well."

Petra put the mug onto Emma's bedside table. "I take it your evening was magical?"

Emma nodded. "Wonderful, thanks. The food was incredible and the company much the same."

"But you didn't invite her to stay overnight?"

Emma folded her arms across her chest. "God, no. What do you take me for?"

Petra shrugged. "Human?"

She couldn't bring herself to say out loud that she wasn't ready to jump into bed with someone other than Brid. "The last thing I'd want to do is have to kick her out in the middle of the night."

"You could have sent me a text. I'm sure Thea could help you shower." Petra giggled.

"Well, it wasn't necessary," Emma said, "though it's worth keeping in mind for the future. Could I really text you to cancel?"

"Yes. I would've just reported that you had a friend staying who could help you. But you're going to be signed off anyway. You're ready to go it alone."

Emma pressed her hand to her chest. "You're going to leave me? What about showering?"

"Trust me, you're doing fine. You don't need me."

Emma sighed. "I guess I feel secure knowing you're out there."

"You have the careline support pendant. Just press that and help will come if anything goes wrong."

Emma reached for her mug of tea. "When?"

"Today is my last visit."

She nearly choked on her tea. "Are you sure I'm ready?"

"More than. Serves you right; you shouldn't have been such a star pupil."

Emma huffed. "I wish you'd told me sooner." It was good news though. She was way ahead of schedule on both physio and healing. Time to stand on her own two feet, now that she could. Time for independence.

Time to be alone again.

She received a piece of good news from Margot, her roommate from hospital. *Hello, darling. Good news, I've been released. They wanted me to go to some shitty rehab centre, no doubt full of mad old codgers. Opted for private carers at home. Healing nicely.*

That's wonderful news, Margot. I'm doing well too, so one day soon we'll have to meet up for lunch and a catch-up.

Absolutely, darling. I'll keep you posted.

Frankly, Emma was surprised. Margot, for all her drama, really hadn't seemed well when Emma had left. But medical professionals knew best, right?

It was only a day to wait until their next date, but Emma found herself consumed by a restless impatience. She tried to occupy her time with checking on their business website. She'd promised Jen she'd keep an eye on things while she was away, but her thoughts constantly drifted back to her evening with Thea. Had she felt this way with Brid? It was so long ago, she could hardly remember those initial dates. It seemed disrespectful to Brid's memory, but she was sure Brid would just laugh and tell her to stop overthinking. For Christ's sake, she was pushing sixty but behaving like a love-sick teenager.

Could she love again? She wasn't there yet with Thea, obviously, but for the first time since losing Brid, she began to consider the possibility of moving toward opening her heart again.

Her phone pinged with a text from Thea. *Don't eat too much. I'm planning on cooking for us later. Do you want to go for a drive before?*

Sounds wonderful. Any chance we could go for a gentle walk? My physio says I have to start weight bearing.

That's brilliant. I'll park up on the front and we can do a little promenading. It's very flat.

Perfect.

See you tomorrow at four. xx

Emma's heart thumped loudly. What did she expect from this next date? She and Thea were going to be alone at Thea's place. They'd already kissed. Now she found herself grappling with a swirl of conflicting emotions, chiefly, fear around intimacy. She couldn't deny the chemistry between them, and the spark had been ignited. But the thought of taking their relationship to the next level filled her with a mix of excitement and trepidation. Was she ready for that next step? Was it too soon? The fear of the unknown loomed large.

She chewed one of her nails. It had been a long time since

she'd had sex, going on three years now. At the beginning of her relationship with Brid, it had been all-consuming. As time went by, it became less important, and in the latter years, it hardly existed. It wasn't because they loved each other less, it was just non-essential. Yes, she was certainly feeling a lack of confidence in that area. She could hear Brid laughing. *Overthinking again.*

She threw herself into her work so everything would be ready when Jen got back. If anyone could help her sort through her complicated feelings, it was her bestie.

***

Thea arrived dead on time the next afternoon, and they drove to the beach. The sun cast a warm glow over the promenade as they strolled along the bustling walkway. The sound of lapping waves provided a soothing backdrop to their conversation.

Thea watched Emma in a sort of mother hen fashion. "Are you sure this isn't too much for you?"

"Stop fussing, Thea. I'm absolutely fine."

"Make sure you stay close to the wall. You can always lean on it if you feel unsteady."

Emma nodded. She could understand Thea's concern as the promenade was alive with activity, with many couples and families taking leisurely strolls as well as children darting here and there along the path. They paused occasionally to take in the sights, or for Emma to take a rest.

Thea pointed in the distance. "Hey, look at the paddleboarders. There are hundreds of them."

"I bet that's something you do." Emma had a feeling Thea could do pretty much any sport she put her mind to. Briefly, the thought of their age difference reared up again. Emma was slowing down a little, while Thea was still in her prime.

"I've had a go at it, but I'm not convinced it's something I want to take up."

Emma laughed, ignoring the niggling doubt. "Well, it's certainly not on my to-do list."

"Is ice cream on that list?" Thea pointed to a van parked a few metres down the road.

Emma raised one of her crutches jubilantly. "You bet."

"What's your fancy?"

"A cone, please."

"Chocolate flake?"

"Oh, yes." Emma rested on a bench whilst Thea queued at the van. She watched Thea laughing with the person in line behind her. Sunlight highlighted her beautiful face and the way her eyes lit up as she laughed. She really was breathtaking, and Emma swallowed hard at the desire to wrap Thea in her arms.

Thea returned with the ice cream and sat down beside her. They sat quietly, enjoying their treat. Thea wiped dripping ice cream from her chin and licked her finger. Desire, long forgotten and only recently reawakened, flared in Emma's chest, and Thea seemed to sense it. She lightly kissed the ice cream from Emma's lips and then turned away to finish her own, a little grin on her lips.

"What do you want from your future?" Thea asked when they started walking again.

Emma pondered for a while. "I didn't come down here with a plan. I suppose I want to do plenty of exploring when I'm back to one hundred per cent. Maybe when I've exhausted that, I'll look for something to keep my mind occupied, something I'm passionate about."

Thea brushed her hand against Emma's. "I'd like to think we could do that together."

"Which part?"

Thea tilted her head. "All of it, of course."

The idea of that filled Emma's heart and mind with joy. The years of Brid's illness meant she'd been focused entirely on that aspect of life. Everything else had been pushed aside, and after Brid's death...well, she hadn't wanted to do much of anything.

Now, though, with Thea there offering more, the buds of spring popped through the dirt that had mucked up her soul.

As they walked, Emma couldn't help but steal glances at Thea. The way she swayed as she walked and the little skips she made when turning to talk with Emma made her smile. They were silly things, but they gave her an all-round feeling of contentment. There was a comfort in her presence, a sense of familiarity that made her feel as though they had known each other for years rather than weeks. Fun and playful banter filled the air with laughter, and it was exactly what she needed from life.

They walked much further than they'd intended, so Thea suggested Emma sit on the bench nearby while she fetched the car. As she waited, Emma's mind drifted through a whirlwind of emotions. The day so far had been wonderful, filled with laughter, easy conversation, and moments of quiet intimacy. But now, as they were about to head back to Thea's home, fears and doubts crept in.

Nineteen years. The age gap was an ever-present whisper in her mind, a reminder of the differences that may pull them apart. In particular, she worried about the next stage of their relationship and felt a pang of insecurity as she imagined the day ahead. She knew that once they were at Thea's home, they'd share a meal, a few glasses of wine...and there would be a possibility of making love, assuming the people Thea worked for weren't there. She longed for Thea's touch yet feared it at the same time.

What if their physical differences became too apparent? What if Thea realised that Emma's body, no longer as supple as it once was, couldn't keep up with her more youthful vigour?

Too late to back out. Thea drew up by the curb side and beckoned her over. Then it was just a short trip to Thea's home.

This was the first time Emma had returned to the scene of her accident, and all the memories flooded back so real, it could almost be happening again. She stared at the house and felt dizzy. She put her head down and took some deep breaths.

Thea pulled up quickly and took Emma's hands in hers. "Jeez. I'm so stupid and insensitive. Forgive me. I didn't think."

"It's okay, Thea. I didn't think it would have this effect on me. It's just shock, I guess."

Thea stroked her back, and all her fears disappeared.

Emma stared up at the glass fronted house, which was more like a mansion. "I'm not sure if I can make it up those steps. I still have a problem bending my knee fully."

Thea touched a remote, and the garage door opened. "You don't have to. There's a lift at the back of the garage. It goes up to all the floors."

Emma laughed, still a little stunned. "Of course there is."

They took said lift up to the main house, and Emma's jaw dropped in awe as she stepped into the huge open space. "Oh my God, this is really something else." She had a hard time taking it all in. "Er, so this is your humble abode, eh? Well, I know it's not yours, but you have the pleasure of living here."

Thea looked a little uncomfortable. "Yes, I feel privileged."

Emma could see the plusses, lots of them. It was a huge space. It had one of those zoned patios where there were loads of areas divided for different occasions. There was a dining zone near the pool, which was obviously for al fresco meals. Then there was another covered dining area where she imagined they could eat in the cooler months. Next to it was a relaxing seating area. It looked comfortable and inviting, with stylish sofas and lounge chairs with beautiful, cosy textiles. She could imagine how romantic the fire pit would be, all lit up and snuggly. Of course, there was one of those twin sun loungers that looked more like a bed, and it even had curtains to block out the sun or for privacy. Beside it, there was a poolside barbecue which resembled a small kitchen. All of it was very traditional, mostly constructed from natural stone, brick, and wood. She laughed. "Yes, I could live here quite easily."

Thea inclined her head. "Could you?"

Emma wiggled her eyebrows. "In my dreams."

Thea shifted from one foot to the other. "Do you want a guided tour first? Then we can chill out with a cool glass of wine."

Emma looked uncertain. "You don't think the owners will mind? I mean, who cares? Yes, please."

"Give me a couple of minutes. I want to light the barbecue first." Thea did whatever she needed to do and returned. "We'll take the lift down to the lower ground floor."

"How many floors has this place got?"

"Three."

Thea led the way, and Emma was torn between watching the sway of her beautiful bum and looking around at the stunning house. The lift door opened into a spacious foyer adorned with marble flooring and a cascading chandelier. It flowed into the living area where high ceilings and an open floor plan created an atmosphere of airiness and luxury. More beautiful designer furnishings were arranged around a sleek fireplace, and there was a state-of-the-art entertainment system. The floor-to-ceiling windows offered sweeping vistas across the beach and sea.

Emma was truly lost for words. Her vocabulary seemed to only consist of two exclamations, *wow* and *oh my God*. She followed Thea to the adjacent room, which could only be described as a gourmet kitchen. It was a chef's dream come true, and she was sure Thea would be in her element. It was clad in top-of-the-range appliances, extensive counters, and a spacious island with bar seating, along with a more formal dining area nearby. She could imagine Thea's employers hosting dinner parties and intimate gatherings. Oh, and there was a humungous walk-in pantry. "This is amazing. I wouldn't have the faintest idea what to do in it, but it looks impressive."

Thea beckoned her. "Come on; next floor."

Back to the lift and out into a hallway. Emma couldn't help but notice the lack of really personal things. Sure, it was beautifully decorated, but there were no family photos, no knickknacks from trips abroad, or even personal items left where they didn't belong. "Exactly how many bedrooms are there?"

Thea cleared her throat, looking almost embarrassed. "Three on this floor. Two for the children and the master suite."

She didn't see the children's rooms, but Thea showed her the master suite. It was a sanctuary unto itself, with a king-sized bed, cosy sitting area, and a spa-like ensuite complete with tub, dual vanities, and a spacious walk-in shower. It smelled like…well, it smelled like the floral shampoo Thea used. Emma figured the wife used the same brand.

"And back to where we began." The lift opened onto the pool terrace. Thea tapped in some digits, and the glass patio doors opened into a comfortable sitting area. "This is my domain." Thea pointed to her right. "There's a kitchen and a bedroom with ensuite through there. It's nothing fancy."

The three floors of sleek sophistication exuded elegance and opulence from every angle. "It's magnificent. There seems to be a lot of security. In fact, it's a bit like a fortress."

Thea frowned. "I think it's typical of any home around here. These days, you have to be so careful. Most homes have alarms, motion detectors, window sensors, and surveillance cameras. I bet your building has much the same."

Emma gave that some thought. "Yes, I suppose it does."

"Come and sit down. I bet you're whacked after that tour." Thea led her to a couple of seats by the cooking area.

Emma laughed. "I'm certainly ready for that drink." She took a seat, and Thea handed her a glass. "Nice," she said after taking a sip. She glanced up at the sky and fanned herself with her hand. "It sure is a sun trap here."

Thea stood and put the sun umbrella up. "It is. Do you know, it's hotter here now than it is in Zakynthos." She topped the glasses up. "Back in a tick. I'm just going to fetch the food." She returned carrying a large tray. "This is something I made earlier."

"Wow, you're so well prepared." Emma laughed. "I guess you

had to be, given your career."

"True. I learned this sort of cooking in Cyprus. They rarely eat indoors and mostly, it's cooked on coals." Thea laid the kebabs on the grill and put the other dishes into an oven which was built in on the side.

The smell of the barbecue was a tantalising blend of rich, smoky, and sweet aromas. Emma inhaled slowly. "Hmm, you're making my mouth water."

Thea looked at Emma, and a tiny grin touched her lips. "Good. That's the idea."

"What's in the oven?" Emma asked, trying to hide the redness she knew must be flooding her cheeks. Thea's flirting had a palpable sensuality.

"Rice and caramelised vegetables."

Emma licked her lips, and her stomach flipped at the way Thea's eyes darkened as she watched her. "Sounds good."

Thea got up and tended to the food, and Emma was content to watch.

"Okay, we're ready here." Thea placed everything on the table. "Help yourself."

Emma wasn't shy, and she did exactly what Thea had instructed, savouring every mouthful. "This is sheer delight. You sure know the way to a woman's heart."

Thea wiggled her eyebrows. "Somehow I got the impression that food would do the trick."

Emma put her elbow on the table and leaned her chin on her hand. "Do you miss army life?"

Thea tilted her head. "Yes and no. I miss the camaraderie. I *don't* miss the unsociable hours."

"Do you still see your army friends?"

Thea's expression grew a little guarded, but she smiled. "My bestie, Quinn, is doing another stint in Cyprus. She's off next month. I'll miss her."

"I imagine you can still keep in touch."

Thea stared into the distance. "It's not the same."

Emma hesitated before asking the question. "Was she your girlfriend?"

Thea tapped her lip with her index finger. "She was my boss, my mentor, my best friend...and yes, we did have a relationship of sorts."

"Friends with benefits?" Emma asked.

"I guess that's what people would call it. It was different though. Closer."

Emma could feel her mouth going dry, and her tongue was having a hard time trying to form words. She felt a pang of jealousy. Is that what Thea was looking for, a replacement for her friend with benefits? She didn't and couldn't respond.

As if realising Emma's concerns, Thea reached across and took her hand. "That's not what I want with you, Emma. I want more. I'll just miss my friend, that's all."

Emma breathed a sigh of relief that almost made her dizzy. "Good, because I don't think I could cope with the former. That's never been my style. And...I guess I wouldn't want to share you. That sounds stupid, this early in our..." She shrugged, unable to find the words she needed.

Thea looked happy with her answer. She kissed Emma on the lips, a sweet and tender kiss full of promise.

They continued staring into each other's eyes, and eventually Thea broke the magic. "I'll tidy this up. I don't like leaving stuff around: too many flies." She laughed. "Sorry, I'm inclined to border on obsessive-compulsive disorder, and my training just made it worse. I try to keep it in check."

Emma got out of her chair. "I'll help you."

"No, it's fine. It won't take me a minute. Go make yourself comfortable and catch the last sunbeams." Thea loaded the plates on the tray and disappeared into the house.

Emma glanced around. The twin sunbed looked incredibly inviting, and she really did need to rest her leg. That was her excuse as she hobbled over to it. She stared at the distant horizon, thinking about the many things she knew about Thea, as well as the things she still didn't know. But there was time. It would be dull to know everything all at once, wouldn't it?

Thea returned to lie beside her and propped her head on her hand as she looked into Emma's eyes.

The sun hung low in the sky, casting a golden hue where they lay on the sun bed and bathing their bodies in the warm glow of the evening light.

Emma's breath hitched at the desire in Thea's eyes. Her pulse began a staccato rhythm that demanded she move, that she engage.

Thea kissed Emma, softly at first, and then more intensely. She slid a hand under Emma's T-shirt and unclipped her bra at the back. She traced her hand around to Emma's breast, stroking and caressing. She kissed Emma's chin and then swept her tongue across Emma's neck. She nibbled gently. "Love at first bite."

Emma groaned.

Thea removed Emma's T-shirt and bra and pulled off her own. She took Emma's nipple in her mouth and sucked hard. She flicked her tongue across Emma's nipple, back and forth. Emma arched, yearning for more and desperately trying to quiet the voice in her head telling her it was wrong, that it wasn't Brid. At the feel of Thea's teeth on her neck, all thought mercifully fled.

They explored each other's curves, their fingers tracing patterns of desire along their skin. Every touch ignited a spark of longing. Their clothing became a barrier to be shed, and they discarded each remaining article with an urgency that mirrored the intensity of their passion. Their naked bodies pressed together, and their hearts seemed to beat in unison as they lost themselves in the heat of the moment. Emma wanted this. She wanted Thea. She wanted to be *wanted*.

Thea moved her hand slowly down Emma's body. She caressed her tummy and rested her hand between Emma's thighs. Emma's breathing became erratic as she parted her legs, and Thea's fingertips teased the skin of her inner thigh.

Emma's breath quickened. "Please, Thea."

Thea slid her fingers inside her, and Emma cried out and bucked forward. It was a perfect rhythm and tempo. She held Thea tightly and dug her nails into Thea's back. "Now, now, now." Thea increased her pace until Emma couldn't take any more. She cried out with pleasure as she arched her body and surrendered to the moment. Their lips met in a passionate kiss, and Emma shuddered with pleasure, spent and breathless in Thea's arms. It had felt so natural, and all Emma's previous worries about sex had disappeared into the clouds.

It was okay. She could let go. She could move forward. Thea was beautiful, smart, kind, and they'd shared a connection from the moment she'd fallen onto her driveway. The new life Emma never thought she'd get was there for the taking.

Chapter Ten

Once upon a time, what seemed like many moons ago, Thea had woven a small web of lies. She'd convinced herself that it was necessary. She had to protect herself and her children and never let the past repeat itself. She'd built a fortress to shield them from dangers that lurked beyond the safety of their home. But the fortress was more than just a physical barrier; it was a mindset, a way of life.

But now, as the days passed, and she spent every minute possible with Emma, the weight of those untruths weighed heavily upon her shoulders. Of course, she'd meant to tell Emma everything, but somehow, the opportunity had never come up, and the fear of losing Emma prevented her from revealing the truth. So she put it off, again and again. She remembered the brief conversation about children. What was Thea doing dating someone who didn't like kids?

After that wonderful night, Thea and Emma spent the next three days and nights together immersed in a whirlwind of intimacy. They explored each other's bodies with a hunger that bordered on obsession. Passion, pleasure, and ecstasy echoed through the walls of their secluded world. A world of their own, in a house Emma thought belonged to someone else.

They revelled in the sheer joy of being together. They cooked, took walks along the beach, and swam together in the pool. They watched the sunset in each other's arms, savouring every precious moment they shared. Thea loved every minute, but she knew full well that there was a ticking bomb in the background, one that could explode and wreck it all. She was falling for Emma, and she was going to have to make a decision about the truth soon.

They lay together on a sunbed wrapped in each other's arms one afternoon, and Thea's thoughts were heavy, though she tried to hide it. She kissed the tip of Emma's nose. "I've been putting it off, but I have to tell you I'm going to Zakynthos on Sunday."

Emma shrugged. "It's okay. I guessed that would be soon." She lay her head on Thea's chest. "How long are you going for?"

Thea whispered, "Two weeks. Then I'll be back."

Emma sighed. "I don't suppose it will be the same though. You'll be looking after the children when you come home." She smiled. "Hopefully, you'll find time for me too."

Thea sprang up and stared down at Emma, the nagging secrets like a serpent ready to strike her heart. "Of course I will. We can do lots of things together."

Emma nodded and laughed, looking surprised. "I know my place hasn't got the luxury you're used to here, but we'll survive. As long as we're together, that's all that really matters."

Thea mentally nudged herself. *Time to be honest.* She wasn't sure how this conversation would go, but there was no putting it off.

She got up and poured two glasses of wine and put them on the table. "Come and sit with me, Emma. There's something very important I have to tell you."

Emma giggled. "Ooh, this sounds like fun."

Thea frowned. "I wouldn't class it as fun. It's actually incredibly serious."

Clearly becoming wary, Emma made her way over and sat on the chair opposite Thea. "I'm ready. Fire away."

Thea's hands trembled as she picked up her glass and drank the lot. A knot of fear tightened in her stomach. "There's no way I can wrap this up in some fancy paper and a ribbon. So here goes nothing." She took a deep breath. "Lyra and Seb are my children, and this is our home. I won the lottery a few years back."

The silence that followed was deafening. Tension hung between them like a veil. Perhaps she hadn't delivered that information quite as subtly as she'd wanted to, but at least it was out in the open now.

Emma blinked rapidly. "Pardon?" She rubbed her hand across her forehead. "Say that again."

"I'm sorry, Emma. I hate myself for lying to you, but I've had big issues in the past, and I had to learn to trust again. I had to be sure you were someone I could let into my life. Into my kids' lives. I thought if you knew, you might see me differently."

Emma drank some wine. She looked confused, and her face was as pale as a ghost in a snowstorm. "Let me get this right. You were worried I was a gold digger."

Thea grabbed Emma's hand, but she pulled it away. "No, no. It had nothing to do with money, not really. It's about my past." She took a deep breath and tried to steady herself. "A woman came into my life a few years ago and tried to kidnap my children after she found out I'd won the lottery. I've been obsessed with what could have happened. I've hidden away, and I've had to learn how to trust again."

Emma shook her head. "So you thought I was after money, *and* I was going to kidnap your children?"

"Don't be crazy, t had nothing to do with that. I'm sorry, I'm not putting this very well. It's a long story, and I need to tell you from the beginning." Thea was grateful Emma hadn't just got up and left. That was something.

"How long have we known each other? It's months, ard so much has happened between us. You didn't think you could trust me in all that time, to tell me the truth? I've never once given you a reason not to trust me. It's not like I'm destitute myself, and I worked damn hard for what I've got. I didn't have a lucky ticket chucked in my lap." She squeezed her eyes shut and rubbed her temples. "Okay, maybe you didn't know you could trust me for the first week or two. But after months together? This is no small thing; this is enormous." She shook her head. "You lied about the most important things in your life. It's like I don't even know you. Who keeps their kids a secret from someone they're supposed to be building a relationship with?"

"I'm falling for you, Emma." It was the first time she'd said it, but she meant it. "I promise, I never meant to hurt you. I tried to tell you on numerous occasions, but it just didn't pan out."

"It didn't *pan out*?" Emma's expression was a mask of shock and disbelief, her eyes wide, as she seemed to struggle to process the enormity of Thea's revelation. "How could you?" she whispered, and her voice trembled. "How could you lie to me like this, Thea? How could you keep such important truths from me? Not the money, but that this is *your* home. That you have children? The fact that you didn't feel like you could trust me with the truth..." She swallowed hard. "That's what hurts."

Thea's heart clenched at the pain in Emma's voice, and the realisation of the hurt she'd caused crashed over her like a tidal wave. "I was scared. I didn't know how to tell you the truth, and I was so drawn to you. Even when you said you didn't want kids, I couldn't just walk away. Maybe I should have, but I couldn't, and I'm glad I didn't. Please, at least let me explain, let me tell you what happened, then you might understand." Emotion welled up, so strong and thick it was hard to breathe.

Emma's eyes flickered. "You've shattered everything I thought I knew about us." She stood, unsteady on her feet. "I have to leave. I have to process this."

Thea took her arm. "At least hear me out and let me explain."

Emma jerked her arm away. "Go and get *your* children, Thea. Forget about me for the time being."

Thea felt her heart breaking as the weight of her betrayal settled heavily upon her shoulders. "I understand if you need time, Emma. But when I come back, please give me a chance to make things right. I'll do whatever it takes to earn back your trust."

Emma cleared her throat. "Whatever. I wasn't even aware I needed to doubt you in any way. Now I don't know what it is you're not telling me, or if what you do tell me is the truth." She fiddled with her phone but gave up as her hands shook. "Can you call me a taxi, please."

Thea obliged, as Emma seemed adamant about leaving and clearly didn't want to be in a car with her. She couldn't make that offer anyway, because she'd never drink and drive.

Emma collected her things and headed for the lift. She didn't turn around and wave or say farewell. She just pressed the button and disappeared.

Thea tried to propel herself forward, but her legs wobbled, and her knees buckled. *Pull yourself together, woman.* She took heaps of deep breaths and made her way to the window. Emma stood on the drive, her shoulders hunched and head bowed. She reached up occasionally as though wiping at her eyes. She got in the taxi that pulled up and was gone.

Thea found herself consumed by a profound sense of loss. The wrongdoing was on her part, and she would never forgive herself for all the lies she'd told. Yes, she'd had her reasons, and yes, they'd felt solid at the time. But if that lack of trust meant losing Emma, what did her reasons matter? If she could turn back the clock, she'd do it in flash, but that wasn't an option. Everywhere she looked was a haunting reminder of the world that had slipped through her fingers, the possible future she'd thrown away.

A knot of nausea churned in her stomach, and Thea stumbled to the bathroom. She collapsed onto the cold tile floor, sobbing and gasping for breath, and clutched at the porcelain bowl for support. She began to shiver and went into a cold sweat. She retched and was physically sick.

She took a shower and got into bed, though she knew she wouldn't find sleep. She'd bombarded Emma with texts and received only one in response.

I trusted you, but you didn't trust me. You chose to lie to me, and now we both have to live with the consequences.

She could hardly blame her. She had nobody to blame but herself. Apparently, rock bottom had a basement, and she'd found it.

As the night wore on, sleep remained a distant and elusive prospect, while the memories of Emma's departure played in an endless loop in Thea's mind. Her inability to trust had hurt Emma, and it burned like a tattoo upon her soul. Even if, in the long run, Emma could understand her reasoning and forgive her, the fact remained that Emma didn't want children. Thea had allowed the attraction to grow knowing full well that it was unfair. Emma's heart had got involved, and by not telling her until it was too late, Thea had made it so she'd have to choose between Thea and her children, and walking away.

And she'd walked away.

Chapter Eleven

EMMA SLUMPED INTO HER chair and sobbed. Oh, what a fool she'd been. She'd never had the impression that Thea was struggling, but she'd never considered that she might be a multi-millionaire: a multi-millionairess with two children. And for all she knew, there could be a husband too.

A thousand thoughts raced through Emma's mind as she grappled with the implications of Thea's lies. Why had Thea kept her life hidden from Emma? What was it she shouted about? Something about learning to trust again and some woman trying to kidnap her children for a ransom. Or was it that Thea withheld the truth because she thought Emma was a gold digger? How dare she? It struck at the core of her identity and integrity.

The woman she had fallen for was not who Emma thought she was. The deep friendship and relationship they had formed had been shattered into pieces.

She couldn't stop her heart from pounding in her chest like it was trying to escape through her ribcage. She closed her eyes and took several deep breaths. She tried to remember the sequence of the meditation she learned after losing Brid. It worked to a degree, enough for her to make a mug of camomile tea and take it to bed.

All Emma could hear were pings on her phone. She was inundated with a barrage of texts from Thea. She quickly scanned them. Apologies, regret, and begging for Emma to hear her out. She wanted to lash out for all the pain Thea had caused her. Instead, Emma chose to respond with quiet dignity. She wanted to take back control.

She tried to sleep, but no matter what she tried, it evaded her. She tossed and turned, her emotions a rollercoaster of grief, anger, and sadness.

Finally, she drifted into a dream, twisted and distorted into nightmarish visions full of torment. She rubbed her eyes and checked the time on her mobile. Six a.m., and all wasn't well. She got up and drew the curtains back. The sun had risen, and the weather forecast promised another hot day. It should be stormy, with thunder and lightning. The sun had no business shining when she felt this way. Her body ached with weariness, and when she stared into the bathroom mirror, a bleary pair of eyes stared back at her.

Tea and toast were all she could manage. What she really needed was to talk to someone, to share her feelings. It was way too early to ring Jen, but she could at least send her an email. Of course, they had kept in touch whilst Jen and her partner, Steve, had been in America, but it was purely small talk and an assortment of photos that Jen shared with her. She remembered the email she'd left in drafts. She retrieved it, read through it, and made a few alterations.

Hi Jen,
Hope you're recovering from your jetlag.
I know you're going to kill me for not letting you know about this, but honestly, darling, I didn't want to ruin your holiday.
A week or so after moving, I had a bit of an accident and came off my bike. Now don't panic, everything is fine. Long story short, I broke my leg but it's healing nicely. I'm still on crutches, but my physio is happy with the way I'm mending. It won't be long before I'm up and running.
During that time, I met a woman. She was someone special, and we developed a relationship. However, I've just found out that she's been lying to me from the moment we met. Consequently, I left, and I doubt I'll ever see her again.
It's quite shaken me up, and I feel like shit now. But don't

*worry, you know me...I'll eventually rise above it and move
on. Miss you though, and wish you were here to talk to.
I'm going out for a drive now, but I'll call you later to have a
natter.
Love you loads,
Emma xx*

She pressed send and felt a little better. Someone out there knew she was hurting, other than the person who'd caused it all.

Right now, she needed to get out. To drive somewhere, anywhere. To try and make sense of everything that had happened. She had a small car, and the lodge manager had made sure to take it for little drives on a regular basis. It would be the first time she'd driven since she'd had her accident, but it was an automatic, and it was well within her capabilities now.

She considered driving to Rocky Cove, the place where they'd spent that lovely day picnicking, but that would only bring back memories of a happier time. Instead, she drove in the opposite direction. She had no idea where she was going; just like she had no idea where her life was going.

She made a right turn and pulled into a car park which overlooked a pretty bay. She took her crutches and made her way to a solitary wooden bench where she let the weight of melancholy settle over her like a heavy fog. The sea stretched out before her, and the sun shimmered on the water, yet she found no solace in its beauty today. Memories of happier times danced at the edges of her consciousness, taunting her with their fleeting glimpses of the joy and laughter that she and Thea had shared.

A gentle breeze rustled through her hair, carrying a faint scent of salt and seaweed. Emma closed her eyes and allowed herself to be swept away by the sadness engulfing her. Her heart ached, but she knew she had to be resilient. She must find a way of overcoming this misery. Maybe it was a sign. Maybe she wasn't meant to date after all. Maybe Brid really had been her one and only.

She walked a little way across the car park when she couldn't take the direct heat any longer and an idea came to her. She may not have her bestie to talk to, but she had made another new contact. Margot wasn't a close friend, but she was easy to talk to, and right now, Emma needed to unload and get another perspective.

She opened her WhatsApp and pressed the telephone icon on Margot's profile. It rang and rang, but nobody answered. She stared into space. She knew Margot's address, well, most of it anyway. She'd drive there. What if she wasn't in? Did it really matter? She had nothing else to do, and nowhere else to go. It sounded a little like being a stalker, but she'd risk that as she was in dire need to talk to the only other person she knew in Westleigh. And Margot would understand.

She entered her address into Google maps and up it sprang. At least she'd got it right. Margot was quite a way out in the countryside, and it took her fifty minutes to get there.

At the bottom of the road was a corner shop. She pulled in and bought a bunch of flowers to take to Margot. It was the least she could do given that she was about to show up uninvited. She turned into Harris Road and drove the length of the road. It was much longer than she'd imagined. Cars were parked on both sides of the street in front of the terraced houses, and it was mostly resident parking apart from a few spaces in the middle, but they were all occupied. It was a shame she couldn't remember the number of the house, but maybe she'd get lucky. When she reached the top of the road, it was a dead end, so she turned around and drove slowly back down it. Each house had a small garden at the front, and like anywhere, some looked after their gardens, and some were overgrown.

Luck was with her. A car pulled out from one of the general spaces, and she slipped into it quickly. She grabbed her handbag, the flowers, and one of her crutches to help her balance. She was parked outside a house with a bright purple door, where a man was crouched down in the garden doing some weeding.

"Excuse me. I wonder if you could help me?" she asked. He neither spoke nor looked up. Perhaps he was deaf. She waited a few minutes then coughed. "Hello. I wonder if you could help me?"

This time, the man looked in her direction. He groaned, held his back, and gently got himself to a standing position. He huffed and puffed. "What you say?"

"I'm looking for my friend who lives on this road. I'm sorry but I can't remember the house number."

"What's 'er name?"

Emma cleared her throat. "It's Margot Templeton-Smythe."

The man laughed. "Never 'eard of 'er."

Emma's shoulders slumped. "All I know is she lives here with her sister and husband."

"What she look like?"

Emma pondered this question. "About my height, late fifties... and she's just come out of hospital."

The man scratched the stubble on his chin. "What you say 'er name is?"

"Margot Templeton-Smythe."

The man doubled up and burst into raucous laughter. "Margot Templeton-Smythe," he said in his best posh voice. "So that's what she goes by these days."

Emma frowned. "I don't understand."

"Me neither, luv. But I reckon the woman you're after is Maggie Smith. Sounds like 'er anyway."

Emma was sure there was a perfectly good explanation. "And she's just come out of hospital?"

"Yeah, fell out the shower," he laughed, "pissed as usual." He raised his hand. "'Scuse my French. Lives with 'er 'usband, Dudley...for 'is sins," he said, still in fits of laughter.

Emma shrugged. "It could be her. Which number does she live at?"

"Twenty-seven." He pointed up the road. "Can't miss it. Orange door and gnomes galore." He chuckled, continuing to shake his head.

Emma forced a smile. "Thank you. You've been most helpful."

"Welcome, luv." He laughed. "You'll 'ear 'er before you see 'er."

Emma was now beginning to regret her decision to visit Margot. Another person who'd been lying about who she was. Heck, her name wasn't even the same. At least Emma hadn't slept with this one. But she was here now, so she might as well go through with it.

Sure enough, just as the man had said, there were the gnomes and the orange door. *Gnome, sweet gnome.* She hoped the man was wrong, but she had a nagging feeling that this day was going from bad to worse.

She pressed the doorbell but couldn't hear it buzzing. She tried again and finally decided to knock. It took a while, but she heard someone shouting.

"'old yer 'orses."

Eventually the door opened. The woman bore a vague resemblance to Margot. But it was only vague. Her hair was matted and instead of the well-groomed woman she'd met in the hospital, she was now faced with an unkempt version, one that looked disturbingly hostile. No hint of Hyacinth Bouquet. She was leaning on a Zimmer frame and dressed in a tight pair of leggings with a yellow sweatshirt. The sweatshirt was heavily stained with a colourful mosaic of spaghetti sauce and breakfast cereal.

The woman stared down at her. "What's up? Cat got yer tongue?"

Emma guessed that must be the problem. "Margot, it's me, Emma."

"Oh, yeah? You from social services?"

"No. It's Emma. We met in hospital. We were roomies, don't

you remember?"

Margot, Maggie, or whatever her name was screwed her eyes up and stared at Emma. "Bloody 'ell."

Yes, Emma thought. That about summed it up.

Margot wiped her nose with the back of her hand. "You should've called me first."

"I tried."

"Er, well, you've caught me at a bad moment." Her eyes were unfocused as she peered more closely at Emma. "You look different in the light of day."

As did "Margot." Emma nodded. "I'm sorry. I shouldn't have come." She thrust the flowers forward. "I hope you make a speedy recovery." She turned and slowly walked back to her car. She shook her head. Her life was surrounded by liars. If she didn't feel so distressed, she'd see the funny side of it, but that was quite a challenge right now.

She couldn't remember when she'd last eaten, and her stomach began to emit a low, persistent rumble, despite her emotional turmoil. The last thing she wanted to do was prepare something when she got in. She knew she'd end up skipping food, but common sense plus experience told her she needed nourishment. She passed a quaint looking café on the side of the road and pulled in. Her appetite was minimal, but she managed a couple of poached eggs on toast and a strong cup of decent coffee.

Emma returned home and sat alone in her apartment, which now felt as though it would swallow her up. She was overcome with loneliness, and tears welled up as she replayed everything going wrong around her.

Her phone pinged. *Oh no, please leave me alone.* However, she peered at the message.

I'm outside. Jen xxx

No, she couldn't be. She re-read the message, and it was definitely from Jen. Somehow, she still thought it was some kind of cruel trick. She opened her door and headed towards the main entrance. As she peered through the window, her breath caught in her throat at the sight of her friend getting out of her car. With a mixture of surprise and gratitude, Emma propelled her crutches as fast as her balance would allow, her heart racing.

Moments later, Emma dropped her crutches and Jen enveloped her in a warm embrace, Emma wrapped her arms tightly around her.

"I'm here for you, Emma," she whispered. "You're not alone."

Tears streamed down Emma's cheeks as she buried her face on Jen's shoulder. The weight of her grief lifted slightly. "I can't believe you're here."

"And I can't believe you didn't tell me sooner."

"Jen, I couldn't. I knew you'd cut your holiday short. It wasn't necessary."

Jen punched Emma's arm playfully. "Well, you should've let me be the judge of that."

"I'm okay. I've coped."

Jen laughed. "Well, I haven't. I need a large mug of proper British tea. I threw some bits into a bag and drove straight down here like a bat out of hell. Yes, I did have a wee stop and some plastic sandwiches, but that was hours ago." Jen picked up Emma's crutches and passed them to her, then she pulled her bag from the boot of her car. "C'mon, I can't wait to see your flat."

Over a supper of local fish and chips, Emma relayed the whole sordid tale. She finished by telling her the story of Margot and the gnomes in her garden.

Jen laughed. "So it was time for you to go gnome."

Emma frowned. "Promise me; no more jokes about gnomes."

"I promise. Anyway, there's more important things to talk about."

Despite Emma being shattered, they sat and chatted into the small hours. She knew that no matter what challenges lay ahead, she wouldn't be facing them alone. She still had Jen, which meant she wasn't completely alone in the world yet again.

Chapter Twelve

THEA STEPPED OFF THE plane onto the tarmac at the airport and felt a sense of calm wash over her—a welcome respite from the havoc that had consumed her in recent days.

She made her way through the bustling terminal filled with holidaymakers and was greeted by a familiar sight that filled her with warmth and joy...the smiling faces of her father and children waiting eagerly to welcome her home. Tears of happiness welled up in her eyes, and she rushed forward to envelop her children in a tight embrace. The weight of their bodies pressed against her chest like a balm to reduce her pain. "Oh, my darlings," she whispered, her voice choked with emotion. "You have no idea how much I've missed you."

Lyra and Seb giggled with delight as they returned her hugs. Their laughter was music to her ears. All her troubles seemed to melt away, replaced by her wild happiness at being reunited with the ones she loved most. She turned to her father, a pillar of strength and love in her life. "Dad, I don't know what I would do without you."

Her father smiled warmly and wrapped his arms around her. "Welcome home, sweetheart. We're so glad you came back early. We've missed you. We can't wait until the day you move here permanently."

"Me neither." That had always been Thea's intention, but she wanted Lyra and Seb to finish their education in England, just like her mum and dad had insisted for her and her brothers. Sadly, there weren't any international or bilingual schools in Zakynthos. They followed a national curriculum, with Greek as the language of instruction, and she knew Lyra and Seb wouldn't cope. They spoke a smattering of Greek but not enough. For English-speaking or international kids, the closest options would be in larger cities on the mainland. It was a difficult situation because she knew that they would love to live there, and Thea missed her family desperately.

They made their way to her father's car, the air alive with the excitement of their reunion. As they headed back home, the familiarity of sights and sounds of her island enveloped her like a warm caress, filling her heart with a sense of nostalgia and belonging. As messy as things were back in England, she could always count on her family. *Unlike Emma, who has no one.* The thought twisted in her soul like an angry snake.

Her father parked the car at the bottom of the track, and the four of them walked hand in hand towards her family's restaurant, which lay nestled between the olive trees and the golden sands. As Thea approached the restaurant, memories of summers spent playing on the beach and evenings gathered around the family dinner table flooded her mind, filling her with a sense of longing for the simplicity of days gone by.

They walked through the outside dining area, which was bustling with the laughter and chatting of happy tourists. Thea glanced around, trying to spot her mother, and was greeted with the comforting aroma of their family's cooking: a fragrant bouquet of herbs, spices, and barbecued foods. There she was. She quickened her pace and ran into the arms of her mother, who was turning the meats and kebabs on the grill.

Her mum's face lit up. "Thea, my darling girl." She pulled her into her arms and smothered her with kisses. "You look terrible. What's happened?"

Mortified, Thea burst into tears.

Her mum gently stroked her hair. "Everything will be fine."

"Oh, Mum, I wish you were right."

Her mum sat her down at a nearby table. "First, we'll feed

you, then you must get some sleep. You can tell me about it in the morning. Let the feeling of home sink in first."

Thea sniffed and tried to force a smile.

Lyra and Seb sat down beside her.

Lyra touched her hand. "What's wrong, Mum?"

"It's the onions." She laughed. "One day I'm going to make the *onions* cry." She shook her head and took both of her children's hands. "And I'm so happy to see you."

That answer would suffice for the moment, but she could tell by Lyra's stare that she didn't believe Thea for one minute.

Before she went to bed, her mum prescribed a large ouzo, which had always been a cure-all in their family. It seemed to do the trick, and she fell into a deep, dreamless sleep.

The following morning, she awoke to the beautiful sun shining through her window. Had it really been only yesterday when she'd woken with Emma in her arms? The ache rushed back into her soul. She showered and made her way down the stairs. Her mum was preparing an assortment of fruit in a large bowl.

Thea looked around. "Where's Lyra and Seb?"

"Your father has taken them fishing." She tilted her head and gazed at Thea "We thought it was a good idea. We're not open until tonight, so I thought we could have a catch-up."

As Thea settled into a chair at the kitchen table, a lump formed in her throat, a knot of guilt and shame that felt like it was choking her. How could she confess to her mother the deception that had torn her relationship apart? And yet, she couldn't keep the truth hidden any longer, not from her family, not from herself.

Her mum spooned some fruit into a small bowl, put a warm croissant on a plate and passed them to her. "Eat."

Thea knew better than to disobey. When she'd finished, she took a deep breath and met her mother's gaze. Her eyes filled with tears. "Mum, I made a terrible mistake." Her voice trembled with emotion. "I lied to Emma. I told her that I was a nanny looking after Lyra and Seb, and that the house wasn't mine, that I just had a room in it. I let her believe that for months, even knowing how she felt about having kids. And now she's gone, and I don't know how to make things right."

Her mum frowned. "But why, darling?"

Thea shrugged. "Because I was scared about the past. I was terrified it was going to happen all over again. What if I trusted someone the way I trusted Riva and put my kids in danger again?"

Her mum continued to chop fruit. "But Emma didn't sound like that sort of person. Did she give you a reason to think she might not be worth your trust?"

"No. Never. I just couldn't trust myself. I couldn't trust that I could read people anymore or make the right choices when it came to them. I told myself I just needed time to be sure. But the more time passed, the harder it became to tell her the truth."

"What happened with that witch... It's okay that it scared you, scarred you. But you've let it change you, and that's not good. You have been overprotective with Lyra and Seb, and you've let fear rob you of that beautiful heart you used to give so freely." Her mum kissed her forehead. "It's going to be okay. We'll sort it all out."

Thea pushed away the bowl of fruit as her stomach turned. "It won't be. She wouldn't listen to the whole story. She said it had to do with the fact that I couldn't trust her, even after all we'd shared. Even after months together, I didn't trust her enough to tell her the truth. She told me to leave her alone."

Her mum's expression softened, and she took Thea's hands in hers. "Oh, my dear," she said gently, her voice filled with compassion. "You've made a big mistake; we all make them from time to time." Her mum laughed gently. "You have no idea about some of the mistakes your father and I have made." She let go of Thea's hand and picked up the knife again. "There are questions you have to answer for yourself. Can you really let someone in again? Or will you always keep a wall up, keep them at a distance in case they hurt you? Do you want Emma to forgive you so you can be together, or do you want her to forgive you so you don't feel guilty? They're very different things." She looked up from the melon. "It's your choice, but it's time for you to find a way to heal, my love."

With her mother's unwavering support by her side, Thea saw a glimmer of hope. It was true, she had things to work through, and she owed it to Emma to figure herself out before she tried to make amends, whatever the outcome might be.

***

As Thea prepared to leave the Greek island and return home, a bittersweet feeling settled over her. It was a mixture of sadness at saying goodbye to her parents and gratitude for the precious time they'd shared together. The two weeks had been one of deep reflection and lots of heartfelt talks with her parents, and she was ready to move forward, as difficult as it might be.

Her mum whispered in her ear, "Everything will work out fine, my darling. I feel it in my bones. Go with the flow."

Only dead fish go with the flow. She didn't say it out loud. "I wish you were coming with me."

Her mum shook her head. "There are some things that you must face alone. I have every faith that you'll put things right between you and your young lady."

Thea chuckled. Her mum still insisted on calling Emma her young lady, but for some reason, it was a nice feeling.

At the gates of the airport, Lyra and Seb embraced their grandparents one last time. Tears welled up in their eyes with the weight of parting. Thea knew how much Lyra and Seb adored their grandparents, and the thought of leaving them behind left her with a deep sense of longing.

"I'll miss you, Yaya and Papou," Seb whispered, his voice quivering as he clung tightly to his grandmother's hand.

"We'll miss you too, my darlings," she said, her voice filled with love as she pulled her grandchildren close. "Remember, we'll always be here for you, no matter how far away you may be."

Seb and Lyra reluctantly pulled away from their grandparents' embrace and made their way through the gate.

Thea couldn't shake the feeling of emptiness that settled in the pit of her stomach. The island had been a haven of safety and love, and bonds had been strengthened. The thought of leaving them behind made her feel as though the rope on her boat had been cut, and she was drifting out to sea. Maybe it was time to move back. Maybe she was floundering out there alone, without her family to steady her.

Seb buried his nose in a book, and Lyra flipped through the movies on the screen attached to the seat in front of her. She couldn't move the children. Not yet. And wouldn't she just be running away from her problems?

Not that Emma was a problem. She was the only thing Thea had been able to think about for two weeks, and she was the reason Thea wanted to heal some of the wounds to her heart and mind. She didn't expect it to be easy, but she was going to do her best to get Emma to hear her out.

When they arrived home, and Thea had settled Lyra and Seb in bed, she opened up her phone. She couldn't believe her eyes when she read the text from Emma.

I need to hear your explanation. Perhaps we can have a coffee together.

It was a little terse, but nevertheless, it gave her hope. Now she had to answer. The children would be back at school, so it wouldn't be too busy.

There's a hotel on the promenade called Vista. There's a small lounge which is usually quiet. Are you free on Tuesday at 11am? She waited for a response, her heart pounding.

See you then.

Thea couldn't shake the mix of nerves and anticipation that filled her as she awaited the meeting with Emma. The text had sent a jolt of uncertainty through her, but deep down, she knew she needed to confront the past head-on.

Tuesday came and with a deep breath, Thea made her way to the agreed meeting spot. There were a few people in the lounge, but she found a table by a window overlooking the sea. Minutes stretched into eternity as Thea's mind raced with a whirlwind of emotions. Perhaps Emma had changed her mind, and then just as doubt began to creep in, she saw Emma approaching, her expression a mixture of apprehension and vulnerability.

As they sat face to face, all Thea wanted to do was to kiss her and take her into a warm embrace. But the wary look on Emma's face told her that wasn't a good idea. "Thank you for coming, Emma. I ordered a pot of coffee; I hope that's okay?"

Emma nodded. "Thank you."

The weight of unspoken words hung heavy in the air, and fortunately, the coffee arrived quickly, and Thea poured some into each cup. "I'm sorry, Emma." Thea breathed deeply and gathered her strength. "I know I hurt you, and I can't begin to excuse the lies I told. But I need you to understand that I was scared... I was scared of losing you, of facing the truth of my own insecurities and fears."

Emma's expression remained unchanged. "Tell me about them."

Thea tucked her shaking hands under her thighs. "I'm not sure where to start."

Emma folded her arms across her chest. "The beginning. It's always a good place."

Thea detected more than a hint of sarcasm in Emma's words. She could hardly blame her. "I always wanted children. I didn't want a husband or a wife, but I wanted children and to raise them on my own. I bought a property, and I had significant savings. When I left the army, the time was right. I think I told you; I went back to work in my family's restaurant and lived in the flat above. When I was ready, I went to Greece for a few years, because

I wanted a Greek egg donor. I had both my children by IVF. I moved back into the flat I'd bought, and I was able to carry on working in the restaurant because my aunt, uncle, and cousins adored children. It's how things are with us; everyone mucks in, so I was never short of babysitters." Thea smiled and paused whilst she topped up the coffee cups. So far, so good. Emma was clearly listening closely, even though she hadn't interjected at all.

"Every week, I played the lottery. Just a couple of lines for a laugh really, because I'm not money-orientated, but I do like to feel financially secure. Like most, I dreamed of the win that would change our lives. And it happened. I had a very big win." Thea cleared her throat as she remembered the day she'd seen the winning numbers on her ticket. "I did all the stuff that others do and looked after my family, not that they wanted it, because they all continued working, but as my mum and dad said, it would make retirement more comfortable. I honestly didn't know what I wanted to do, so I stayed put and carried on living virtually the same life. I needed time to think about our future. After all, there was no rush. As usual, I went to the local gym every day, and that's where I met Riva. We got on so well right from the word go. We seemed to have so much in common. You know how it is."

Emma stared directly at Thea. "Yes, I know exactly what you mean."

Thea winced but kept talking. "I trusted Riva, and she was brilliant with Lyra and Seb. I'd known her for a couple of months, and she often sat with them while I popped out, and I had no problem with that. I did get a little suspicious at one point though, because I saw her with this guy, and she kissed him. When I confronted her about it, she told me it was her brother. I didn't give it too much thought after that. In hindsight, alarm bells should have rung. Anyway, a couple of weeks later, I had the flu. I felt bloody awful, and Riva made me soup and stuff and looked after Lyra and Seb. She was an angel, or so I thought. It was a beautiful day, and Lyra and Seb wanted to go out and play in the park. She offered to take them, and I let her." Thea wiped her clammy hands on her jeans and took several deep breaths.

Emma's expression turned to one of concern. "Shall I get you a glass of water?"

Thea shook her head. "Thanks, Emma, I'll be fine in a minute." She composed herself. "I dropped off to sleep and when I looked at the clock, nearly two hours had passed. Then there was a knock at the door. Lyra ran into my arms, crying. Seb was only four and a half, and he was sitting on his tricycle, giggling as though it was all a big joke. I think he was totally oblivious to what had happened and was just excited that he'd been able to ride in a police car. A policewoman and a guy from the National Crime Agency asked if they could come in. It transpired that Riva and her so-called brother, who was actually her boyfriend, had been under surveillance. Their plan was to kidnap my children and hold them to ransom. The boyfriend had tried to get some help from his friend. Although the guy was a bit of a villain, he didn't want anything to do with kidnapping. He'd gone to the police, and they'd been watching them ever since. When they saw the pair headed for the airport with my children, they put a stop to it."

Emma shook her head. "Oh my God, you must have been distraught."

"It turned out they'd targeted me. They'd found my name on the lottery winners' register and decided they'd get a healthy ransom for my kids. Riva was a lie, and I was dumb enough to believe everything she told me. She used my Facebook profile to find out the things I liked, and they built a kind of profile for her so I'd think we had all these things in common. That way they could take the kids without a huge uproar, whereas if they just snatched them off the street, the police would be looking for them instantly. They also wanted to see if I'd give Riva access to my bank account." Thea felt sick at the reminder of how gullible she'd been.

"I was frightened and angry, but most of all I was overwhelmed with a sense of vulnerability. It's hard to explain. It turned me from a normal trusting person into an obsessive maniac. The kids were fine, and I hadn't lost any money. But the what-ifs haunted me, and I didn't trust myself anymore. My mum and dad came right away. They wanted me to go back with them, but I didn't want to run away. Eventually, Quinn came to my rescue, and she helped me move to Westleigh. I thought things would get better, but I got worse. I built my fortress, determined not to let anyone into our lives again." Thea held her head in her hands and let the tears run down her face.

Emma got up and sat beside Thea. She wrapped her arm around her. "But I'm not Riva. You should have told me. I would have understood your concerns. And you would have left it to me to make the choice about whether or not I wanted to date someone with kids."

Thea looked around at Emma. "Do you think you could get me that water now?"

Emma came back with a jug of water and two glasses. "Would you like something stronger? Maybe a brandy?"

Thea smiled wanly and shook her head. "No, honestly. I'm okay." She took a long drink. "I tried to tell you. Remember when I came to yours early on? I was about to confess, and your physio rang. I put it off and put it off. Then I found I was covering myself from every angle. The longer I lied, the deeper the hole became. When our friendship turned into more, and my feelings for you grew, I was terrified of losing you. It was wrong, and I'm sorry." She'd said what she had to say, and Emma's arm felt so good, so right, around her shoulders. "Please forgive me," she whispered. "I don't want to lose you."

Chapter Thirteen

As the pieces of the puzzle fell into place, Emma's heart softened with understanding. She recalled the moments when Thea had seemed guarded, and the hints of hesitation in her eyes whenever the topic of her personal life arose. She remembered the time when she'd told Thea about the nurse who'd turned up outside her flat. Thea had gone berserk, telling her that she was a stalker. Emma realised now that Thea's lies were born not from a desire to deceive, but from a desperate need to protect herself and her loved ones.

Emma's anger dissolved, giving way to empathy. Thea had trusted someone, and it could have destroyed her children's lives. Trusting after something like that would be incredibly difficult.

She took Thea's hand in hers, a gesture of understanding and forgiveness. "I wish you had told me sooner," she said softly. "But I understand why you found it so difficult."

Thea looked like a weight had been lifted from her shoulders. "I love you, Emma. I need you. Do you think you could give me another chance?"

A knot of anxiety tightened in Emma's chest. She knew she had to have this difficult conversation with Thea. She and Jen had spent long days and nights discussing Emma's doubts and fears. She took a deep breath and gathered courage to tell Thea the truth, even though she knew it would hurt them both. "I have to be honest with you. Lyra and Seb are young, and there's a nineteen-year age gap between us. I can't take on the responsibility of raising your children at my age."

Thea's shoulders dropped, and tears filled her eyes. "I'm not asking you to raise them. I just want you by my side. Couldn't we try it?"

"It wouldn't be fair to come into their lives, realise I couldn't cope, and leave. I wouldn't think you'd want that either."

"You're not even willing to try?"

Emma's heart ached at the thought of not seeing Thea again. "I wish things were different, but I have to be true to myself, and I honestly don't think I can handle children."

"I understand," Thea said quietly, her voice tinged with sadness. "It's a lot to ask of anyone."

No relief came from being honest, and as tears tracked down Thea's cheeks, Emma felt awful. She wanted to hold her, take it all back, say she was willing to see if it was possible...but there were no more lies to be told, no more omissions or broken promises.

As she watched Thea walk away from the hotel, her head bowed, Emma wondered if she'd made the right choice.

***

The next few weeks passed by slowly, and Emma felt swamped with doubt and regret. She was haunted by thoughts of Thea. Each day was like an eternity, and she was plagued by self-doubt and second-guessing her decision.

She was unable to shake off the emptiness of her existence. Not so long ago, she'd contemplated the idea of opening another nearly new shop in Westleigh to fill the void in her life, but now her heart simply wasn't in it. Despite wanting to throw herself into a new venture, the thought of the day-to-day responsibilities of running a business left her uninspired.

As each day passed, Emma found herself consumed by a sense of listlessness. When Jen video-called her that evening, she told her about the meeting she'd had with Thea and the decisions she'd made.

Instead of the support she'd expected, she was met with a

blunt and cutting response.

"You're an idiot," Jen said. "You let go of someone who loved you, who cared for you, and who wanted to build a future with you. She made a mistake, but damn, you kind of can't blame her for being a little messed up over that whole thing. And you're not going to let her in because of what? Fear of the unknown? Couldn't you at least have given it a go?"

It was like a slap in the face, and Emma wasn't sure how to respond. "We talked about this. I didn't want to start something that maybe I couldn't finish. You know how I am. Remember, Brid and Colly both said I was lacking in depth. And children require caregivers to have at least a little of that."

"Bugger that, Emma. That's a load of shit. Both Colly and Brid were control freaks, and it was a way of getting at you. As far as Thea goes, she was prepared to take the risk, and they're *her* kids. You could have taken a run at it."

"It wouldn't have been fair."

"That's a cop out, and you know it. You threw away something precious, Emma, and now you're paying the price."

Was Jen right? Had she been a fool to let her fears dictate her actions? "Well, it's too late now. I can't turn the clock back." Nor did she know if she wanted to. Maybe it was just better to deal with the heartbreak now than it would be later when there were attachments all around.

"No. But you could get in touch with her and say you're missing her."

Emma harrumphed. "She's probably moved on already."

"Ha," Jen said. "I never put you down as a defeatist."

"I'm a realist, Jen." She paused. "I'll give it some more thought though."

"Make sure you do. I want a full report after the weekend. Talking of which, I have to go and throw some clothes into a bag, Steve and I have rented a motorhome."

Emma laughed. "What happened to luxury hotels?"

"Boring. We want something different. Well, more to the point, some friends have just bought one, so we're going to meet them at a site in the Northumberland National Park. Who knows? If we take to it, we may just buy one."

"Wow. Well, have fun, and I'll talk to you next week."

Jen blew a kiss and hung up.

Emma envied Jen's life, just a little. She and Steve were so carefree, and they loved being in each other's company. She wanted that too. Spending what years she had left alone sounded pretty awful. Perhaps Jen was right. Maybe she should face her fears head-on. But her fears were logical, weren't they? How was she supposed to do away with logic?

The following morning, Emma looked into the fridge and found an uninspiring array of nothing but rotting fruit and vegetables. She cleared it all out, made a list, and headed to the supermarket.

Emma navigated the aisles, her mind preoccupied with her grocery shopping. She was suddenly startled by a voice calling her name. She turned around and found herself face to face with Thea. Her heart raced with a chaotic blend of emotions. "Thea." There was no denying the thrill that rushed through her when she looked into Thea's beautiful eyes. "It's so good to see you."

Thea tentatively hugged Emma and kissed her on the cheek. "I've so missed you."

Emma's heart lurched. "I've missed you too."

"Hey, where are your crutches? Have you thrown them away?" Thea asked and laughed.

"Yep. Right out the window. All back to normal now." She grimaced. "Well, I need to get some exercise and strengthen my leg, but that's just a question of time."

"That's fantastic."

Two children raced up the aisle with armfuls of fruit and came to a standstill when they saw their mother talking to a stranger.

Thea grinned. "This is my daughter, Lyra, and my son, Seb."

Emma's gaze shifted to the two children standing beside Thea, their faces alight with curiosity. "Hi, Lyra. Hi, Seb. It's good to meet you both," she said, offering them a tentative smile.

Lyra beamed. "Are you Emma?"

"Er, yes, I am."

"Do you like bike riding, Emma? We're going on a bike trail and picnic tomorrow. You should come too."

Thea clipped Lyra on the head playfully. "Lyra! You're embarrassing Emma. She probably has plans."

Emma's heart skipped a beat at the unexpected invitation but she wasn't sure how to respond. Did Thea want her to accept? Did *she* want to accept?

Seb motioned with an orange. "It's going to be so much fun."

There was something about their warmth and kindness that drew her in and made her feel welcome. In that moment, she decided she very much wanted to go. "In that case, I'd love to join you."

"Yippee!" Lyra and Seb said in unison.

Emma covered her mouth. "I've just remembered that I never collected my bike. I hope you haven't sold it?" she asked, only partly kidding.

Thea's grin spread. "As if. I'm sure Lyra and Seb will polish it up for you and oil the chain."

Lyra's eyes sparkled. "We can do that this afternoon when we do ours."

"So we'll pick you up at eleven tomorrow morning. Is that okay?" Thea said.

Emma nodded. "Fantastic." She looked down at Lyra and Seb. "And thank you so much for the invite." She wheeled her trolley away and called over her shoulder, "See you tomorrow." *What have I done?* She felt a sense of excitement and anticipation building within her. Maybe, just maybe, this was what she needed.

Chapter Fourteen

ON THE MORNING OF the bike ride, Thea was up early, preparing everything for their coming day together. Excitement and fear made her nerves tingle. She couldn't help but laugh at the way Lyra had jumped into action and invited Emma for their day out. She would've liked to have asked herself, but coming from Lyra, Emma clearly had a hard time refusing. What a little angel she was.

This was only the beginning, and she was aware how difficult it would be to let go of the past and the old wounds that had held her captive for so long. She did feel that she had begun to heal, and with that came a newfound sense of hope and possibility.

Her thoughts were interrupted by the sound of her children bounding down the stairs.

Seb was the first to arrive in the kitchen. "Are you ready, Mum?"

Thea patted the stool beside her. "Breakfast first."

Seb and Lyra hopped onto the stools and wolfed their cereal down.

Thea tutted. "If you get indigestion, don't blame me. Have you got all your gear together?"

Seb nodded, his mouth crammed full of a banana.

"Now listen, you two. Some rules for the day. Firstly, remember Emma has only just recovered from a nasty knee injury, so I don't want you racing away like a crazy pair of hyenas."

Lyra nodded.

"And watch your manners. Don't start interrogating Emma at every given opportunity." She directed this statement directly at

Lyra. "Remember what Yaya and Papou always say."

Seb piped up. "Seen but not heard."

Thea raised her eyebrows. "Yeah. Some hope."

Lyra patted her mum's hand. "Bubbles! Everything will be fine."

Thea laughed. "Bubbles?"

Lyra put her hands on her hips. "It doesn't matter whether you shout it or whisper it, the word bubbles can never sound nasty."

"Where the heck did you get that from?"

"Grandma Yaya."

Thea held her hands up. "Surprise, surprise." Her daughter was more like Thea's mother than she'd ever been.

Was it too soon for her and Emma to try again? A lot of water had gone under the bridge, and it needed to settle and flow freely.

Thea tooted on the horn outside Emma's apartment, and Emma hesitantly climbed into the front seat of the car. As she settled into the seat, she was greeted by a chorus of enthusiastic voices from the back seat.

Emma returned a smile. "Hi, kids. It's good to see you again."

Thea couldn't help but notice how quickly Emma's tension seemed to melt away with the warmth of their greeting. Emma didn't really have much choice, as Lyra and Seb engaged her in lively conversation, telling her about the trail that lay ahead.

As they chatted throughout the journey, Thea felt a sense of joy as her children excitedly shared stories about their latest exploits in Zakynthos with their grandparents. She was so proud of her children, and Emma didn't seem at all uncomfortable.

When they arrived at their destination, Thea unloaded the bicycles from the rack, and they geared up with helmets, shoes, and rucksacks. The four of them waited, poised at the trailhead with their bikes at the ready awaiting instructions from Thea.

Emma stared into the distance. "What's the trail called, and what's the distance?"

"It's called the Lily Pond trail, and it's eleven miles." Thea said.

Emma frowned. "Each way?"

Thea laughed and patted Emma's shoulder. "Round trip. Don't worry, we'll take it easy. Seriously, Emma, if at any point you feel it's too much, just tell me. Promise?"

Emma nodded. "Don't worry, I will. I'm no hero."

"Come on, let's go, Mum," Seb shouted.

Lyra and Seb took off along the bike trail, and their laughter echoed through the trees like a melody. They bounded ahead with Lyra leading the way and Seb following closely behind, his little legs pedalling like fury to keep up with his older sister. She could hear his laughter mingling with Lyra's as their spirits soared on their adventure into the great unknown.

It wasn't easy for Thea to let them go, and when the trail twisted and turned, and they disappeared out of sight, she began to panic. "Not so fast," she shouted. The ache and fear in the pit of her stomach was like a razor wire cutting through her every nerve ending.

Emma seemed to recognise how anxious she was. "Thea, you go ahead. Don't worry, I'll catch up."

Thea took a deep breath. "No. I have to let them spread their wings. How's your leg holding up?"

"Pretty good actually, for a first time." Emma pointed to the side of the track. "Look, the squirrels are running alongside us."

Thea laughed. "Yeah. I told them we were coming. I said it was a special occasion."

"It is, isn't it? I mean, here I am, out on an adventure with you and your children. I have to say, they're enchanting."

Thea laughed. "Enchanting? I think they're scheming little buggers."

"Well, they brought us together again, so they must be very special."

Thea wanted to leap off her bike and kiss Emma. And why shouldn't she? *Because you should take it slow. Because she might not want you to. Because... No.* No more excuses, no more wasting time. She cycled quickly around the corner, pulled up and leaned her bike against a tree.

Emma came to a standstill. "Are you okay?"

Thea put her arms around Emma and kissed her gently. She'd liked to have done more, but her children were only a few hundred yards ahead of them. "I've missed you."

Emma stroked Thea's cheek. "I've missed you too. Maybe we need to talk some things out when we're alone."

"Whatever you want. But right now, let's make a pact. If either of us have any doubts, whatsoever, about anything, we sit down together and talk about them."

Emma hugged her tightly. "I agree."

Thea grabbed her bike. "Best find my little angels." She heard some giggles and found them hiding behind a tree. "How long have you two been there?" she asked.

Lyra grinned. "Just got here. We wondered where you were, so we backtracked."

Thea was sure they'd seen everything, but they had to get used to it. After all, Lyra had instigated this adventure, and she was sure her daughter and friends knew all about kissing. She wasn't sure about Seb, but she suspected he found it all uncool.

It wasn't easy or necessary to hold much conversation, but as they cycled along the winding path, all the tension that had once lingered between them melted away. The trail unfolded before them leading them deeper into the heart of nature's embrace. They passed through meadows carpeted in wildflowers and dense thickets alive with the cheerful chatter of songbirds.

"Mum, Emma. Come and look at this," Seb shouted excitedly.

Thea and Emma came to a halt and propped their bikes up against a fence. Both her children were kneeling on the grass and pointing. Nestled within the gnarled roots of an ancient oak tree was a hidden treasure, a secret doorway.

Emma's face lit up with joy as she crouched down beside them. "Wow! It's a fairy door." She beckoned Thea. "Look, it has little carvings on the door."

Thea took out her phone and photographed this magical moment of Emma and her children crouched together studying the fairy door. Emma looked genuinely happy, almost as if she were experiencing the joy of childhood for the first time.

Emma stooped lower and whispered to Lyra and Seb, "What do you think is behind the door?"

"Do you think fairies live behind it?" Seb whispered, his voice filled with awe.

Emma nodded. "Of course. It's a portal to adventure. But only if you're brave and you believe in magic."

Lyra's eyes sparkled. "Could we try it?"

Emma nodded. 'As long as we do it carefully. We don't want to frighten the fairies, do we?"

Lyra tugged on Seb's sleeve. "Do you want to do it?"

Seb grinned. "Yes!"

The three of them exchanged a knowing glance before Seb gently pulled the door open.

Emma peered inside and whispered, "Do you see the soft golden light? It's illuminating a hidden pathway. Shall we step inside?"

Lyra and Seb nodded eagerly.

"Follow me." Emma inhaled deeply. "Can you smell the scent of the forest and the wildflowers?"

"And look, there are fireflies dancing in the air," Lyra said.

Seb nodded. "They look like tiny stars."

Emma put an arm around their shoulders. "Look at the pixies; they're playing hide and seek behind the toadstools. And the fairies are dancing with the elves."

The children laughed, and Thea wiped a small tear away from her cheek. Her heart skipped a beat as she listened to Emma's storytelling.

Emma tilted her head. "What is it they're saying?" She cupped her palm behind her ear. "They want us to dance with them." She took Lyra and Seb's hands as they stood and danced around in circles.

Thea said nothing, just clicked away on her camera as she captured the enchanting moment and listened to their laughter ringing out like music in the stillness of the forest.

When the dancing stopped, Emma squatted down on the ground. "I think it's time to bid farewell to our friends."

Seb and Lyra joined her as they waved bye-bye and closed the door to their fairytale world.

Thea cleared her throat. "I don't know about you lot, but I'm starving."

"Yes," they roared and jumped on their bikes and pedalled like crazy along the trail.

And then, they stumbled on another hidden gem nestled amidst the trees: a lily pond shimmering like a mirror in the sun.

They dismounted and headed to the water's edge. They spread out their picnic blanket on the soft grass underneath a weeping willow tree and feasted upon crusty baguettes, juicy strawberries, and home-made lemonade.

Laughter and conversation filled the air, and Thea felt the wounds of the past were slowly healing with all their newfound friendships and shared pursuits. She felt deep gratitude to her children for making the day so relaxed and full of fun. She covered Emma's hand with her own and gave her a smile she hoped telegraphed all the love she was feeling.

They cycled back to the car, and Thea loaded the bikes onto the rack.

As they drove back home, animated chatter filled the car, and it also filled Thea's heart with love. Even Seb joined in with the happy conversation instead of having his nose stuck in a book.

As they pulled up outside Emma's apartment, Thea's heart sank. Was that it then? Was it a one-off? Would Emma depart, never to be seen again, or was this a new beginning?

Emma leaned over the seat, and although it was a little tricky, she managed to give Lyra and Seb a great big hug. "Thank you for inviting me, and for the absolutely wonderful day."

Her children looked sad. Perhaps they thought that it was a one-off too.

"It's my birthday tomorrow," Seb said, springing to Thea's aid. "Will you come to my birthday party? We're going to swim and have a barbecue after. Please say yes. Mum looks really happy when you're around, and she's been really sad for a long time."

Thea didn't know what to say. Did they really think that? Seb wasn't one to hold back, and it hurt to think that's what they thought.

Emma whooped. "Your birthday! How old will you be?"

"Seven." He gave her a proud, toothy grin.

"Wow. How exciting. But don't you want to spend it with your school friends?"

"I'm going to do that next week. We're going to the climbing centre. We couldn't do it this weekend because of the holidays." He shrugged. "It's fine. And it means I get *two* parties."

"In that case, I'd love to come. Thank you, Seb."

Seb and Lyra glanced at each other. Thea laughed inwardly. *Scheming little buggers.* She was sure they'd hatched this plot earlier in the day. Still, she didn't want Emma to feel pressured.

Emma waved to them and got out of the car. "See you tomorrow."

Thea got out and stared up at Emma's bike on the rack. "Shall I take it back and leave it in the garage with ours? I'm sure we'll go on another soon...if you want to."

"I'd love to. Thanks, Thea, I had so much fun today."

Thea grinned. "I think we all did." She stuffed her hands in the back of her shorts' pockets and rocked back on her heels. "I hope Seb didn't push you into that. Children can be very cunning, as I'm finding out. My two seem to have hidden depths."

"Honestly, I want to come. But thank you for checking."

Thea breathed a sigh of relief. "Fantastic. Shall I pick you up?"

Emma shook her head. "I may take a steady walk. Either that or I'll get a taxi. What time?"

"About four. Don't forget to bring your swimsuit."

Emma smiled. "Wonderful. Until tomorrow then. And thanks so much for today; it's been fabulous."

"Thanks to you." Thea tilted her head. "You know, you were so great with Lyra and Seb."

"I surprised myself too. They're lovely children." Emma stepped forward and kissed Thea on the cheek. "See you tomorrow."

Before she had a chance to grab Emma and give her a proper kiss, Emma had disappeared through the side gate with a quick wave. Thea got back into the car with a wide grin on her face. It was early days, but she hoped against hope that today had given them both an opportunity to mend what had been broken.

Chapter Fifteen

EMMA REFLECTED ON THE day spent with Thea's children. She couldn't help but feel a sense of astonishment at how smoothly everything had gone. She'd been apprehensive about being with them, and she'd anticipated challenges in making a connection, but to her surprise, they had effortlessly found common ground.

It was strange really. She'd never given much thought to her early years, and yet it all came back when she saw the fairy door. She'd recalled the adventures with her parents on their escapades to the woodland nearby, and how her dad told her stories of what was beyond the door. He took them there in their minds and cast a magical spell. It had become so vivid, and she found herself wanting to go back there and share those memories with Lyra and Seb.

Through laughter and nostalgia, she had discovered that, despite the vast differences in their ages, they weren't so dissimilar, because no matter what age you are, you can still daydream. Their shared love for imaginative storytelling had brought down her barriers and allowed them to connect on a different level.

As Emma reflected on the enjoyable time with Thea's children, she reminded herself of the purpose of getting to know them. It was for Thea, and it was because she loved Thea and couldn't see a future without her. Amid the laughter and the play, Thea was always in her thoughts.

It must have been difficult for Thea to trust Emma with her children. She'd been through so much heartache in the past, and Emma hadn't really given that enough consideration. All she'd thought about was her, and it made her feel incredibly selfish. Emma sat on her patio, cradling a mug of camomile tea. The sun had dipped below the horizon. She loved this quiet time of day, yet her mind was far from serene. Thoughts of the future, with all its uncertainties and fears, weighed heavily on her.

Yes, Lyra and Seb were wonderful kids, bright and full of life. She adored them, truly. But their presence was a constant reminder of the life ahead, one that filled her with unease.

Thea was thirty-six, in the prime of her life, while she was approaching fifty-six. The gap between them was more than just a number. She was falling for Thea, but that didn't silence the questions that kept her awake at night.

What's really bothering me? The age gap thing wasn't just about her and Thea, it was about the children too. She'd be nearly seventy by the time they were in university or starting a career. What if she wasn't around long enough to see them graduate? To see them start their own families. What if she wasn't able to keep up? What if her health declined, and she became a burden?

Her mind was full of what ifs, and she couldn't answer them on her own.

Despite all her anxieties, the first thing she thought about when she woke up was Thea's beautiful smile. The next thing she thought about was Seb and how excited he'd be about today. She should get him a birthday card. It was way too late to buy a present, and she had no idea what a seven-year-old would want anyway.

She drove to the town centre and walked the short distance to the card shop she'd found on Google. She chose a suitable card and left. There was a Waterstones bookshop opposite; Thea had said how much Seb loved a good read, and Emma wondered if she could find him something. She found the children's section, but that was about as far as she got. She had no clue what to buy. She knew he liked the Enid Blyton adventure books, but surely he'd have every single one of those.

A woman approached her. She looked young, but maybe she was close to Thea's age. The thought made her wince a little.

The woman smiled. "You look like you could do with some help."

"You're not kidding. I have no idea where to start."

She laughed. "Give me some clues."

"Well, I'm looking for a birthday gift for my friend's seven-year-old boy. He reads a lot, mostly he's into *The Famous Five*."

The woman swooned. "Oh, such awesome memories. I have all the sets of books, and my children have read them all." She stroked her chin. "My son is seven, and he's just finished *The Boy Who Made the World Disappear* by Ben Miller." She beckoned Emma over to a table display. "Here it is." She handed the book to Emma. "Honestly, he really enjoyed it." She reached across the table and picked up a box. "Actually, we've got a box set on offer. I mean, what more could a young boy want than three magical adventure stories?"

Emma glanced at them. "I have no idea if he'll like them. But nothing ventured, nothing gained. I'll take the set. Thank you so much for your help."

She gave a thumbs up. "I think he'll love them. If he doesn't, he'll never tell you." She laughed. "But of course you'll know."

Emma couldn't help but hope he did like them. If she was going to make this foray into the world of parent-adjacent relationships, she wanted to make a good impression from the start.

It was a little overcast, but nevertheless it was warm, and the weatherman had predicated there'd be no rain until tomorrow. After all the cloudless days they'd had, today was a little gloomy by comparison, and she'd so wanted a perfect day for Seb. Her slow walk took her twenty minutes, and she stood by the gate, feeling more than a little apprehensive. The last time she'd been here hadn't been a happy time, but she had to put that out of her mind. She rang the buzzer, and the side gate opened. Within minutes, Thea came dashing down the drive.

She flung her arms around Emma and nearly crushed her. "You came."

Emma stepped back. "Of course. Did you doubt it?"

Thea shrugged. "I wasn't sure. I kept looking at my phone thinking I'd get a text saying you couldn't make it."

Emma shook her head. "Actually, it didn't cross my mind." She pulled Thea close and kissed her. "Come on, let me see the birthday boy."

When they got out of the lift, they were greeted by two screaming children running towards them. They came to a standstill before crashing into Thea.

Seb was beaming. "You came!"

It seemed like everyone doubted she'd grace them with her presence today. Had she given that impression? She hoped not because she really needed to get to know them better, and more to the point, she wanted to be there.

"Happy birthday, Seb." Emma handed him his card, and he tore it open. She held onto the gift, wanting to occupy her hands with something.

"Thanks, Emma, that's so cool. We're having Coke; do you want one?"

Thea laughed. "I'm sure Emma would like something a bit stronger."

"No, honestly, I'd love a Coke right now." She winked at Thea. "I don't want to drink and swim, but do ask me again later, please."

Seb returned with a can of soda. "Do you want a straw?"

"No, this is fine, thanks."

Seb bounced on his heels. "We're going to play games in the pool soon."

"Great." Emma wasn't sure it was. It was one thing escaping into fairy stories, but she wasn't sure about games. Kids games were a distant memory, and she sure as hell didn't want to make a fool of herself. Not at her age.

She passed the present to Seb. "I know you like reading, but

I'm not sure if these are your kind of books."

Seb's eyes lit up as he eagerly unwrapped his gift and carefully took the books out of the box. "Oh, wow." He nudged Lyra, and she read the titles out loud.

"*The Boy Who Made the World Disappear*," she said and flipped to the next. "*The Day I Fell into a Fairytale*, and *How I Became a Dog Called Midnight*." She turned back to Seb. "They're supposed to be really good." She handed them back to him. "Can I read them after you?" She giggled. "Or maybe before because you still haven't finished your other book."

Seb snatched them from her. "I'm almost through that." He clutched them to his chest. "They're mine, and I'm reading them first."

Lyra held her hands up. "Okay, if you say so."

"I do." Seb sprang off his chair and gave Emma a massive hug. "Thanks so much, Emma. They look really cool."

Emma wasn't sure if they did, but Seb seemed willing to give them a shot.

Thea stroked Emma's arm. "That was so kind."

Emma liked the feel of Thea's hand on her arm. She would like to feel a kiss too, but this was neither the time nor the place. Was it? Probably not. Did you kiss in front of kids? Not yet? Ever? She wished she had a guidebook, and she glanced over to the double sunbed. Once upon a time, no guide had been needed.

Seb clapped his hands. "Time for the pool!" He grabbed Emma's hand. "C'mon, Emma."

Emma took a deep breath. It didn't look like she could avoid this without looking like a killjoy. "Give me five. I'll just go and put my swimsuit on."

Thea jumped up. "You can use the bedroom to change." Thea tugged down the side of her shorts to show a bikini bottom and a tantalising bit of flesh. "I've already got mine on." She grinned, seeming to know what Emma was thinking. "Let me show you where it is."

Thea guided Emma to the bedroom with a playful glint in her eye. "Here's the room," she said, opening the door with a flourish. "Need any help with that swimsuit?" Her smile widened.

Emma rolled her eyes but couldn't help laughing at her mischievous grin. Before she could respond, Thea pulled her close and kissed her, her lips warm and firm against hers.

Emma eventually pushed her away gently. "Now bugger off, or we'll end up playing games of a different sort."

Thea winked. "Now that sounds like fun."

"Go!"

Thea grinned and shut the door behind her.

A few minutes later, Emma returned with a towel wrapped around her shoulders. Everyone else was in the pool, so she slipped it off and left it on a chair. Why did being in a bathing suit in front of other people make her feel so vulnerable? The lines and creases of time had etched themselves onto her once youthful skin, a stark reminder of the years that had passed. There were small imperfections that seemed to scream at her as she'd looked in the wardrobe mirror. At this stage of life, she couldn't help but feel a pang of insecurity, the kind that comes with the awareness of ageing. It wasn't just about the physical changes, but the constant struggle to accept and embrace herself as she was now.

And there was Thea, looking gorgeous, and tanned, and fit, and it made Emma feel even more conscious about the ageing of her own body. She tried to shake off the thought. Today wasn't about that. She tentatively made her way down the steps into the pool. Her leg was almost as good as new, but it still felt a little stiff, and she was aware of how the scars must look. When she emersed herself, she did a few stretches then joined the gang.

Seb swam over and splashed water over her. Emma cupped her hands in the water and totally drenched him.

He giggled with delight. "Come on, we're going to play Monkey in the Middle."

That sounded a bit ominous. She'd always been self-conscious and was terrified of being chosen to be the monkey.

Seb threw a ball at his mum. "Mum's the monkey."

Thea raised her arms. "I vote it should be you, Seb."

Seb shook his head vigorously. "It's my birthday. I get to choose."

Thea made her way to the centre of the pool. She cracked her knuckles and flexed her arms. "Okay, you guys. I'm ready."

Thea threw the ball to Emma. "Give it your best."

Emma polished the ball with her hand and winked at Thea. She threw it high towards Seb, and he leapt out of the water and caught it. Thea swam towards him and tried to grab the ball from his hands, but he tossed it to Lyra. And so, it continued.

Their laughter echoed around the pool as they dodged and weaved, trying to outmanoeuvre Thea. With each attempt, there was a mixture of anticipation and hilarity as they watched their mum sneakily trying to steal the ball. The slight touches, the way Thea pressed her breasts to Emma's back when she went to tackle her, and the way she made sure their bodies slid past one another constantly were making her crazy in the best way, and Thea's knowing smile made it clear she knew exactly what she was doing.

Thea finally sat on the pool step, out of breath. "Okay, you guys win. Is anyone hungry yet?"

They all shouted at once. "Starving."

They all climbed out of the pool, and the kids ran over to the table filled with nibbles and drinks. Thea, her wet body glistening in the sunlight, draped a towel over Emma's shoulders. "That was fun," she murmured, her gaze dropping to Emma's lips.

"I'm going to combust. If we hadn't been in water, I'd already be ash." Emma let her hand slide over Thea's hip.

"Hungry!" Seb shouted from the table, his mouth full.

Thea laughed and backed away. "We'll come back to this later."

As the tantalising aroma of barbecue filled the air, Thea, with the help of Emma, grilled up a feast fit for a king, complete with juicy burgers, sizzling sausages, and mouthwatering grilled vegetables. Their tummies grumbled as they eagerly awaited the delicious meal. Emma sat there, eating and laughing with the others, and felt a belonging she hadn't felt in a very, very long time.

Seb held his tummy. "What's for dessert?"

Thea raised her eyebrows. "I'll have to see if I can rustle something up. We might end up with ice cream." She disappeared and returned carrying a big birthday cake with candles. It was decorated with a large number seven, surrounded by books made from sponge and icing.

They all sang the birthday song, and Emma's heart lurched a little at how happy the little family unit looked.

Seb blew out the candles and grinned. "I've made my wish."

They stuffed their faces with wedges of cake, and Emma did her absolute best not to notice the way Thea licked the icing from her lips, or the way she cleaned it off the fork with her tongue.

When they'd finished, Seb hugged his mum. "Thanks for today." He hesitated for a second, then turned to Emma and hugged her too. "And thanks for coming. It's nice to see Mum laugh."

Emma hugged him back, overwhelmed and uncertain how to reply with anything meaningful. "No problem."

Eventually, Thea and Emma cleared away, and Emma loaded it into the dishwasher. It was simple family life, and it felt good.

When Emma turned around, Thea engulfed her in her arms. "Thanks for making this day complete."

Emma tilted her head. "I've had a fabulous time, I really have."

"You sound surprised."

"I guess I am. I haven't spent much time around children, and you know it never figured in my life plan. But I think it's something I've missed out on."

Thea kissed Emma's forehead, her nose, and then her lips. She pulled her closer and their eyes locked. Their lips met again, and the world seemed to fade away. The kiss became deeper, and their tongues mingled into a tender exploration. Their bodies pressed together in an embrace that needed no words. Nothing seemed to matter except the intoxicating exchange of love and desire. They finally parted, and Emma felt breathless and flushed. Had they been alone, she knew they'd have ended up in bed, making love. However, there was a silent promise of more to come.

Thea frowned. "I'm sorry, Emma. I so want you, but right now, I have two children to look after."

Emma kissed Thea lightly. "I know. C'mon, let's get back and enjoy the rest of the evening." She made light of it, but deep down, it was something she'd have to seriously consider. Yes, she was having a wonderful day with Seb and Lyra, but at times like this, she wished it was just her and Thea. And if they followed this path to something serious, then it would rarely be just the two of them. Could she be okay with that?

The sun began to set. It wasn't the best of sunsets due to the cloud cover, but nobody seemed to mind.

Thea placed a mask across Seb's eyes. "No peeking, okay?"

Seb chuckled. "You're not going to throw me in the water, are you?"

"Not a chance. Close your eyes."

Emma watched as Thea disappeared to the other side of the pool. There was a raised rockery, not very big, but enough for her to organise her surprise.

"Okay," Thea shouted.

Lyra removed Seb's mask, just as the bright rainbow colours of a rocket sailed through the sky above them. It made a whooshing sound and exploded into a magical shower. It was followed by a ten-minute spectacular display of fireworks that painted the night sky with vibrant colours.

Emma looked at Seb. His eyes widened with wonder as he watched the dazzling show unfold. She was sure his heart, just like hers, was filled with joy and gratitude, though, for very different reasons.

The night drew to a close, and the last sparks of the fireworks faded from the sky. There was a little chill in the air, so Thea lit the chiminea. The kids had hot chocolate, and Thea and Emma moved on to cognac.

Emma nudged Thea, and they smiled as they watched Seb nod off then force himself awake.

Thea stood. "C'mon, you two. Time for bed. It's been a long day."

There were groans from both children, but they didn't protest too much.

Lyra took Seb's hand. "Will you come tuck us in?"

"I need a bedtime story, Mum. You promised; it's my birthday." Seb rubbed at his eyes.

"Okay. I'll be down in fifteen minutes. Change into your PJs and brush your teeth." Thea shrugged after they'd headed inside. "Sorry. It'll only take about ten minutes. I'm sure he'll be asleep in no time."

Emma touched Thea's shoulder. "It's Seb's birthday. You take as long as it takes. It's been a terrific day, so I'm going to make tracks myself."

Thea frowned. "Are you sure?"

"Positive."

Thea looked at Emma. "I want you to stay," she said quietly, stepping closer.

Emma bit her lip, her heart pulling her in two directions. "I want to stay too," she said, "but it will be difficult in the morning. Are you ready to have that conversation with your children yet?"

Thea nodded, understanding the unspoken complexities.

"Then let's take things slowly," she said, offering a small, hopeful smile. "I have a regular taxi guy now, so I'm going to see if he can pick me up." Emma fired off a quick text.

Thea pulled her close and hugged her tightly. "I want you to be in my life. I want you to be in my children's lives too."

Emma kissed Thea on the lips. Her phone pinged, and she had to pull away. "That's my taxi."

"Hmm...shame."

Emma nodded toward the house. "You have a story to read."

Thea pulled a funny face. "I guess so. Anyway, the kids go back to school on Tuesday. Can I take you for lunch?"

Emma nodded. "That would be lovely."

"Great. I'll text you. And thank you for today. You made it perfect." She took Emma's hand. "I'll walk you to your taxi. I don't ever want to see you running from me again."

"How about running to you?"

Thea grinned. "Definitely."

Thea walked her to the gate, and she waved as the taxi drove away until Thea was out of sight.

Chapter Sixteen

Seb's birthday party had been a great success all round. Thea had watched Emma's response to everything they'd done, and it really seemed like she'd genuinely enjoyed it as well. Was it possible that, with time, Emma would become even more accepting of her children, and they'd be able to spend more quality time together as a family? Or was that a pipe dream?

She'd had such a long period of keeping others at a distance that it had become a habit, a bad one. However, the two outings as a group had certainly been a shift in Thea's journey towards learning to trust again.

Yes, it was a significant step in her personal growth. It had been difficult to open herself up to someone new, because it wasn't just going to affect her life but also those of her children. She'd weaved a web like a cocoon, trying to protect them from the world, but she'd never given much thought to how it was affecting them. She laughed. It seemed like Lyra and Seb were more aware than she'd given them credit for. They'd obviously given it a lot of thought, and she was certain her mum had a lot of input too.

She nodded, as if discussing the situation with someone else. Her willingness to give Emma a chance gave her hope for a better future, for all of them. The hurt, fear, and trauma of the past had to heal. Now was the time to move forward, and she wanted to do that with Emma.

On Tuesday, Lyra and Seb were back at school and all she could think of was her lunch date with Emma. They'd been texting each other almost constantly, sending little gifs and jokes, and there'd even been a few spicier conversations that had sent Thea to the hidden toy drawer in her bedroom for a little relief. And yet, as she headed out to lunch, it still felt like a first date. She wanted it to be a new beginning.

They'd agreed to meet at midday and when she arrived in the parking lot, Emma was waiting. She looked great, dressed in cropped white jeans and a navy T-shirt. She pulled her in close without so much as a hello and kissed her with all the pent-up passion she'd been feeling since their make-out session on Saturday. She wished she had the nerve to suggest they go back to her house, but she really didn't want to rush Emma again.

Once Emma was inside, Thea shut the door and got into the driving seat.

They chatted and with shared laughter and stolen glances, the bit of awkwardness began to fade.

Emma continued to look at Thea as though it was impossible not to. "Where are we going?"

"I found this wonderful pub overlooking a bay. It's got good food and incredible scenery."

Emma placed her hands in her lap as if she wasn't quite sure what to do with them. "What's it called?"

Thea laughed. "The Quiet Woman."

"Aha. Either that's a hint or there's a story behind it."

"Apparently, the pub owner's wife, Esme, was a right old nag. Hounded him day and night. He could never do anything right. There were smugglers in the village, and they set traps and lured cargo ships into the cove. The waters there are rocky and dangerous. Ships crashed into the rocks and the smugglers killed whoever was left alive and took the goodies. The pub owner let them stash their loot in his cellar.

"Later, he left a note for the Excise Men telling them what was happening and told them the smugglers would return the following night to collect their stash. He signed the note in his wife's name and told them her husband was innocent. Then the pub owner told the smugglers he'd seen the letter and that the authorities were onto them. The smugglers took their loot and hid it in the caves. When the Excise Men arrived at the pub, there was nothing to be found. They questioned the pub owner's wife, but she couldn't talk. The smugglers had cut her tongue out. So he got rid of the smugglers using his pub and the wife who constantly nagged him."

Emma hugged herself. "That's terrible." Then she stared at Thea through narrowed eyes. "Is that true, or did you just make it up?"

Thea burst into laughter. "I made it up." She held her hands up. "But it could easily be true."

Emma punched Thea's arm playfully. "I was almost taken in."

"You're no different; you weave stories for children."

Emma crossed her arms over her chest. "That's totally different."

Thea didn't think it was, but she wasn't about to argue the point. Emma looked cute when she was defensive.

They pulled up in the car park of the Quiet Woman, and Thea took Emma in her arms and kissed her. "I love your fairy stories. Life should be about happy things, about dreaming."

Emma tilted her head. "As long as some dreams can become a reality."

Thea nodded. "As long as you believe." She let go of Emma, got out of the car and opened the passenger door. "Come and look at this view. I assure you it's not a dream." She grabbed her arm and led her to the view.

Emma gasped. "They don't come much better, do they? We're so lucky to be blessed with such a coastline."

After they'd stood on the edge of the cliff, taking in the serene expanse of the bay, they strolled hand in hand into the quaint pub and settled into a cozy corner which overlooked the views.

Thea looked at the menu. "They do great pies here. The steak and Guinness one is a feast, and the fish pie is also yummy."

Emma scratched her chin. "Perfect for the winter, but I think I'm going for the ploughman's. Those local cheeses sound amazing."

Thea smiled. "Good choice. I'll go and order. What would you like to drink?"

"Diet Coke, please."

Thea went to the bar and ordered, then returned with their drinks. She placed her elbows on the table and rested her chin on her hands. "I've so missed you."

Emma stared into Thea's eyes. "Likewise."

Thea leaned over and took Emma's hand. "I'm forever juggling my life around Lyra and Seb. I know it leaves very little room for romance. Do you think you can handle that?" She knew this had to be addressed. Thea longed for moments of intimacy and connection that didn't involve TV programs blaring in the background or reading bedtime stories. It may be okay now, but eventually she knew she couldn't keep prioritising everything else over their relationship, if they were going to have one.

Emma frowned. "I didn't think I could, but maybe I need to adjust my thinking a little. I know your children will always come first, but I also know that I want to be with you. I want to find that balance."

Thea beamed. "No kidding?"

"No kidding." Emma squeezed Thea's hand. "For my sins, I need you in my life."

Thea could hardly believe it. "I promise you, we'll find more time for us," she said with determination. "We'll schedule regular date nights. I'll get a babysitter."

Emma shook her head. "A little at a time. You don't have to rush anything after what you've been through. I'd never put you in that position."

Thea bit her lip. Was she rushing things? "Seriously, Emma, I have to move on. I'm not saying I won't have a meltdown when I'm not around them, but I really must change."

Emma stroked Thea's cheek. "Let's take it slowly. We can go out for a drink or a walk and gradually extend the time." She took a deep breath. "Honestly, that's probably for the best for me too. Better to ease in, you know?"

"I agree. Thank you for understanding."

Emma opened her mouth as if she was going to ask something, then stopped.

"Go ahead. Ask me whatever."

"Okay. Have you told Seb and Lyra about them having a donor father?"

"Yes. You know how inquisitive Lyra is. I never lied to her and always tried to answer everything as simply as I could."

Emma's eyes widened. "How did you go about it? It's such a complex subject."

Thea laughed. "Would you like a blow-by-blow account?"

Emma smiled. "Oh, please, you do so tell a good story."

Thea rolled her eyes, smiling. "Lyra knew a fair amount, whereas Seb didn't, but by telling them together, I was sure Lyra would delve into it later, and maybe that would help Seb to understand too. I told them when we were in Zakynthos. It seemed appropriate because their donor was Greek. We sat in the shade of the olive trees, and I told them how they came into the world." She laughed. "Lyra just wanted to know if the donor was a nice man, and Seb thinks he's a superpower kid with a great origin story."

Emma hadn't looked away throughout the tale. "Were you nervous about telling them?"

Thea nodded. "I'd worried about having that conversation practically from the moment they were born. But so far, that explanation has held, and there haven't been any further questions. If they ever want to look for the donor, we'll cross that bridge down the line."

"Wow, what a story. I have to say I admire you for having children on your own, and you've certainly done a great job,

Thea."

Her heart swelled with pride. "Thank you. I've been very lucky, and of course, I've always had the love and help from all my family."

The barman arrived with their lunch. "Two Ploughman's, ladies."

Thea paused in between mouthfuls. "Anyway, back to the previous conversation about doing stuff together. I thought we'd start this weekend. That's if you're not doing anything?"

Emma winked. "I think my diary is free."

Thea leaned back. "Seb and Lyra are going to the climbing centre. It's Seb's birthday treat so he's invited a few friends, and I don't need to be there. I'll drop them off and pick you up on the way back. How does that sound?"

Emma didn't answer right away, as she was eating the last piece of cheese. She wiped her mouth with her napkin. "I'm good with that. Do you want me to prepare a picnic or something?"

Thea shook her head. "No. We'll go back to the house." She grinned. "I thought we might spend a bit of that quality time together."

Emma wiggled her eyebrows. "Sounds interesting."

"I want to pick up where we left off. We might not have the house to ourselves all the time, but we can make the most of the moments we do." Thea leaned closer, already desperate to make that happen.

Emma touched Thea's hand. "I can't wait."

"I promise I'll make it interesting, as long as you stay for the weekend."

Emma jerked her head back. "The whole weekend. Are you sure?"

"We have all day. Perhaps it'll be best if I sleep downstairs, and you take the upstairs room...until I've had *that* conversation with Lyra and Seb."

Emma nodded. "I agree. Believe me, as long as we're together, that's all that matters." She continued to look contemplative.

"What's up? Come on, tell me. We said we'd never leave things unsaid. We agreed we'd always discuss stuff that concerned us."

Emma took a deep breath. "I keep trying to put it to the back of my mind, but I really need to talk to you...you see, I can't just let this age-gap thing go. It worries me. I did a calculation, and I'll be nearly seventy by the time they're in university or going into whatever career they choose. I may not even be around to see them graduate. And I doubt I'll see them start their own families. I'll be so much older, and I won't be able to keep up with you or them. The last thing I want is to become a burden if my health deteriorated."

Thea took Emma's hands and squeezed them tightly. "Emma, none of us can predict the future. The kids are so fond of you already, and we're going to make the most of the time we have together. We'll deal with all your concerns *if* and *when* they happen. We'll face whatever comes our way, together."

Emma didn't look totally convinced. "Thank you for that. I wish I had your confidence."

Thea frowned. "Believe it or not, I have my fears too. You may think that I'm too young, too inexperienced, and you may also get fed up with the children."

"I promise that if ever those thoughts cross my mind, I'll tell you."

Thea lifted Emma's hands to her lips and kissed them. "None of us know what the future holds, but we can't let fear dictate our present."

As their lunch date came to an end, Thea dropped Emma back home. They reluctantly parted ways with a lingering embrace. "I'll pick you up about eleven on Saturday." She kissed Emma again. As their lips touched, it felt like an electric spark igniting between them, sending shivers down her spine. The intensity seemed as though it was consuming them both.

Thea watched as Emma disappeared through the doors,

giving a last wave before she went out of sight.

Thea made her way to pick up Seb and Lyra, her mind buzzing with thoughts of the weekend ahead. She couldn't shake the feeling of excitement that bubbled up inside her, like fizzy wine beneath the surface.

When she arrived at the school gates, she was greeted by the joyful laughter of Seb and Lyra, their bright smiles a welcome distraction from the ache of separation from Emma. This slow burn romance was going to be harder than she thought possible. She threw herself into the role of mother with renewed vigour, determined to savour every moment with her children, even though her mind was on other things.

As the day turned to dusk, Thea and Emma exchanged playful texts, each message a reminder of the feelings that united them despite the physical distance between them. Thea hoped that it wouldn't always be like this. Maybe one day, they'd go to sleep and wake up together. The thought made her stumble a little. Was she really already thinking about them moving in together? She'd never been a U-Haul lesbian, but she saw the positive side of it now.

As the sun rose on Saturday morning, Thea's heart raced with anticipation. She'd been eagerly awaiting this day, and she hoped that Emma was feeling the same way.

Seb could hardly sit still in the back seat of the car. "This is going to be awesome. So many people said they're coming."

"Of course they are. Why shouldn't they?"

Seb looked out the window. "They call me the bookworm."

Thea shook her head. She wanted to hug her son, but she was driving. "Listen, Seb, everyone is different. So, you like reading, but it doesn't mean you don't like other things."

Seb nodded. "I love books, but I can't wait to get on that climbing wall."

He didn't need to invite his sister, but he had, and Thea was happy about that. "Are you looking forward to it, Lyra?"

Thea glanced in the rearview mirror. Lyra had a dreamy sort of look.

"I think it'll be fun."

Seb giggled, and Lyra elbowed him in the ribs. Of course, Thea knew who he'd invited, she'd checked the invitation list. It was thoughtful of him to invite Lyra's friend, Adam, but she was sure he'd done it to keep her out of the way.

Seb began to hiccup loudly, and Lyra slapped his back. Thea wasn't going to let on, but she knew the reference as she'd remembered Seb had said that Adam looked a bit like Hiccup in *How to Train Your Dragon*. She stifled a laugh, because she didn't want to make Lyra feel self-conscious.

She dropped them off at the entrance and hugged them both. "Have a wonderful time. Now remember, Fee will be picking you up. If she's not there, just stay put and call me. Don't go looking for her."

Seb put his small hands on his hips. "If she doesn't, Jason and Davey will be with us. I don't think she'll forget her kids."

Thea stuffed her hands into her pockets. "All right, smarty pants. Have fun and see you later."

A smile tugged at her lips as she set out to pick up Emma, her excitement mounting with each passing mile. As she approached the layby at the side of Emma's apartment, she couldn't help but feel a surge of warmth as she saw Emma standing by the side of the curb with a small bag.

Thea jumped out of the car and greeted Emma with a tender embrace. They shared a kiss before setting out on their journey.

As they drove towards their destination, the air crackled with tension. They entwined their hands and stole glances at each other when they thought the other wasn't looking.

It had begun to rain, and they dashed inside the house and up to the covered terrace.

"Coffee?" Thea asked.

"Yes, I'd love one, please."

Thea returned with two mugs of coffee and sat beside Emma. As much as she wanted to lead Emma off to the bedroom right away, she also wanted to take it slow and build up to it. They sipped their coffee, and Thea put an arm around Emma's shoulders. She pulled her close and kissed her, tenderly at first but then with more force. She pulled back and stared at Emma as she stroked her neck. "I want you. Can we go to bed?" Thea waited until Emma nodded then took her hand and led her towards the bedroom. She lifted Emma's tee and Emma raised her arms. After she'd unzipped Emma's shorts, she pulled her own shirt and shorts off.

Her feelings for Emma weren't like anything she'd felt before. She'd had a variety of girlfriends, but they were generally short term. The only long relationship of sorts she'd had was with Quinn, but that was pure sex. But this was special; she'd waited a lifetime to experience this, and in fact, she wasn't sure how she was supposed to feel. All she knew was it felt good.

Emma stepped out of her shorts and fell back onto the bed, and Thea joined her. She ran her fingers through Emma's hair and kissed her neck, then moved upwards and kissed her mouth, gently at first then harder. She parted Emma's lips, and their tongues touched and entwined. Thea pulled back and stared into Emma's eyes. "I love you, Emma. Don't ever leave me." Thea spread small kisses along Emma's cheek and down her neck. She squeezed her breast then flicked her tongue across her nipple, and Emma gasped loudly. She slowly caressed Emma's tummy as she stroked her skin and rested her hand on Emma's thigh.

Emma's breathing became heavier as Thea removed her panties. She sucked on Emma's nipple as she parted her legs and gently stroked Emma's clit. Emma moaned and pressed herself against Thea. She slid two fingers inside her and found a gentle rhythm. As Emma's breathing became erratic, Thea increased the pace and drove deeper inside.

Emma cried out, "Yes. Now."

Emma clenched her fingers and arched her back as Thea felt her juices flowing over her fingers. Emma's body relaxed, and Thea wrapped her arms around her, holding her safe in a tender embrace.

She sighed. "Hmm. That was so perfect." She gazed into Thea's eyes. "I love you, Thea."

"Then I'm very lucky. I know I don't deserve your love."

Emma kissed Thea and hugged her tightly. "I've only given my love to one other woman. Believe me, you deserve love, just as I do. We've both waited a long time for this."

She leaned her head on Thea's shoulder, and they slept in each other's arms, their bodies fitting together like two puzzle pieces finding their perfect match.

Hours passed in a blissful haze as they lost themselves in the ecstasy of their lovemaking. Their bodies moved in perfect harmony as they chased the elusive peak of pleasure together which almost consumed them both. They lay tangled in each other's arms, their bodies spent, but their hearts full of love.

Eventually, Thea kissed the tip of Emma's nose. "Are you hungry?"

Emma laughed. "No more, thanks. Any more, and I'll pass out."

Thea chuckled. 'I mean for food. Because I'm starving."

"Now you come to mention it, I could eat a small horse."

Thea threw the duvet off and pulled Emma up by her hands. "Let's go shower first."

Despite Emma's assertion, she was more than happy to enjoy Thea yet again in the shower as hot water and suds made them slide together perfectly. And Thea was happy to let her. From now on, she'd always think of this moment when she showered, the moment of almost surreal pleasure when she gave herself to Emma's touch.

Whilst they sat and ate in the kitchen after, they chatted constantly. Emma glanced at her watch.

Thea glared and laughed. "You got a hot date or something?"

Emma punched her, playfully. "No. I was just checking the time. I don't want you to be late picking the children up."

"I'm not. My neighbour Fee is collecting them. Seb invited her children, and she offered to bring my kids home with her."

Emma raised her eyebrows. "Are you okay with that?"

Thea sighed. "It took a bit of getting used to the idea, but I have to start somewhere."

Emma got up and walked around the table. She kissed Thea gently. "I think that's a very brave thing to do."

Thea grinned. "It's taken me out of my comfort zone, but at least my mind's been occupied."

Emma's eyes sparkled. "So that means we have some more time alone?"

Thea nodded.

Emma took Thea's hand. "In that case, I have some further business to discuss in the bedroom."

Thea jumped up. "Yay!"

As the late afternoon approached, their lovemaking grew more languid as they explored each other's bodies, finding ticklish spots, asking about scars, and finding the spaces that made their breath catch. Thea fell into it and could have wept with how good it felt to feel so safe, so sexy, so satiated.

But she also couldn't deny that she was getting a little edgy as she watched the hand of the clock click on five p.m. Of course she hadn't given any deadline, and the climbing instructors had told her they'd all be having toasted sandwiches and juice after. But he'd said they should be finished around five. However, she was sure that her neighbour, Fee had everything under control.

It wasn't long after when she heard a car horn. She rushed to the window and saw her children getting out of Fee's car and let out a big sigh of relief.

"They're back," she shouted to Emma. She went to the control panel and buzzed them in the front door, and it wasn't long before they arrived on the pool terrace.

They both ran into Thea's arms, and she hugged them as though they'd been away for a year and a day. Then they ran to Emma and gave her a hug too.

Thea placed her hands on her hips. "C'mon then, tell us all about it."

It was hard to interpret everything with both of them talking at the same time, and their faces were flushed with excitement as they recounted all the tales of their climbing exploits.

Eventually, when Lyra paused for breath, Seb flopped into a chair. "What's for dinner? I'm starving."

"I thought you'd eaten at the centre?"

"That was yonks ago, Mum. We broke for a snack, then rested whilst they lectured us on the bigger wall, then it was all go. I'm *so* hungry."

Thea scratched her chin. "I thought we could have something easy tonight. Maybe a pizza or a Chinese."

"Pizza," Seb and Lyra shouted.

Thea turned to Emma. "Are you okay with that?"

"I love pizza."

"Okay, pizza it is. I'll throw a salad together whilst you three choose your toppings." Thea opened a bottle of wine and together, they shared a scrummy meal, laughter ringing out like music as they relished each other's company. She marvelled at how seamlessly Emma had integrated into their lives, how naturally she laughed with them, her presence a comforting addition rather than a disruption. It struck her how her children didn't even seem surprised by her being there; it was as if they had always known her. They had accepted her so easily, without question, their instinctive trust a silent testament to Emma's kindness and warmth. *Trust, ha!* Hadn't they accepted Riva too? Well, children don't always have great instincts, but in this case, she thought they'd got it spot on.

Lyra wiped her mouth with the back of her hand then licked

off the tomato sauce. "Not as good as Yaya's, but still good."

Emma looked confused.

"You'd best explain who Yaya is," Thea said.

Lyra's eyes lit up. "Yaya is Greek for grandmother. We're Greek, you know, just like our mummy and our biological daddy. We don't know him, but he was a donor who helped make Seb and me. I think he was a kind person."

Thea could tell that Emma was trying to suppress a giggle. Luckily, she succeeded.

"That's a wonderful story, Lyra. Your mum tells me you visit your grandparents often."

Lyra shuffled around in her seat and looked quite serious. "As often as possible. I wish we lived there."

Seb pouted. "Me too."

"Mum says when we're older, but Seb and I would prefer to live there now. Nearly all our family are there. Have you ever been to Zakynthos?"

"Sadly, I haven't. I've been to Corfu, Rhodes, and Athens though. Your mum says it's not far from Corfu."

Lyra grinned and squeezed her shoulders together. "It's so much nicer." She jumped up. "I'll show you." She returned clutching an iPad and sat beside Emma. Seb jumped up and stood behind her seat. "This is Yaya and Papou's restaurant. Our two uncles, Nicholas and Christos work there too." She pointed. "That's them."

Emma leaned in closer. "It looks wonderful, and it's right on the beach."

"It's *our* beach, isn't it, Mum?"

Thea waggled her head from side to side. "Sort of. Our ancestors have lived there forever, so they have certain rights to that part of the beach."

Lyra flicked to the next photo. "This is the main beach, but we're on the other side. It's like a little bay."

Seb tapped Emma on the arm. "The main beach is called

Tsilivi. It's mostly sandy, but there are a few pebbles. But on our beach, it's pure sand."

Emma tilted her head. "It sounds idyllic."

Seb nodded. "It's like something from a perfect story. Like the home you keep trying to get to."

Thea was a little shocked at Seb's statement. She knew they both loved the island, but she'd never realised they thought of it as home. "What are you two planning to do when you move back home, as you put it?" She looked from one to the other. She was sure they hadn't given it much thought.

"I'm going to sell houses and possibly take tourists around the island," Lyra said.

Seb jumped in. "And I'm going to buy my own boat and take people diving."

Thea raised her eyebrows. "Not climbing?"

Seb looked thoughtful. "Maybe."

Emma laughed. "Wow. It sounds like you two have your future mapped out."

Seb and Lyra beamed, and Lyra continued to flip through photos.

Thea huffed. "All this fancy education you're getting, and that's what you really want to do?" Part of Thea was disappointed, but a big part of her was thrilled at the thought they had already given to their future. Of course, when you were their ages, you had all kinds of ideas about the future. They'd likely go through a million more career options by the time they were of an age to actually choose a path. She'd have to give this revelation a lot more serious thought though, if they truly considered the island home.

Emma leaned back in her chair and took a sip of her wine. "And when are you next off to this little paradise of yours?"

"Autumn half term in October," Lyra said.

Thea shrugged and raised her eyebrows. "Why don't you come with us?"

Seb and Lyra whooped. "Oh, please, Emma. Say you will. We

can show you everything. There's so much to see." They danced around her and pleaded.

Emma rubbed her forehead. "Oh, I don't—I don't know." She stared across at Thea, and there was real panic in her eyes. "I haven't had a holiday in years, but I don't think I can just up and go like that."

Thea winced. She shouldn't have put Emma on the spot like that, but the idea wouldn't let go. She waited to see what Emma would say, not wanting to add any more pressure.

Emma raised her hands in capitulation, and the panic in her eyes seemed to recede a little. "I think I'm outnumbered."

It wasn't long before Thea packed the kids off to bed. She needed some time with Emma. She topped up their glasses and slumped back into her seat. "Wow, I can't believe it. You're coming with us."

Emma clasped her hands in her lap. "Are you sure this is what you want?"

Thea leaned over and kissed her gently. "Sure? There's nothing I want more."

Emma frowned. "What about your mum and dad? What are they going to think? Isn't it a little soon to take me home to meet the family?"

Thea laughed. "They'll be over the moon. They know all about you anyway. And it's not until October. There's plenty of time."

Emma nodded slowly. "But do they know how old I am?"

"Of course they do. They couldn't give a toss. It's not about age, Emma, it's about whether we make each other happy."

"And we do seem to." While the words were positive, she still sounded unsure.

"Listen, Emma. I ballsed this up once, and I don't intend to let you go again. You've become a massive part of my life...and you can see, Seb and Lyra adore you."

"For your information. I think they're pretty wonderful too."

Thea took Emma's hand. "Let's go discuss this in bed."

As they lay there, wrapped in each other's arms, Thea went over some of Emma's concerns in her mind. What would happen if Emma was overwhelmed by her family? There were so many of them, and they could be a bit full on. She'd deal with it. They'd have an exit plan, maybe a signal or phrase. As long as they were together and they had each other's support, Thea was convinced everything would flow like water. As long as Emma didn't panic and want to run. She didn't have any experience with big family situations, and while she was getting used to being around Seb and Lyra, would she cope with being away with them? Thea swallowed hard and lightly kissed the top of Emma's head. *Please let her be strong enough to stay with us.*

Chapter Seventeen

September flew by in a whirlwind and Emma couldn't help but feel thrilled and anxious about the upcoming vacation with Thea and her children. The mere thought of being together on an island sent a flurry of butterflies dancing in her stomach. Of course, she would be surrounded by Thea's family, but by all accounts, they seemed like a chilled bunch of people who were happy to look after the kids. That meant she and Thea would have some alone time, which hadn't been as infrequent as she'd feared, but it definitely meant spontaneity couldn't be a big part of their relationship. She was careful not to overstep too, and that wasn't always easy. She had thoughts about parenting stuff, opinions on what the kids were doing when they made Thea a little crazy, but she made sure not to voice them. She wasn't a co-parent. Thea had been raising them on her own so far and probably didn't want Emma interfering. That left Emma in a limbo of sorts, where she wasn't always certain how to respond. She tried to set that anxiety aside and hope that it would work itself out in the long run, but she had a feeling that talking it out might be better...at some point.

In the weeks leading up to their holiday, Emma and Thea stole every spare moment they could together. Whether it was cozy dinners, shared times with Seb and Lyra, leisurely walks or outings, they cherished every moment they shared. Emma savoured it all, knowing that very soon she'd be whisked away to a paradise of sun, sea, and sand, and their alone time might drop dramatically.

Emma eagerly counted down the days on her calendar and

with only a week to go, she was in a state of chaos. What if Thea's parents didn't like her? What if it became awkward, and she wanted to leave but couldn't get away? What if it all became too much?

When Thea video-called her that evening, she was wandering aimlessly from room to room.

Thea chuckled. "You're running around like a headless chicken. What the heck is the matter?"

"Sorry. There are so many preparations to make."

"Like what?"

"Lists. I have about ten lists so far, and they're growing."

Thea shrugged. "Just chuck some things in a bag with your passport."

"I suppose that's what you do. It's your second home, and you know it like the back of your hand."

"But seriously, Emma, what are the lists for?"

"Shopping. I need a new wardrobe. I have suntan stuff to buy. I need creams in case I get bitten by mosquitos. A new suitcase. My nails need a manicure and varnish. My hair needs cutting, and other things too."

"I wish I'd never asked," Thea mumbled, chuckling. "But apart from that, you're okay?"

"What if your family don't like me?"

"They will."

"How do you know?"

"Because I love you, and they will too."

"You have an answer for everything."

It didn't matter what Thea said, Emma couldn't shake off that lingering sense of apprehension. Meeting Thea's family for the first time weighed heavily on her mind. She wanted to make a good impression, but she wasn't sure if she'd fit in, and it was a daunting prospect. However, there was an undeniable sense of joy bubbling within her, and despite her apprehensions, she couldn't wait to escape to the tranquil shores of the Greek island that Seb and Lyra called home. No, she couldn't let her fears hold her back. This holiday was a chance for her to deepen her bond with Thea and become a part of her world in a way she had never imagined before.

However, Emma wrestled with the gnawing guilt of moving on, her heart heavy with memories of her late wife. Each step towards something new felt like a betrayal, yet a glimmer of hope flickered within her. She imagined Brid's smile, her encouraging nod, and held onto the belief that she would want her to find happiness again. So she tried to embrace the excitement of her next adventure, trusting that Brid would be happy for her. She knew Brid would say that the past was the past, and it was time to move on.

The day was upon them, and as the sun rose over the airport tarmac, Emma, Thea, Seb, and Lyra stood in line waiting to board their flight to Zakynthos.

They found their row, and Seb and Lyra squabbled about who would have the window seat.

Lyra gave in. "Fine." She grinned. "Mum can sit in the middle, and I'll take the aisle seat next to Emma."

Seb frowned. "Can't Emma sit in the middle of us? I want to sit next to her too."

"Stop arguing, you two. I'm sitting in the aisle, and Emma will be on the other side. That's what it says on our boarding passes, and that's it. You'll have plenty of time with Emma once we get there. Give her some peace, eh?"

Seb and Lyra pouted but soon settled down in their seats.

Thea glanced at Emma and raised her eyebrows. "Bloody children. Who'd have them?" She winked. "You okay?"

Emma breathed a tiny sigh of relief. The kids had been bouncing off the walls all morning, and she had to admit that it was a little exhausting. "Great, thanks. How long is the flight?"

"Three and a half hours. There's a time difference so we should get there about twelve thirty."

Emma pointed at Seb with his nose pressed against the window. "He's mesmerised."

"He'll soon get bored. Then he'll want his book."

She was right, and it wasn't long before he began to fidget. "You did order breakfast, didn't you, Mum?"

"Of course. I can see the stewardess loading up her trolley, so it won't be long."

Thea was always so patient. Was that something that came with the territory? The four of them feasted on an assortment of Danish pastries and croissants with jam. After breakfasting, Seb and Lyra read their books, and Emma and Thea relaxed into their seats, the hum of the engines lulling them into a sense of tranquillity.

Thea chatted quietly about her plans for their vacation. "There are so many wonderful beaches I want to show you. There are about fifteen of them and loads of little coves to escape to. I want to show you Turtle Island too; it's part of the National Marine Reserve." Thea seemed to disappear into a world of her own. "Maybe we'll rent a boat, or maybe take a kayak."

"I've read about the turtles. I can't wait for that."

Lyra leaned across. "Can we come too?"

Thea tutted. "How many times have you seen them?"

Lyra grinned. "I can't remember, but it's never enough."

"We'll see," Thea said.

Emma was reminded once again that a relationship with a mum was a relationship with the kids. Leaving them behind all the time wasn't an option. She nodded to herself. So be it.

The hours passed quickly, and the plane began its descent toward Zakynthos airport. Emma felt a rush of excitement course through her. This was it: the beginning of their family adventure. The thought made her breath catch.

Seb and Lyra bounced in their seats. "We're here. We're home."

They gathered their belongings and made their way off the

plane, stepping into the warm Greek sunshine. The sight of the swaying palm trees, and the scent of seawater brought a wide smile to Emma's face. This was the easy part. Very soon she'd be meeting Thea's father, who was coming to collect them.

As they stepped into the arrivals hall, Seb and Lyra tore off towards a man standing with his arms open. Once he'd hugged them, he turned to Emma and Thea.

"Yassou!" he exclaimed as he enveloped them in a warm embrace. "I'm so happy to meet you, Emma. We've heard so much about you."

His embrace was strong and comforting, as if he really meant it. "Thank you, Mr Fontini."

He waved his hand. "No, please call me Dimitris. We are friends now." He ushered them out of the hall. "Come, my car is just across the road."

Seb ran alongside his grandfather, and Dimitris ruffled Seb's hair and gave Lyra a playful wink.

"Kalos irthate! Welcome home, my little adventurers."

On their journey, Seb and Lyra regaled Emma with tales of the island's beauty and history, pointing out landmarks along the way. Emma and Thea exchanged smiles. Emma was grateful for the opportunity to share this experience with Thea's children, and at last to meet Thea's parents...even though she was scared shitless.

Dimitris parked and unloaded the luggage, and they all walked up the track towards the restaurant. In the distance, Emma could see a group of people and heard the animated chatter and laughter coming from the diners. Then she saw a woman dashing at full speed down the hill.

Her arms were wide open, a smile spreading across her face. "Welcome, Emma. I'm Maria, Thea's mother and these two little rascals' grandmother. It's so wonderful to meet you."

Emma returned the embrace as much as she could. It had been a long time since she'd been greeted that way. She remembered her own parents had always shown their emotion, but that was many years ago, and she certainly hadn't felt any warmth from her sister. However, she could sense the genuine affection in Maria's hug, and it was a wonderful feeling. "It's so good to meet you at last, Maria."

Thea coughed loudly. "Where's my hug then?"

Maria swung around. "Oh, my darling daughter. How could I forget you?"

They hugged for what seemed like an eternity.

When they'd finished, Maria linked arms with Emma and Thea, her eyes sparkling with excitement. "Come, come! We're preparing a feast for us all. You must be starving after your journey." Maria chatted animatedly about the dishes they had prepared, describing each one with passion and pride. She turned to Emma. "Please excuse Dimitris and me. We have to finish looking after our diners, but they'll be leaving soon, and we'll close the restaurant. Then we shall have our own family party."

Emma couldn't help but smile as a sense of comfort and belonging washed over her from the welcome she'd received.

As they walked through the outdoor terrace, they were greeted by the welcoming chatter of diners and the tantalising smells of grilled seafood and aromatic herbs.

Maria led them to a long table on the other side of the bustling terrace. She touched Thea's cheek. "There's wine on the table. Help yourselves, and we'll be back soon."

All hell let loose when four children careered across the terrace, shouting at the top of their voices. Seb and Lyra ran to greet them.

Thea held her hands up. "Whoa there, you lot. Where's your manners?"

The four children came to a halt, then Thea bundled them into a huddle and kissed each one. They stared up at Emma shyly. "This is my friend, Emma. Emma, these little horrors are my nieces and nephews.'

The four children giggled. "Hello, Emma."

"Hello back. Who is who?"

The eldest boy stepped forward. "My name is Gregorious. This is my sister, Zoe, and these are my two cousins, Sophia and Elena. Are you Aunty Thea's girlfriend?"

Emma wasn't quite sure what to say and glanced at Thea, who just quirked an eyebrow and grinned. "Err...yes, I suppose I am."

Thea laughed and clipped him behind his ear playfully. "Go help Papou with the luggage, you lot. Then you can play." They all ran off and Thea shouted, "Seb, Lyra, change your clothes before you go on the beach. And stay with your cousins."

"Yes, Mum," they shouted back.

Thea grinned at Emma, then took her in her arms. She kissed her gently. "So, what do you think so far?" she asked.

Emma stared back with wide eyes. "Scary and challenging. But they're all lovely," she added and smiled. Emma glanced to the beach and the sea beyond. "You weren't exaggerating. It's beautiful beyond imagination."

Thea rested her head on Emma's shoulder. "I don't know about you, but I need a quick wash and change of clothes.'

Emma agreed and followed Thea around the side of the restaurant to a small annexe at the back.

Thea opened the door. There was a cosy sitting area with a sofa and a couple of armchairs. One window looked out onto a small patio which overlooked the beach, and the side window had a view of a wooded area. Behind the furniture were two single beds.

"I'm afraid it's not plush," she said and wiggled her eyebrows, "but we can push the beds together later."

Emma spotted their luggage. "Don't your mum and dad mind us sharing?"

Thea grinned. "It was Mum who suggested it. She did ask if you'd prefer a room of your own, but that would have been above the restaurant—way too far for me to sneak up to. At least here, we get some privacy. Not to mention, we're adults, not teenagers, and it isn't like they don't know we're sleeping together." Thea lifted the suitcases onto the beds. "C'mon, best get a move on before I throw you on the bed too."

"Sounds tempting, but somehow, I think they'd come looking for us."

Emma and Thea took a very quick shower and went back to the restaurant. The desire for privacy and some quiet time with Thea warred with the idea that the family would be wondering where they were, and that caused a hot flush.

It was a hive of activity. All the diners had gone, and the family were running back and forth, covering the table with masses of food.

"Hey, little sis," someone shouted.

Two men and two women came dashing towards them. One of them swept Thea off her feet and swung her around, then put her down. Thea laughed uncontrollably as they pushed her from one to another and smothered her with kisses and hugs.

The taller man opened his arms. "I'm Thea's elder, most handsome brother, Nicholas. This is my lucky wife, Anna. This here is my little brother, Cristos, and his wife, Katerina."

They swarmed Emma, hugging and kissing her cheek as though she was a long-lost friend. She did her best not to look completely overwhelmed.

Cristos poured large glasses of wine and passed them around. "I'll just go and help Mum and Dad with the food. Katerina, can you call the children?"

Katerina yelled at the top of her voice, and the children came running.

The food arrived. Plates of mezze, grilled octopus, moussaka, kebabs, assorted barbecued meats, and a fresh Greek salad adorned the table. As they all dug into the delicious feast, laughter and conversation filled the air, weaving a tapestry of love and connection. Emma did try to keep up, but the conversation flowed fast, and there were several going at once, so she just laughed when she thought she was supposed to. The kids were clearly in their element, and Thea practically glowed with happiness. It was beautiful, if chaotic.

The evening was full of merriment and eventually, way after midnight, they fell into their beds.

Emma woke up and looked at her watch. Six thirty a.m. She turned over and tried to get back to sleep but failed. She glanced at Thea, but she was dead to the world, likely the result of too much ouzo last night. Emma had resisted and stuck with wine, though she promised herself she'd give the ouzo a go at the next opportunity.

She peeked through the curtain to see a beautiful day dawning. She decided to take the opportunity to explore and walk along the beach. She put some clothes on and quietly slipped out of the room. She strolled through the olive groves and inhaled deeply, taking in the distinctive earthy-fresh aroma mixed with hints of sweetness and bitterness. It felt a little like her life. There'd been the sweet and the bitter. She was back to the sweet again, but she couldn't help but wonder if that pattern would repeat, and that she'd lose it all again. An early fear raised its head. What if she got attached to these wonderful people, and it all fell apart? Ending up alone again after that... She didn't know if she'd be able to recover.

Wanting to push those thoughts away as she reached the beach, she held her arms out and ran towards the water's edge as though she was flying. The rhythmic sound of the waves lapping against the shoreline created a soothing melody. With each step, she felt a sense of calmness that only the ocean could provide. Yes, she now lived by the sea in England, but there was nothing quite like the beauty of Ionian Sea and the Mediterranean.

Lost in her thoughts, Emma hardly noticed the figure approaching her until they nearly collided. She stumbled backward, startled, only to find herself face to face with the familiar smile of Maria.

"Emma, what a pleasant surprise!" Maria said, her eyes sparkling with genuine delight. "No one else in the family gets up at this time if they don't have to."

Emma returned the smile. "I didn't expect to see anyone here. I think I'm still on UK time."

"I often come down to the beach for my morning walk," she said, gesturing to the expansive stretch of sand before them. "It's such a peaceful place to gather my thoughts."

Emma nodded, though her thoughts had been less gathered and more strewn. "I couldn't agree more. There's something incredibly calming about the ocean."

"Indeed," Maria said as she fell into step beside Emma. "There's a lovely little café just around the corner. Shall we have some coffee?"

Emma smiled. "That would be lovely."

Maria linked arms with her as they continued their walk along the shoreline.

Over coffee, the conversation flowed effortlessly between them as they chatted about everything from the beauty of nature to the challenges of everyday life.

"This must have been a big step for you, to come and meet Thea's family. I hope we haven't frightened you off."

Emma touched Maria's hand. It wasn't something she'd normally do, but somehow it felt normal. "On the contrary. You've all made me feel so welcome."

Maria squeezed Emma's hand. "Good, because I know you mean a lot to Thea." She sighed. "I'm so sorry Thea lied to you. You know, she's not that sort of person really, but since the episode with that woman, she became someone we hardly recognized. My own daughter, and I didn't have a clue how to cure her fears. It's taken a long time. It was you, Emma, who brought her to her senses, and I'll be eternally grateful for that."

Emma gave a nervous chuckle. "Actually, it was Thea who came to my rescue. Joking apart, as soon as I heard the truth, it all slotted into place. I think she's beginning to trust again. I hope so, anyway, because she's become a big part of my life too."

Maria frowned, her gaze searching. "Can I ask a personal question? How do you feel about Seb and Lyra? It's obvious they've become very attached to you."

Emma rubbed her forehead. "To be honest, I was apprehensive at first. You see, I've never been around children. But I adore them, and they've made that so easy for me to do. I still worry, and I still have some questions about how things will work, but..." She shook her head. "It's hard to imagine not being part of their world."

"I can see how fond they are of you, and that makes me so happy." Maria frowned. "We all miss them so much though. School holidays just aren't enough. I've tried very hard to persuade Thea to come and live here permanently."

Emma's palms sweated, and she wiped them discreetly on her trousers. The fear of losing Thea and her children weighed heavily on her mind. Would they leave? "I know," she said. She didn't want to continue this conversation. It made her feel incredibly vulnerable.

As if realising, Maria checked her watch and sat upright. "Oh my God, look at the time. They'll all be wanting breakfast, and here I am, burdening you with stupid talk of my dreams." She placed some money under the coffee saucer and got up.

Emma followed and once again, Maria linked arms as they strode back along the beach. Maria told her the story of how she'd met Dimitris in England and how she'd fallen in love with both him and the island of Zakynthos.

As Emma gazed around her, she could fully understand why.

Chapter Eighteen

THEA YAWNED AND STRETCHED, then extended her arm across to the other side of the bed. She quickly jolted awake when she felt that Emma wasn't there. She called out, thinking maybe Emma was in the shower, but there was no reply, so she jumped out of bed. Emma's clothes were missing from the chair, so she figured she'd woken early and gone for a walk.

She parted the curtain and saw Emma disappearing through the olive grove. She could have dressed quickly and joined her but dismissed the idea. Maybe Emma needed to take a walk on her own, so it was best to give her some space. *Wait. What's this?* Her mother slipped out of their house and into the grove, clearly moving quietly. Since when had her mother gone for early morning walks? *Since she saw Emma heading that way, that's when.*

Thea watched closely as her mum headed to the left. Thea knew exactly what she was doing: taking the short cut to make a turn by the sand dunes and then head back. "Oh," she'd say to Emma, "what a chance meeting." *The crafty bugger.*

Thea returned to bed and checked her email, but her thoughts continued to drift back to Emma. Was she okay? What was she thinking? Eventually, she got ready and walked over to the house to wake Seb and Lyra up, but they'd beaten her to it and were already playing some game on the beach with their cousins.

Cristos sat on a wall watching over them. He waved when he saw Thea approaching. "Hello, little sis." He patted a spot next to him. "Come and join me."

Thea kissed him on the cheek and sat by his side. "Thanks."

He turned to her. "For what?"

"Watching over them, of course."

Cristos shrugged. "They don't really need it. They know the rules, and they never wander off. They stick together. But I know how you feel...so here I am." He winked at her. "This is it then? The real thing."

"What?"

"Emma, that's what. She's a real keeper. If I were you, I'd ask her to marry me."

Thea punched Cristos on the arm. "You crazy brother. We've only known each other for a few months."

"Wow, that long. When I met Katerina, I knew within the week. I'd asked her to marry me by the end of the month."

"Yeah, and she said yes. Poor Katerina." Thea laughed.

Cristos sighed and looked up at the sky. "We could do with another wedding. I just love the romance of it all."

Thea raised her eyebrows. "You always have been a big softie."

"The love of your life doesn't come along very often. That's all I'm saying."

"Can I borrow your jeep tomorrow?"

"Don't change the subject, sis, but yes. Are you taking Emma for a tour of the island?"

Thea nodded.

"Seb and Lyra can spend the day with us."

Thea hugged Cristos. "Aww, thanks, bruv. You're a little gem."

Thea thought about what her brother had said. She loved Emma, and Emma surprisingly loved her back. But it wasn't without its complications. Was Emma willing to take on her and her children? She'd had years of experiences, some of them dark and difficult. Did Emma truly understand what she was stepping into? And then there was her family, a close-knit but sometimes overbearing presence. She'd plunged Emma in at the deep end. A holiday with them was one thing, but one day, Thea hoped to move back to the island. Would Emma be able to cope with that?

Could she adapt to the slower pace of island life, which was even slower when the tourists were gone? Somehow, she couldn't see Emma crocheting tablecloths as the locals did. Thea's heart ached with the weight of uncertainty. She longed for a future where their love could flourish without the shadows of doubt, but reality was rarely that simple.

Emma and her mum wandered in, with Emma looking thoughtful. Her mum winked at Thea and began to bustle about the kitchen.

"Everything okay?" she asked, after giving Emma a quick kiss on the cheek. "I was surprised you were gone when I woke."

Emma smiled, but there were shadows in her eyes. "Everything's good. I just wanted some time to think and breathe in the morning quiet."

Thea nodded, and they were swept into family conversation, but she could feel the way Emma seemed distant and lost in her thoughts.

After their breakfast of yoghurt and fruit, Thea and Emma packed their bags and headed off. They stepped onto the warm sand of the beach, and a gentle breeze whispered through the air, carrying the salty scent of the sea and the promise of a day filled with tranquillity and relaxation.

Thea found the perfect spot by the water's edge. She spread out two colourful beach towels, and Emma nestled beside her.

Emma laid back and folded her arms behind her head. "It's so beautiful here."

Thea turned onto her side and looked down at her. "It's perfect, now that you're here." She kissed Emma on the lips. "I thought we'd just chill today. Cristos has loaned us his jeep for tomorrow, so we can tour around the island."

"That's brilliant. I'd love to go and see that shipwreck. Is that on the agenda?"

"Of course, but not tomorrow. We have to take a boat to see that." Thea breathed in deeply. "Tell me truthfully, are my family too much for you?"

Emma put her arms around Thea's neck and kissed her. "Absolutely not. I love them. It's odd; I feel like I've known them all my life. Or perhaps I've just been waiting for them."

Thea's smile spread across her lips. "That's the best thing anyone's ever said to me." *What a relief.* Still though, she couldn't help but feel like Emma was holding something back.

For the rest of the day, they simply relaxed, alternating between sunbathing, taking dips in the refreshing sea, and strolling along the shoreline hand in hand. They were enjoying each other's company without any distractions, sharing stories and dreams. Thea didn't tell Emma about her big dream. She thought she'd wait a while until Emma had settled into her family's life. To see if it could work. To see if Emma could ever share her dream.

Later, back at the restaurant, they joined Thea's family for a meal prepared by Anna and Katerina, which was an array of delicious fresh fish dishes caught earlier that day by Nicholas. In the background, Seb, Lyra, and their cousins ran around excitedly, their laughter filling the air as they chased each other around the terrace.

As the night came to a close, Thea couldn't help but feel gratitude for the perfect day they had spent together. She felt rejuvenated and closer than ever to Emma and her family. Seeing her kids so happy, so free, took her back to what they'd said about this being home. There was no question they were completely in their element. And being able to make love to Emma and wake up wrapped in her arms gave her a kind of contentment she'd never experienced. Somehow, she had to find a way to combine the two things.

The following day, they packed their rucksacks and set off in the jeep to explore. It wasn't a clear blue sky, but it was perfect for a sightseeing tour. Thea turned to Emma. "I hope you're not going to be too mad at me. I know you wanted to go to see the shipwreck at Navagio Beach, and I wanted it to be just the two of us." Thea cringed a little. "Mum and Dad are closing the restaurant for the rest of our holiday, so Nicholas has offered to take us all in his boat to see it. I hope you don't mind."

Emma looked bemused. "That sounds fabulous, and don't be silly, I'd love to share it with them. I don't always need to have you to myself, you know. Trust me, Thea. I promise I'll tell you if I want more alone time with you."

Thea stroked Emma's leg. "Thanks for understanding."

"Where are we going first?"

"I thought I'd give you a general tour of the island. Visit some villages, take a swim in a secluded cove where I can have my way with you, have some lunch, more sightseeing, etcetera. Not necessarily in that order."

They took a leisurely drive north up the coast. There were still a fair number of tourists around, but the pace suited them fine as it enabled Emma to get a flavour of the awesome scenery. Thea so wanted to create a good impression...for many reasons.

Emma clutched Thea's leg. "Darling, this is amazing. I can't ever remember seeing such beautiful scenery. Is the island all like this?"

Hmm. I like being called darling. "Yes, mostly. There's seventy-six miles of stunning coastline, but not all of it has white sand beaches. The western side is more rugged, with craggy cliffs and dramatic rock formations, but it still has some brilliant beaches. It's all incredible, even though I've seen it so many times."

When they got to the northern tip, they headed slightly inland towards Volimes. It didn't take long, and they parked on the edge of the village and walked up the hill.

Emma crooked her arm in Thea's. "So what's so special about this village then?"

"It's the most important village in the north. I like it because it's full of pride and tradition. They produce oil, and honey, and spices. There's a lot of handicrafts like tablecloths and centrepieces, and in the winter, they make handmade carpets. They supply them all over Greece."

As they wandered through the cobblestone streets, they stopped and admired the local handicrafts, and Thea chatted with the friendly villagers in Greek.

Emma nudged Thea. "Wow, I'm impressed. So you're fluent in Greek?"

Thea shrugged. "I learned it as a child. It's so easy when you're small. To be honest, I'm a bit rusty. I should swot up on it more... especially if —"

"Especially if what?" Emma's entire body stiffened, and she gently pulled her hand from Thea's.

Thea spread her hands in front of her. "For the future."

Emma nodded slowly. "How much into the future?"

"I honestly don't know, Emma." She didn't. That much was the truth, but more and more, she was becoming drawn to the island. She could see herself living happily here, but only if Emma was there too. They'd built and crossed many bridges, and she sincerely believed Emma felt at home with her family...but to ask her to live here, to ask her to move when she'd only just settled in Westleigh seemed like it might be out of the question.

Emma absently picked up a jar of honey from one of the local stalls.

Thea whispered in her ear. "Don't even think about it. Mum would kill you. She thinks she makes the best honey in the whole of Greece."

Emma laughed and put it down, and the tension seemed to ebb a little.

They wandered back to the jeep. Thea pulled a couple of cold drinks from the cooler and handed one to Emma with a smile. They clinked their cans together in a silent toast before taking long, satisfying sips.

Thea opened the passenger door. "I thought we'd head down the coast and find a taverna somewhere, then we can aim for a nice beach and take a dip." She wiggled her eyebrows. "And maybe more."

Emma stroked Thea's arm. "Now that sounds like a great plan."

After feasting on local fish, they continued their journey south. "We're heading for Pelagaki. It's one of my favourites. It's a bit of a hike down to the beach but well worth it."

It took over an hour to get there, and Thea stopped the jeep next to the small café. "Do you want a cake or anything?"

Emma shook her head and placed her hand over her stomach. "No way, thanks. I feel I've already put on weight with all this wonderful home cooking."

Thea patted Emma's tummy. "I like a bit of meat on my women."

Emma stared at her wide-eyed. "Women?"

Thea laughed and ducked away. "Whoops, slip of the tongue." She quickly grabbed the rucksacks and moved out of Emma's reach. She threw one to Emma, and they put them on their backs. "We'll need our sea shoes, because it's pebbly."

Emma stood at the edge of the cliff. "Oh my God. What a magnificent view."

"Yeah. We're blessed with them. Wait until you get down there." She led the way down the steep steps, and eventually they arrived on the beach. Very few people were there due to the accessibility.

Emma stood, staring in wonder. "I can't wait to get into that clear blue sea."

They dumped their gear in a shady spot by the cliffs. Thea stripped off to her bikini, but Emma wore her one-piece swimsuit. She knew Emma was self-conscious about her body, but one day, she'd convince Emma how beautiful she'd look in a bikini. Yes, one day she hoped to fill Emma with confidence so she knew just how gorgeous she was. They put their sea shoes on and ran to the water's edge.

Emma laughed, an open and beautiful sound, as she looked into the water. "I can see the fish from here."

They ran into the sea hand in hand. They swam for a while, and Emma marvelled at the scenes of the cliffs behind her. She put her arms around Thea and kissed her deeply. "This day has been remarkable. Thank you."

"I want to show you as much as I can, and this is just the beginning."

Their laughter mingled with the sound of the waves. Thea couldn't take her eyes off Emma, captivated by her beauty and the depth of the love she felt. They played around in the water, splashing each other. Every gesture, every laugh, and every glance Emma gave her felt like a treasure. She felt overwhelmed with love, and as the water enveloped them, she drew Emma close and made love to her in the embrace of the ocean. After, she held her close in her arms, full of awe and tenderness, none of which she'd ever experienced before. She felt complete and could no longer imagine her life without Emma.

With a contented sigh, they both settled onto their towels, basking in the warmth of the afternoon sun.

"Thea," Emma said, her voice soft yet tinged with a hint of uncertainty. "We need to talk."

She turned to face her, her heart tightening at the seriousness in Emma's eyes. "What's the matter?"

She hesitated, the words seeming to weigh heavily on her tongue. "I need to know where we stand, especially when it comes to your children. What do you see my role being in their lives?"

Thea took a deep breath, her mind racing. She had been so caught up in her feelings for Emma that she hadn't fully considered the practicalities of their relationship. Her children were her world, and she knew that any future with Emma had to include them.

"Emma," she began, taking her hand. "You mean everything to me. I can't imagine my life without you. My kids are my life, and I want them to know and love you as much as I do."

Emma squeezed her hand, her eyes searching for reassurance. "I want to be there for you and the kids, Thea. But I need to know what that looks like. I don't want to overstep, but I also don't want to be left in limbo, unsure of my place."

She nodded, understanding her need for clarity. "I want you to help me raise them, to be there for the big moments and the small ones. But I also want us to take this step by step, to make sure we do what's best for them."

Emma nodded. "I just need to know that we're on the same page."

"We are, Emma. We're a team, and we'll figure this out together." Thea leaned in and pressed a gentle kiss on her lips. "I know the future is uncertain, but for the first time, I feel ready to embrace it, and I hope you do too. You've given me a new lease on life, and I'm determined to make the most of it, for both of us and for the children. I guess we'll have to navigate the challenges ahead one step at a time, and we'll talk everything through. I promise."

"I know it's not going to be easy, but as long as you make sure we do it together." Emma smiled contentedly and rested her head on Thea's shoulder.

They agreed they'd stay there for the rest of the afternoon; it was way too magical to leave.

As they congregated around the table that evening, an mated chatter filled the air. Thea and Emma exchanged knowing glances, and she knew, like her, Emma enjoyed the love and warmth of their family. They dug into the meal with gusto, savouring every bite and sharing stories of their tour of the island.

As the evening wore on and the stars began to twinkle overhead, contentment, warm and deep like the Med, filled her. Not only did they have each other, but they were surrounded by joy and love.

After making love once more, Thea tenderly caressed Emma's curves, her eyes lingering on her with a gentle intensity.

"I love your body."

Emma shifted uncomfortably. "Don't look. I'm all wrinkly, and my skin is ageing." She turned away slightly, as if she wished Thea would stop staring.

Thea gently took her hand. "Emma, you're ravishing. Every line tells the story of your life. I see only beauty in you."

"But what happens when—"

"Emma, tell me something. Ours is the same age gap as you and Brid. Did you look at her and see a wrinkled ageing body?"

"I suppose beauty is in the eye of the beholder."

Thea pressed a finger on Emma's lips. "Exactly, and I'm the one beholding. So trust me when I tell you that I see your beauty."

Emma leaned into her and snuggled in closely. "Thank you, my darling. You say all the right things."

The following morning, everyone gathered around the table for a late breakfast, feasting on feta cheese, eggs, cold cut meats, and bread, followed by a selection of seasonal fruits and yogurt.

Emma shook her head and whispered to Thea. "Do you always eat this much for breakfast?"

"Mostly. Greeks like their food." She laughed. "Maybe we'll have to work it off in the bedroom," she said and bit into a hard-boiled egg.

"Shush." Emma nudged her and put her finger over her lips.

It was too late. Everyone had heard, though they didn't comment, but their smiles said it all.

"Thea," her father said, his deep voice commanding attention as he set down his coffee cup, "I was thinking that you should take Emma out to see the turtles this afternoon. The forecast is good for today, but it's going to be overcast for the next few days."

"That's a great idea, Dad." Thea glanced at Emma to gauge her reaction.

Emma's face lit up with a radiant smile. "Oh, could we, please? I'm longing to see them."

Thea's father tilted his head. "There's no guarantee, but if you take a kayak and follow one of the main boats, you might get lucky."

Emma clapped her hands. "Oh, I do hope so."

Lyra and Seb pouted. "Can't we go too?"

Cristos coughed, loudly. "You said you wanted to go climbing today."

Seb and Lyra jumped off their chairs and flung their arms around their uncle Christos. "We do, we do. We can see the turtles next time."

Thea frowned. "What's all this about climbing?"

He half covered his mouth with his hand and whispered, "It's a steep hill, sis, that's all. All of us are going. You can come too if you prefer."

Thea and Emma shook their heads vigorously.

After clearing the breakfast remnants, Thea and Emma took a walk along the beach.

Suddenly, without explanation, Emma pinched Thea's arm.

"Ow, that hurt. What have I done wrong now?"

Emma stopped in her tracks and rested her hands on her hips. "Your public displays of affection and your innuendos, that's what."

Thea roared with laughter. "They don't have a problem with it. We've always been a very open family. My parents are incredibly forward thinking. Not all Greeks are, but I'm blessed."

"Maybe you are, but I'm still self-conscious about it."

Thea took her into a cuddle. "Aw...I'm sorry. I promise I'll be a good girl."

"Stop being so patronising." Emma pushed her away. "Anyway, when did they know about your sexuality?"

"I plucked up the courage to tell them when I was fifteen. There was no awkward silence or hesitation...just an overwhelming sense of support. They said they all knew, hugged me, and told me they loved me for who I was, and that would never change. They were happy because I was true to myself, and all that mattered was my happiness."

"You're so lucky to have had such great communication with your family."

Thea nodded. "We've all been brought up to believe in the importance of acceptance, kindness, and the rights of every individual to live their truth. After I'd told them, they made sure to educate themselves about LGBTQ+ issues and tried to understand the challenges I might face, so they could support me."

Emma shook her head. "I have to say, they are a remarkable family."

"They sure are a family in a million. They've even been with me to Pride parades, and they're always the first to speak out against discrimination and prejudice. The restaurant became a safe haven for others in the community too." Thea spread her arms out, palms up. "It's exactly the same here too; everyone is welcome and accepted. There are loads of brilliant reviews from the LGBTQ+ community for places all over the island."

Emma rubbed Thea's arm. "That's a lovely story. Nevertheless, it'll still take me a while to get used to public displays of affection. I'm so self-conscious."

Thea kissed her. "Just be yourself. You don't have to change, because I love you as you are."

They continued their walk hand in hand along the beach, and Thea discovered that every day, she loved Emma more for being herself.

Later in the day, Thea and Emma took off in search of the turtles. It was a short drive to Agios Sostis. Thea placed a small cooler bag in the kayak, and then slipped on their lifejackets. She looked at her watch and glanced over at the boat they'd be following. "Shouldn't be long now."

"Whilst we're waiting, tell me a bit about the turtles. Why are they called loggerheads?"

Thea cocked her head. "Locally, they're known as caretta

caretta, and they have incredibly large heads, powerful jaws, and pointed beaks. They can't withdraw their heads into their shells, but the adults are protected from predators by their thick shells and the thick scaly skin on their heads and neck. And of course, they are *seriously* big. About three feet long, but there are some that have been known to measure nine feet."

Emma's mouth opened. "You're kidding?"

"Nope. Most of that is their head. I haven't seen one that big, but I have seen some huge ones. They're awesome. When they mate, they circle each other like this." Thea danced around Emma, and she laughed. "Then they nuzzle, bite, and make demonstrative head and flipper movements." Thea ducked and dived around Emma, flapping her arms and protruding her head. When she moved in close and lightly bit Emma's neck, she got a quiet moan for her efforts. She laughed. "Phew, all this talk of mating is turning me on."

"You can forget that, because the boat is moving off without us."

They jumped into the kayak and paddled towards the boat and trailed behind it at a safe distance.

Emma glanced around. "There are quite a lot of boats. Is it safe for the turtles?"

Thea frowned. "The short answer is no. It's not too bad at this time of year, but the summertime is crazy. They get way too close to the turtles and scare them. They also invade their territory on the beach." Thea sighed. "Sometimes, I don't like humans. They don't have any respect for animal life and nature. All they want is a good photo to show their mates. Tourists have even been known to try and steal the baby turtles. Fortunately, the World Wildlife Fund have a lot of volunteers, and they guard the hatching area."

"That's terrible, but sadly, that's how we are. On a lighter note, have you ever seen the hatchlings?"

Thea beamed. "Yes, years ago before Seb and Lyra were born. We went with one of the WWF volunteers who is a friend of Nicholas. I tell you; it was amazing. They're less than two inches long when they hatch."

"Lucky you." Emma leaned over the kayak, scanning the water.

"Yes. Very lucky." Thea peered ahead. "The boat has stopped. That means they must have spotted one. Keep your eyes peeled." She took a deep breath when she saw the tell-tale sign. "Okay, it's coming up on our right. Keep still, and it'll stick around. Don't put your hands in the water; they do bite, and they can crush pretty hefty shellfish with their jaws. We have to be careful because they may look invincible, but they're really sensitive and get stressed out easily."

Emma gasped and positioned her phone. She whispered, "It's there. Right alongside us. It must be a good three feet!"

"Yep, that's about the average." She crooked her neck as she watched the boat ahead. "Let's paddle slowly forward. I think they've spotted another."

And there it was. This one was even bigger and lifted its head out of the water.

Emma covered her mouth with her hand. "Oh my God. I think I might pass out, I'm so excited."

"I'll paddle around so you can get a better view and more pics. Now that is a big bugger. Just look at the size of his flippers."

Emma hardly spoke. She seemed totally mesmerised by the spectacle. When she wasn't clicking her camera, she was whooping quietly. They hung around, watching and waiting for more, but no others appeared, so they headed back to the beach.

When they got back, Emma said. "I think that has to go down as one of the best experiences I've ever had."

Thea winked at her. "Better than sex?"

Emma laughed. "I did say *one* of the best experiences."

They continued their tour of the island after some more kissing in the shadows of the hill, and Emma seemed to bathe in the beauty around her. She'd fallen in love with the turtles, and

Thea loved her more and more for that. The whole experience had brought back wonderful memories for her, and she was beginning to question whether she could leave them all behind again. But if she couldn't, then what did that mean for her and Emma?

Chapter Nineteen

Magic. Every moment and every bit of scenery was pure magic. Every single second was a grand journey of discovery. And by all accounts, Emma still had a lot more to see. Over the past few days, Emma had done a lot of thinking about her conversation with Maria. It was obvious that all the family wanted Thea there and to see Seb and Lyra growing up in Zakynthos.

She knew Thea had reservations; she wanted to give Seb and Lyra the best education, and that didn't seem possible in Zakynthos. But was it fair to deprive them of the life they wanted? To deprive them of the company of the family who adored them.

It all appeared to be coming to a head, and she could see Thea grappling with it every time a family member brought up the issue, but where did that leave Emma? Was she even part of the equation? Somehow, she thought she was, but for Christ's sake, she'd only just moved to Westleigh. Was Thea expecting her to uproot and start again? That was such a crazy idea. People would think she'd lost the plot!

But who are those imaginary people? She only had one close friend, and that was Jen, and she knew what she'd say. "Go for it." Zakynthos was only a three and a half hours' plane journey from the United Kingdom. It wasn't a million miles away from civilisation. They could even have a long-distance relationship for a while, if it came to that. People did that kind of thing all the time...

She punched the cushion and leaned back in her chair, overlooking the olive grove. There were certainly worse places to have a mid-life crisis. She couldn't name a place where she felt more at home, and it was so tranquil. She thought about the summer months, and how the island would be heaving with tourists. Was that a bad thing? Certainly not for the islanders, as that was their number one source of income. Thea's family made their living from tourists, although she knew they didn't do it for that reason; they did it because they loved that life. She was certain they could all retire comfortably as the business had always thrived. And Thea's lottery win meant she could take care of the whole family if necessary. No, they seemed to thrive on work, and the more they did, the happier they were.

It was funny how quickly Emma had become so fond of them all. They were the family she'd never had. All those years, there'd been something missing in her life, a bond and people who looked out for each other when they needed it. The Fontini family were just those people.

Had Brid looked after her? No, that hadn't been the same. She and Brid had been independent people with different interests, and they came together when they weren't doing other things with other people. They sort of looked after each other, although she did recall that mostly she was the one who propped Brid up. Brid was a bit needy, but it hadn't really mattered at the time. It was funny; she'd never given it that much thought until now. What would it be like, to have someone who wanted to be around her, who wanted to give her attention and make sure her needs were met? Someone she could do the same with. It was hard to fathom.

"Cooee, Emma. Where are you?"

"Here," Emma replied.

Thea burst through the door. "I was getting worried. What are you doing?"

Emma tilted her head. "Thinking. Looking at the view."

Thea waggled her eyebrows. "Do you fancy some thinking in bed?"

Emma grinned. "Go on then."

Thea picked her up, and she screamed with delight as she threw her on the bed. Thea kissed her with force and began to remove Emma's clothing. "So this is what I've been thinking about."

Their love-making lasted a few hours, and they lay in each other's arms totally spent. Emma couldn't think of a time she'd been happier. All the worries from earlier were left behind in a sex haze.

As the days of their holiday on the island drew to a close, a bittersweet feeling settled over her. Time seemed to be slipping through her fingers like grains of sand. They had shared so many unforgettable moments and created memories that would last a lifetime; enjoyed lazy days spent lounging on the beach and exhilarating experiences exploring hidden caves and rocky cliffs. Each moment became more precious as they savoured the final days of their stay, but they still had one big adventure to look forward to.

The second to last day, they headed off for a family outing to Agios Nicolaos, where the family kept their boat, and parents, brothers, and wives came together with all the children. They loaded the boat with everything they needed for a day of exploring and sunbathing. The chaos wasn't nearly as overwhelming as it had been when Emma had first arrived, and the whole thing just made her smile.

Nicholas handed out life jackets to everyone. "Okay, you kids. I know you're excited, but we don't want to lose any of you overboard. We may feel differently later, in which case we'll leave you on the shipwreck, but for the moment, sit on the centre seats and don't mess around."

The children obeyed as they argued about who should be left behind.

Thea beckoned Emma to the front of the boat. "We get the best seats today as it's your first visit."

The engine burst into life, and the boat bobbled gently in the lapping waves towards the Blue Caves. "Why are they called the Blue Caves?" Emma asked.

"The geological formations are all natural archways which have been carved out of the cliffs by years of erosion, and when you get inside, you'll see why they're called the Blue Caves. Better you see it than me explain it."

As they sliced through the waves, Emma marvelled at the beauty that surrounded them. The cliffs rose majestically from the sea, their rugged edges kissed by the sun. Emma pointed up towards the seabirds that were swooping and soaring overhead, their cries echoing off the rocky walls.

Soon, the mouth of the first cave loomed before them, a gaping maw in the side of the cliff.

"Stay seated, everyone. The caves are very low in places," Nicholas called out.

He slowed the boat down as they floated into the darkness, the only light coming from the shimmering blue waters below. Inside, the air was cool and still, and the waves gently lapped against the rocky walls. As they ventured deeper into the cave, the true magic of the caves revealed itself. Shafts of sunlight filtered through the stone and into the water, casting ethereal beams of blue light that danced across the walls. The children whooped with excitement.

Emma grasped Thea's hand. "Wow. This is truly magical."

"It is. It doesn't matter how many times I see it; it still amazes me." Thea squeezed her hand. "Now you know why I couldn't explain it. It's pure, unadulterated beauty."

As they emerged from the first cave, they were greeted by another, even larger cavern ahead. Nicholas steered the boat onward to explore every hidden corner of the underwater wonderland.

For an hour or so, the boat seemed to lose itself in the maze of caves and grottoes that dotted the coastline. Everyone watched in awe as the vibrant marine life darted between the rocks. The boat headed out of the last cave, and they all took a final glance back at the caves.

"Fasten your seatbelts, everyone; we're off to Shipwreck Cove," Nicholas said, imitating a pirate's accent.

Emma leaned back and admired the scenery, the craggy rocks, and the deep cerulean colours of the Ionian Sea. "What's the story of the shipwreck?"

"Can I tell Emma, Mum?" Lyra asked.

Thea got up and took Lyra's hand. "Okay, come over."

Lyra sat beside Emma. "They say that the ship was caught in a bad storm. It couldn't see where it was going, and it ran aground in the cove." Lyra lowered her voice. "Rumour has it that the ship was smuggling drugs, and that's why the beach has a nickname of 'Smugglers Cove.'"

"When did it happen?" Emma asked.

Lyra shrugged. "Oh, years ago. A long, long time ago. I think it was in the late nineteen hundreds, like 1980."

Emma feigned shock, though the dated reference made her wince a little. "My, that sure is old history. I think I was about ten years old then."

Lyra frowned. "Really? You were around then?"

Emma groaned. "I'm afraid so."

Maria cupped her hands around her mouth. "You're not alone, Emma. Dimitris and I were both in our teens."

"Everybody is so *old*. Anyway, it was never proved, so the captain and crew never went to jail. It's been rotting on the beach ever since." Lyra smiled.

Emma looked out at the water and then back at Lyra. "Thank you. I can't wait to see it, especially now that I know the story." Emma's breath caught in her throat as she gazed ahead again. "Oh my God." She pressed her hand across her mouth. "It's spectacular." She turned to Lyra. "It's massive. How big is the ship?"

Lyra scratched her head. "Erm—"

"It's one hundred and fifty-seven feet," Seb shouted from where he was clearly desperate to be part of the conversation.

"It looks so incongruous," Emma said. "I mean, I know that ships and sea go together, but it looks like someone just dropped it there as an attraction."

"Welcome to Shipwreck Cove, Emma," Nicholas said.

Cristos lowered the dinghy into the sea. "I'll have to make several journeys, but the plan is I row you all over to the beach. Dad will pick a good spot, and we'll set up camp." He beckoned his parents forward. "Old folk and women first."

Dimitris punched his arm. "Less of the old folk. I could give you a run for your money."

Cristos pushed his chest out. "I might put that to the test later."

"Anytime," Dimitris said, slapping his son on the back.

Emma would put her money on Dimitris any day.

Dimitris helped Maria into the dinghy, then did the same for Emma too. Thea, of course, didn't need any help. She dropped into the little boat as though she'd been born to it. Cristos took the oars and rowed them towards the beach. He dropped them at the water's edge, then turned back for his next trip.

Emma shaded her eyes with her hand. "The sand is so white, it's blinding." She peered across at the shipwreck. "That is so eerie. I can't wait to see it close up."

"It is pretty spectacular, isn't it? But you'll have to wait for the children. They want to show you around."

"I can't wait." Emma crouched down, scooped up a handful of sand and let it run through her fingers. "It's so fine; it's like gold dust."

In the meantime, they carried bags, umbrellas, and towels towards the bottom of the cliffs. Thea hammered in the umbrellas in chosen spots and spread the towels out beneath them. Soon, they had a little family village set up.

Maria patted the rock next to her. "Come on, Emma. Take a pew and let them do the work."

Emma perched beside her. "This is heaven, Maria. You're so lucky to have all this beauty on your doorstep."

Maria winked. "It could be your doorstep too, my lovely."

Emma raised her eyebrows. "Tempting." And that was true. The more she saw, and the more time she spent with Thea's family, the more this felt like home. Normally, she'd tell herself that she was seeing things through rose-coloured glasses, that this was a holiday romance in all senses. This time though, she felt like the dream had become a reality.

Maria put her arm around Emma's shoulder. "You know something, Emma, I do believe you've fallen in love with Zakynthos…just as I did. I can see it in your eyes."

Emma tilted her head. "You might be right." She laughed. "However, I fell in love with your daughter first."

Maria stroked Emma's back. "And she with you. You fit together beautifully."

Emma leaned her head on Maria's shoulder. She'd never shown this sort of emotion, and yet here she was, getting all close and feeling comfortable as though it were the most natural thing in the world. "I feel like I'm in paradise."

Once everybody was brought to shore, they settled down to their picnic feast and washed it down with a white retsina wine. Of course, it was followed by baklava, Emma's favourite dessert. The heady combination of nuts, honey, citrus and spices sandwiched between crispy filo layers was enough to persuade Emma to move to Zakynthos, though she feared she'd soon have to buy a new wardrobe.

The adults rested and chatted until the food had settled in their stomachs, but the children ran off towards the shipwreck.

"Be careful." Dimitris frowned. "Don't go on the wreck until we're with you."

"Don't worry. They wouldn't dare." Cristos threw a meatball at his father, who caught it in his mouth. "Well done, Dad."

After about half an hour, they all strolled over to the wreck.

It was a rust bucket, but truly magnificent. Emma was enthralled and photographed it from every angle. Then she joined Nicholas and the children on the wreck as they pranced around acting out their pirate escapades. Emma let go of her self-consciousness and joined in the fun, much as she had at the fairy door in the forest. She caught Thea's eye and smiled, and her heart swelled as Thea smiled back and blew her a kiss.

It was a warm afternoon, and it wasn't long before everyone ran into the sea to cool off. Then they lay on their towels, enjoying the last hour before their journey back.

Eventually, Anna, Nicholas's wife, broke the silence. She sat up with a mischievous grin. "I have an idea." She reached into her bag and pulled out a frisbee. "How about a game?"

The children heard her and sprang into life and dragged each and every one of them up from their relaxation.

Emma laughed as all the children tugged on her arms and pulled her up. "Okay, okay," she shouted.

With a flick of the wrist, Anna sent the frisbee sailing through the air, and the children chased after it, their laughter mingling with the sound of lapping waves.

Seb caught the frisbee and sent it skimming through the air towards Emma. She stuck her hand up and caught it, but Thea grabbed Emma's waist and pulled her to the ground. They wrestled playfully in the sand as Thea attempted to steal the plastic disk from her. The family gathered around laughing and cheering Emma on. Eventually, Thea feigned defeat and lay panting, as if she was out of breath. Emma reached for her hand and pulled her up, and as she did so, Thea pulled her close and kissed her.

"Aww..." Anna said and kicked Nicholas on his shin. "How come you never do that anymore?"

Nicholas laughed. "Wait until they've been together as long as we have."

Emma sent the disk flying, and everyone ran and played like

children, the cares of the world melting away with each moment of joy and laughter shared between them all.

After their fun and games, they rested a while before making a move. Thea put her arm around Emma, lay her head on her shoulder, and sighed. "I can't tell you how much I'm going to miss this."

The children overheard and dropped beside them on the sand. "Why can't we stay here, Mum? Oh, please, please!"

Their wide eyes and hopeful voices tugged at Thea's heart, making the impending departure feel even more bittersweet.

After packing their belongings, Cristos rowed them all back to the boat.

Later that evening, Emma lay in Thea's arms and sighed. "Hmm...this has all been such a tonic."

Thea kissed her forehead. "For me too. I haven't shown you a fraction of the island. It's flown by so quickly, way too quickly."

Thea was right, and yet all their days had been filled with simple pleasures and cherished traditions, sometimes with Seb and Lyra, and sometimes alone. But each occasion had been gloriously happy, and she wouldn't have changed anything. It turned out the balance between alone time and family time wasn't all that difficult to find after all. But then, that's what it meant to be on holiday. It was reality that made it more difficult.

After making love, they nestled in each other's arms, and their breathing slowly returning to normal. Emma rested her head on Thea's chest, listening to the steady thump of her heart and feeling the rise and fall of her breathing. Thea's fingers trailed lazily up and down Emma's arm. It was soothing and comforting. "I love you, Thea," she whispered.

Thea's arms tightened around her, and she kissed the top of her head. "I love you too, Emma. More than anything."

Emma drifted off, safe and warm in the embrace of the woman she loved. She didn't want this feeling to ever end.

Chapter Twenty

When Thea woke the next morning, Emma wasn't by her side once again. She smiled. Emma had taken to walking each morning whilst she was sleeping. She wasn't sure if Emma met up with her mum on her walks but knowing her mum, it was more than likely.

The smile disappeared when she remembered this was their last full day on the island. Tomorrow night, they'd be on a plane bound for England. She sighed, her heart heavy with sadness.

This holiday had been so different from the usual. It had been complete, because not only was she surrounded by her children and family, but also Emma had been there too. She'd noticed a big difference with Seb and Lyra, who seemed to have thrived and forged deeper bonds with their cousins and other island children too. Their laughter filled the air as they played in the sand, chased after seagulls, and had endless adventures. She smiled. The boundless imagination of youth was a beautiful thing to see. If only they could stay. It was a selfish thought. How could she expect Emma to give up her life in England, all on a whim? Especially for a woman she'd only been dating for a few months, and who had children she hadn't been sure she wanted to be part of her life in the first place?

Thea got up and showered, her thoughts too heavy for the beautiful day. She pushed them aside and immersed herself in the family breakfast time. The kids went a little quiet as talk turned to packing and flight times.

Thea, Emma, Seb, and Lyra spent their day playing in the surf, building sandcastles, and collecting seashells. It was as though they were wrapped in a cocoon of happiness, and as the sun began its descent, they gathered driftwood and kindling for the bonfire they planned to have on the beach that night. Thea breathed it all in, wan`ting to remember every second as the moment began to feel fragile.

After another sumptuous meal together, the family moved chairs and blankets down to the water's edge, where all the children had built a large, vaguely haphazard bonfire.

Her dad lit the fire, and it wasn't long before it roared and crackled to life, its flames dancing and flickering in the moonlight. The family sat around the fire, their faces illuminated by its warm glow, and their bodies mellow from the retsina wine. Thea took in the faces of all the people she loved, gathered in that one space. They were all getting older, and it would be months again before she saw them.

Her dad handed out Coke for the children and ouzo for the adults. He raised his glass. "Let's drink to the happiness of this holiday together...and here's to many more."

Everyone raised their glasses and drank, and they were immediately refilled.

Thea's mum took another drink. "Of course, it doesn't have to be the end of a holiday." She stared at Thea. "You could make it permanent, and move home."

Everyone glared at Thea's mum, as though it had been agreed that wouldn't be said out loud.

Seb and Lyra looked at her, waiting for her to respond, their expressions hopeful.

Her dad nudged her mum. "Maria, stop meddling."

Her mum shrugged. "I'm only voicing all of our thoughts."

Thea tipped the contents of her glass into her mouth. "Don't, Mum. You're only making this harder for me. It's bad enough as it is. And you know how I feel about Seb and Lyra's education."

Thea's mum held out her glass. "Top me up, Dimitris."

"I think you've already had enough," he muttered but did as

he was told.

Her mum put her glass down and held her hands on her lap. "There's an international school opening after the Christmas holidays."

Thea stuttered. "What? Where?"

Seb, Lyra, and the rest of the family looked back and forth from Thea's mum to Thea. It looked like they were watching a ping pong ball.

"In Zakynthos town."

Thea spread her fingers. "It's irrelevant, and there's no point in even thinking about it. They'll have a waiting list of about three years if they have a good reputation."

Her mum dipped her chin and took a deep breath. "I put their names down the moment I knew it was opening."

All the children gasped. The rest of the family looked as though they already knew what she'd done, and most of them found something to look at other than Thea.

Thea stared at her. "What?"

Her mum locked up. "Well, I didn't think it would hurt. Like you say, there's a long waiting list, so they're not going to worry one way or the other if someone changes their mind."

Thea rubbed her forehead. For once, she was lost for words.

Her mum took Thea's hand. "I understand it's a big decision, Thea. But I truly believe that this island would be a wonderful place for you, Emma, and the children to build a life together." Her mum looked over at Emma. "Emma, what do you think?"

Thea shook her head. "I can't believe you're doing this. How could you put her under that kind of press—"

Emma took Thea's hand. "It isn't out of the question."

All eyes were on Emma, but nobody said a word. You could hear a pin drop in the sand.

Thea stared at her, emotion making it hard to breathe. "Are you saying you'd be prepared to live here with me?"

"I have no ties to England, but I've developed lots here."

Thea stood and began to pace. "You'd go stir crazy, Emma. It's an island; there's nothing to do. It's a *tourist* island."

"Exactly! We could start a business together." She shrugged. "I've been thinking about it. It's not as though I haven't done it before."

"What? I don't mean this as an insult, but there's hardly a demand for skiwear or designer clothes here."

"Obviously. I was thinking more on the line of accommodation."

Thea raised her eyebrows. "We're inundated with hotels."

Everyone's gaze returned to Emma.

"I know. But there's no glamping."

Thea laughed. "Glamping? Where?"

Emma pointed to the olive groves. "There. If it was an option. I mean, there's a lot to consider, and plenty to research. But it would be something we could build together, and it would provide a steady income. I mean, I know you don't need it, but I'll need something to do."

"Are you serious?" She stared at Emma. "You're serious, aren't you?"

Emma nodded. "Deadly."

Thea looked from her brothers and their wives to her mother and father. "Is there something I'm missing here?" She peered at her mother. "It's you, isn't it? You've been plotting something, or is this something you've hatched between you on your morning walks?"

Emma got up and took Thea's hand again. "It was my idea. I shared my thoughts with Maria, and she thought it was a marvellous plan."

I bet she did.

Emma tugged on her hands to get her to focus. "Can't you see? I've fallen in love with everything. You, your family, and the island. We could really make this work." She hesitated. "If you want to. If you're ready to take that step. I know it's a huge one."

Once again, everyone's gaze turned to Thea. Cristos noisily

munched on crisps, his eyes wide.

Thea looked down at the sand, trying to make sense of it all, trying to understand what was happening.

"You're mad at me, aren't you?" Emma asked.

Thea looked up. "Mad at you?" She broke out into a massive grin. "I'm mad *about* you, you crazy woman." She picked Emma up and swung her around and around. "Yes. Yes, let's do it."

The peace shattered as everyone cheered. Eventually, she put Emma down, and Seb and Lyra rushed over and hugged them both.

Seb looked up at his mum. "Can we really live here, Mummy?"

Thea picked him up and kissed him on his forehead. "I don't see why not." She looked from Seb to Lyra. "Is that what you really want?"

Lyra clung onto her. "More than anything. More than life itself."

Everyone roared with laughter, including Thea. "That's a bit dramatic, but you've convinced me."

"Yay!" Seb and Lyra shouted in unison.

Everyone rose and hugged Thea, Emma, and the children, and the air was full of celebration. Their chatter continued amongst themselves, giving Thea and Emma time to talk.

They sat down a little away from everyone else, and Thea put her arm around Emma's shoulder and drew her closer. Oh, how she loved this woman. Not only had she returned her love, but now she was making it possible to fulfil her dream too. It filled her with a sense of hope and excitement. Thea could hardly believe it. "Are you sure you're ready for this? It's a big step," she asked, searching her face for any doubt.

Emma smiled. "I love you, and I love your children. This feels right. It *is* right." Her voice was steady, and her sincerity shone through.

"What about your apartment?"

Emma wrinkled her nose. "It was just a box I slept in. I never got attached to it. I did think about renting it, but I think I'd prefer to sell. After all, this is our future."

"Our future is looking awesome." It was all so much to take in. It had happened so quickly, and yet, like Emma, Thea knew it was right.

Everyone drifted back to the restaurant, leaving Thea, Emma, and the children snuggled together on a rug by the fireside. Seb and Lyra huddled against them, their eyes heavy with sleep, their shared warmth a testament to the bond they shared, just as Thea shared with her own brothers. The fire crackled and popped, giving a comforting sound in the quiet night.

As the night wore on, the fire began to die down, leaving behind glowing embers. They gathered their things, wrapped the children in blankets, and made their way back to the house, the children fast asleep in their arms. They tucked them into their beds, kissed them, and whispered goodnight. Emma did it all as though she'd been doing it since the day they were born.

As they lay in their own bed, they replayed the day's events together.

Thea pulled Emma close and wrapped her arms around her. "Thank you for today," she whispered. "It was everything I wished for."

It had been the most perfect day of her life. And it was only going to get better.

Epilogue

The months flew by as everyone worked tirelessly to bring Emma's vision of the glamping site to life. The decks for the yurts had been erected, and the family pitched in to complete it all, including the children, who helped after school and on weekends.

Amidst all this activity, Thea, Emma, and the children were house hunting, and it wasn't long before they found the most charming villa nearby. The villa made it easy for the kids to get to school but also gave everyone a little space, which was needed after they'd stayed with her parents for a little past the length of time that was comfortable.

When the yurts were finally assembled, Emma added her personal touches to the interiors, creating a warm and inviting atmosphere.

Thea looked around, feeling particularly proud of what they'd accomplished. "I have to say...this looks so cool. I could easily move in here."

"I think we'll certainly have to christen it," Emma said, winking.

"I can't wait. We'll cook, drink ouzo, and make love under the stars."

Emma laughed. "Preferably not on the evening when all the children are planning their sleepover."

"Definitely not."

Emma and Thea's new chapter on the island began with a mixture of excitement and planning. They dove headfirst into transforming their dream into reality, creating a luxurious glamping experience nestled among the olive grove in its natural beauty.

It was hard work, but as word spread about their unique offering, their business began to thrive. Guests were enchanted by the combination of rustic charm and modern amenities, and soon, reservations poured in from all over the world. Thea, with her knack for hospitality, made sure each visitor felt like part of the island family, while Emma's eye for detail ensured that every yurt was a haven of relaxation and style.

Their glamping site became more than just a business; it was a community. Guests rebooked for another year, drawn by the warmth and authenticity that Emma, Thea, and their family infused into every aspect of their venture. Locals, too, embraced the newcomers, appreciating their commitment to preserving the island's natural beauty and culture.

Life on the island wasn't always easy, but it was richly rewarding. Their decision to move had not only been the right one but had also given them a life filled with purpose and happiness. Together, they had created not just a business, but a legacy—one that celebrated the love they had for each other and the idyllic island they now called home.

Everything had fallen into place. As they sat on their balcony in their new home, sipping champagne and looking out at the azure sea, Seb and Lyra bounded onto the balcony.

"Can Raiden come for a sleepover?" Seb asked.

"And can we have a puppy?" Lyra added.

Thea and Emma laughed and ruffled Seb and Lyra's hair. "One step at a time, sweeties. Let's get a little more settled first, then we'll talk about sleepovers and puppies."

They ran back inside, arguing about what they'd name the new puppy.

Thea topped them up and raised her glass. "Welcome to our new life," she said, her voice filled with awe.

Emma leaned into her. "Here's to new beginnings."

And with that, their adventure truly began.

~ THE END ~

Thank you so much for reading my latest story. I'd love if you
could pop a review on Amazon for me—my book gurus tell me
that's the best way to get other people to read my books!
And if you'd like to keep up with my author life and general
ramblings, perhaps you'd consider signing up to the Butterworth
Books newsletter? (bit.ly/ButterBookers). I don't have my
own mainly because I'm too busy running around the South
Coast enjoying retirement, and it's so much easier to send my
occasional scribbles to my gurus to put out into the world!

Ciao,
Karen Klyne

Other Great Butterworth Books

Caribbean Dreams by Karen Klyne
When love sails into your life, can you climb aboard?
Available from Amazon (ASIN B09M41PYM9)

Encrypted Hearts by E.V. Bancroft
Even amid the chaos of war, love is the hardest code to crack.
Available from Amazon (ASIN B0DKG7BHMJ)

Unwritten by Helena Harte
No strings is fun 'til it unravels.
Available from Amazon (ASIN B0DGQFFHYB)

Chucking Putty at the Queen by Simon Smalley
A heartbreaking, humorous, and courageous exploration of what it takes to be ones authentic self.
Available from Amazon (ASIN B0DGGBV22W)

The Promise by Addison M Conley
When the world keeps pulling you under, who do you reach for?
Available on Amazon (ASIN B0DDY9FH6Z)

Back to Back by Jo Fletcher
."When Fred and Ruby's worlds collide, can love rise from the rubble?"
Available on Amazon (ASIN B0D6M499K2)

Sanctuary by Helena Harte
Passions ignite and possibilities unfold. Welcome to the Windy City Romances.
Available from Amazon (ASIN B0D4B42RRW)

Heart of the Storm by Ally McGuire
Sometimes a storm is just what you need to clear the skies ahead.
Available on Amazon (ASIN B0CYTSQXWW)

Brave Enough to Love by Valden Bush
In a dance between truth and sacrifice, can they rewrite the rules of love?
Available on Amazon (ASIN B0CQP8PMVB)

Dead Ringer by Robyn Nyx
Three bodies. One killer. No motive?
Available on Amazon (ASIN B0CPQ8HFK7)

Medea by JJ Taylor
Who will Medea become in her battle for freedom?
Available from Amazon (ASIN B0CK2FB7GW)

Virgin Flight by E.V. Bancroft
In the battle between duty and desire, can love win?
Available from Amazon (ASIN B0CKJWQZ45)

Fragments of the Heart by Ally McGuire
Love can be the greatest expedition of all.
Available on Amazon (ASIN B0CHBPHR6M)

Stunted Heart by Helena Harte
A stunt rider who lives in the fast lane. An ER doctor who can't take chances. A passion that could turn their worlds upside down.
Available on Amazon (ASIN B0C78GSWBV)

Here You Are by Jo Fletcher
.Can they unlock their hearts to find the true happiness they both deserve?
Available on Amazon (ASIN B0CBN935ZB)

Dark Haven by Brey Willows
Even vampires get tired of playing with their food...
Available on Amazon (ASIN B0C5P1HJXC)

Green for Love by E.V. Bancroft
All's fair in love and eco-war.
Available from Amazon (ASIN B0C28F7PX5)

Call of Love by Lee Haven
Separated by fear. Reunited by fate. Will they get a second chance at life and love?
Available from Amazon (ASIN B0BYC83HZD)

Stolen Ambition by Robyn Nyx
Daughters of two worlds collide in a dangerous game of ambition and love.
Available on Amazon (ASIN B0BS1PRSCN)

Cabin Fever by Addison M Conley
She goes for the money, but will she stay for something deeper?
Available on Amazon (ASIN B0BQWY45GH)

Breakout for Love by Valden Bush
They're both running from their pasts. Together, they might make a new future.
Available from Amazon (ASIN B0CWHZ4SXL)

The Helion Band by AJ Mason
Rose's only crime was to show kindness to her royal mistress...
Available from Amazon (ASIN B09YM6TYFQ)

That Boy of Yours Wants Looking At by Simon Smalley
A riotously colourful and heart-rending journey of what it takes to live authentically.
Available from Amazon (ASIN B09V3CSQQW)

Sapphic Eclectic Volume Five edited by Nyx & Willows
A little something for everyone...
Available free from the Butterworth Books website

Of Light and Love by E.V. Bancroft
The deepest shadows paint the brightest love.
Available from Amazon (ASIN B0B64KJ3NP)

An Art to Love by Helena Harte
Second chances are an art form.
Available on Amazon (ASIN B0B1CD8Y42)

Music City Dreamers by Robyn Nyx
Music brings lovers together. In Music City, it can tear them apart. Available on
Amazon (ASIN B0994XVDGR)

Let Love Be Enough by Robyn Nyx
When a killer sets her sights on her target, is there any stopping her?
Available on Amazon (ASIN B09YMMZ8XC)

Dead Pretty by Robyn Nyx
An FBI agent, a TV star, and a serial killer. Love hurts.
Available on Amazon (ASIN B09QRSKBVP)

Nero by Valden Bush
Banished and abandoned. Will destiny reunite her with the love of her life?
Available from Amazon (ASIN B0BHJKHK6S)

Warm Pearls and Paper Cranes by E.V. Bancroft
A family torn apart by secrets. The only way forward is love.
Available from Amazon (ASIN B09DTBCQ92)

Judge Me, Judge Me Not by James Merrick
One man's battle against the world and himself to find it's never too late to find, and use, your voice.
Available from Amazon (ASIN B09CLK91N5)

Scripted Love by Helena Harte
What good is a romance writer who doesn't believe in happy ever after?
Available on Amazon (ASIN B0993QFLNN)

Call to Me by Helena Harte
Sometimes the call you least expect is the one you need the most.
Available on Amazon (ASIN B08D9SR15H)

What's Your Story?

Global Wordsmiths, CIC, provides an all-encompassing service for all writers, ranging from basic proofreading and cover design to development editing, typesetting, and eBook services. A major part of our work is charity and community focused, delivering writing projects to under-served and under-represented groups across Nottinghamshire, giving voice to the voiceless and visibility to the unseen.

To learn more about what we offer, visit: www.globalwords.co.uk

A selection of books by Global Words Press:
Desire, Love, Identity: with the National Justice Museum
Aventuras en México: Farmilo Primary School
Times Past: with The Workhouse, National Trust
Young at Heart with AGE UK
In Different Shoes: Stories of Trans Lives

Self-published authors working with Global Wordsmiths:
Steve Bailey
Ravenna Castle
Jackie D
CJ DeBarra
Dee Griffiths
Iona Kane
Maggie McIntyre
Emma Nichols
Dani Lovelady Ryan
Erin Zak